FROSTED BY THE GIRL NEXT DOOR

Visit us at www.boldstrokesbooks.com

By the Authors

Jaime Clevenger and Aurora Rey

Published by Bold Strokes Books
A Convenient Arrangement
Frosted by the Girl Next Door

Published by Bella Books
Love, Accidentally
New Leash on Love

Aurora Rey

Cape End Romances
Winter's Harbor
Summer's Cove
Spring's Wake
Autumn's Light

Built to Last
Crescent City Confidential
Lead Counsel (Novella in The Boss of Her collection)
Recipe for Love: A Farm-to-Table Romance
The Inn at Netherfield Green
Ice on Wheels (Novella in Hot Ice collection)
The Last Place You Look
Twice Shy
You Again
Follow Her Lead (Novella in Opposites Attract collection)
Greener Pastures
Hard Pressed
Roux for Two

Renovation Romances
Sweat Equity
Good Bones

Jaime Clevenger

Published by Bella Books
The Unknown Mile
Call Shotgun
Sign on the Line
Whiskey and Oak Leaves
Sweet, Sweet Wine
Waiting for a Love Song
A Fugitive's Kiss
Moonstone
Party Favors
Three Reasons to Say Yes
All the Reasons I Need
Just One Reason
One Weekend in Aspen
Over the Moon with You
Under the Stars with You
Houseswap 101

Published by Spinsters Ink
All Bets Off

FROSTED BY THE GIRL NEXT DOOR

by

Aurora Rey and Jaime Clevenger

2024

CREDITS
EDITOR: CINDY CRESAP
PRODUCTION DESIGN: SUSAN RAMUNDO
COVER DESIGN BY INK SPIRAL DESIGN

Acknowledgments

We'd like to thank Bold Strokes and Bella for letting us team up once again and the wonderfully talented and astute Cindy Cresap for her editing brilliance. Mostly, though, we want to thank the readers. We love going on these adventures with you.

CHAPTER ONE

"Oh, my God. Go." Tara McCoy made a shooing gesture. "I got it."

Shawn lifted both hands in defeat. "I'm going, I'm going. Just, you know, be nice."

Tara let out an indignant huff. "What is that supposed to mean?" She knew full well what Shawn meant.

"You can be a little intense is all. You know. Chop-chop."

"The fact that I don't dawdle with customers and trade town gossip does not make me intense." She frowned. "Or unfriendly."

Shawn didn't even pretend to buy it. That was the problem working with a sibling. Or at least one of the problems. They knew too much to let you slide on anything. "I know you care about customers. But the little old lady who comes in to buy herself a treat to perk up her afternoon deserves the same level of care and attention as one of your brides."

"Even if the bride is ordering four hundred cupcakes?" She didn't know why she asked. She knew Shawn's answer to that, too.

"Even then."

One of the drawbacks to taking over the family bakery was the family part. Shawn was perfectly content to run things the way they had always been run. That meant simple recipes and a laid-back, coffee-shop vibe that had as much to do with being a place to go as a place to buy cupcakes. There was nothing wrong with that of course, but Tara wanted more. Shawn had been willing to let Tara spice up the recipes, but she'd dug her heels in on any other changes. Which made turning Coy Cupcakes into a high-end dessert destination an uphill climb.

"If you keep pouting, I'm not going to go," Shawn said.

"It's a dentist appointment. You have to go." Shawn wouldn't actually skip. But pushing Tara's buttons and pointing out that for all her pastry chef training, she wasn't the best at everything? That happened at least once a week.

"I guess it's only an hour." Shawn let out a world-weary sigh. "Promise to stay up front and smile if anyone comes in."

Tara shook her head. "Go."

Shawn finally did, and Tara stood behind the counter with her arms folded. She tapped her foot and looked around. It was one in the afternoon on a Wednesday. Chances were high no one would come in anyway. She fussed with the arrangement of things in the display case for a minute and gave the front glass a wipe down even though it didn't need it.

She checked her email, but no new inquiries had come in since she checked that morning. And, of course, she'd replied to all those that had been there then. She tidied the business cards she'd designed and insisted live at the front register for anyone who happened to pop in but might be considering a larger, custom order in the future. Then she checked that there were spare rolls of receipt tape and Coy Cupcakes stickers tucked under the counter. She might give Shawn a hard time about being casual, but Shawn didn't mess around.

This is ridiculous. It was one thing to be friendly. It was another to waste time. And Tara McCoy did not waste time.

She propped open the swinging door that separated the kitchen from the front of the shop and went back to the batch of chocolate cupcakes she'd been swirling with salted caramel buttercream. And since she could have fun, dammit, she flicked on the little speaker she kept tucked on the shelf in the corner.

She frosted that batch and decorated them with chocolate curls, then bagged up the brown sugar Swiss meringue buttercream that went with her riff on pineapple upside down cake. Those got piped with a simple cloud and topped with a perfectly caramelized dried pineapple flower. Satisfied with the results, she put a half dozen of each on the trays she'd special ordered to dress up the display case and carried them out.

She slid one tray into the open spot in the case and set the other under a vintage glass cake dome. She jutted her hips side to side and gave a little twirl. Because she could be fun and productive at the same time, thank you very much. Pleased with herself as much as the cupcakes, she strutted her way back to the kitchen because she did, in fact, feel good as hell. She picked up the piping bag of frosting and told it so, asking how it was feeling for good measure.

"Hello?"

Tara spun around, frosting still in hand.

"Sorry, I didn't mean to interrupt." The stranger—customer— gave an easy smile that seemed more flirtatious than apologetic.

She dropped the piping bag, swore, and picked it up. Then she set it on the table and hurried out, pulling the door behind her to at least muffle the music. "No, no. I'm sorry. I wasn't expecting anyone."

The customer's brow lifted. "No? Are you not open?"

"I mean, right at that moment. It's usually pretty slow between lunch and when school lets out. I was just, um, doing some frosting." Why couldn't she stop talking? Because feeling like an idiot flustered her, obviously. And the fact that she'd been caught by a legit hottie wasn't helping matters.

Stranger McGoodlooking hooked a thumb in the direction of the door. "I could come back later."

Tara laughed, though it came out a little too loud to pass for cool. "It's fine. Um. Are you interested in some cupcakes today?"

"I think I am."

They made a show of perusing the case, giving Tara the chance to peruse them. Tall and kind of lanky, sandy blond hair and hazel eyes. Jeans and a heathered gray sweater that was technically casual but looked expensive. Definitely not local. Which was fine by her. Shawn might like the local clientele, but she knew the bread and butter of a high-end cupcake shop were tourists and catered events. "What can I get you?"

"What would you recommend?"

If they were trying to put her at ease, it was well played. She could talk cupcakes in her sleep. "Well, if you like chocolate, the salted caramel is my favorite. We also do a lemon drop that's really nice."

"Cool, cool. I might have to try one of each."

Tara grabbed a box and remembered Shawn's instructions to smile. "Coming right up. Can I get your name?"

"Um. Casey." The customer—Casey—offered an almost sheepish smile. "Stevens."

She barely resisted a face-palm. Names might be standard fare for phone orders and wedding consults, but they definitely weren't part of counter service. "Sorry. I'm used to talking with customers on the phone more than out here."

Casey offered an affable nod. "I don't mind. It's nice to meet you."

Tara nodded, happy for the graceful smooth over. "Well, it's nice to meet you, too. I'm Tara."

Casey pointed at the case. "I shouldn't, but since we're on a first-name basis, can you put one of those red velvet ones in there, too?"

She added it to the box. "You absolutely should."

"Way to twist my arm, Tara."

Tara blushed, though she wasn't sure why. Feeling flustered for an entirely different reason, she totaled up the order and spun the screen around for Casey to swipe her card. "Thanks for coming in today. We hope to see you again."

Casey's smile turned sly. "I think you will."

Before she could decide whether to take Casey's answer at face value, or ask her to elaborate, Shawn strolled in. "Look at you, helping customers like it's your job."

Casey glanced briefly at Shawn before giving Tara a playful look. "Do you not actually work here?"

Tara ignored Shawn, who would doubtlessly tease her later, and went for her own version of a playful smile. "Of course I work here, but Shawn here keeps me locked in the kitchen most of the time."

"Only because you're the better baker." Shawn turned to Casey. "My sister makes the best cupcakes. You're in for a treat."

"I can't wait." Casey took the box Tara had set on the corner. She headed for the door but stopped when she got to Shawn. "You should let her out more. I bet customers would come for the entertainment as much as the cupcakes."

Casey didn't elaborate or give Shawn the chance to reply. She simply offered a wave and was gone. Tara stared after her, unsure whether to be amused or mortified.

"What was that about?" Shawn asked.

Tara blew out a breath. "She may have walked in on me dancing like a fool and singing into a piping bag."

"I'd have paid money to see that," Shawn said without missing a beat.

She and Shawn didn't have a teasing sort of relationship, so the quip left her as stilted as getting caught by Casey in the first place. "Stop."

Shawn hung her jacket and came behind the counter. "I'm serious. You're fun when you let loose."

That was Shawn code for "you're usually so uptight." Which, to be fair, she was. Ten years in high-pressure pastry gigs could do that to a person. But that was done. She was home now. And she might be trying to up the ante of what Coy Cupcakes had to offer, but there was no point acting like she was in competition with anyone but herself. "Well, leave me in charge of the register and who knows what might happen."

"We'll have to get you your own tip jar." Shawn laughed. "Seriously, though. Thanks for covering for me."

"No big deal." Even if she managed to embarrass herself in front of the one—totally gorgeous—customer who happened to stroll in.

"It looks like you distracted her enough to leave her phone." Shawn held up a sleek device in a case that had more to do with looks than protection.

"Crap." She grabbed it and sprinted out to the sidewalk. Unfortunately, there was no sign of its owner.

"She'll come back," Shawn said. "There aren't that many places she could lose it."

That was true. Unless it was summer or peak ski season, Rocky Springs rocked the sleepy small-town vibe during the week. "Why don't I hold onto it? We don't want someone knocking it to the ground in the after-school rush."

Shawn gave a rather obnoxious knowing nod. "And when she comes in, should I send her right back?"

It might be silly, but she liked the idea of seeing Casey again. Even if only for a minute. "You do that."

CHAPTER TWO

Casey patted her pockets again, knowing she was simply wasting time. Clearly, her mind was on vacation. "Dammit. How could I lose my phone?" And now she was talking to herself.

She closed her eyes and took a deep breath, trying to retrace where she'd gone that morning and when she'd last taken out her phone. Aside from snapping some pictures of the town—which was only one main street six blocks long nestled right at the base of a mountain—she hadn't used her phone for hours. Twenty-four to be exact.

She'd been avoiding social media, emails, and texts quite effectively since she'd arrived in Rocky Springs and even congratulated herself on the fact that she'd been offline for a whole day. But now she needed her phone. She had no idea where she was supposed to meet Kit and no way of getting in touch with her. Where the hell had she left it?

After a moment of indecision, she turned and walked back into the store she'd just stepped out of. The lady in the jewelry shop was sweet enough to offer to call her number but neither of them could hear any ringing and no one answered the line.

She thanked the jeweler and left, walked past two storefronts, and then paused again. Maybe losing her phone was karma for how much she'd cursed being tethered to it these past few months. With all the drama that had gone down, she'd been overwhelmed with friends sending check-in texts not to mention all the notifications that popped when someone dropped her name in an online post. Those notifications had eased up at least.

She scanned up and down the street trying to recall the places she'd stopped. Her phone could be at the park. She'd spent an hour there simply relaxing in the sunshine and people watching. Or she could have left it in one of the dozen shops she'd poked around in. On a day where she'd promised herself to do nothing, she'd walked a lot. Her stomach rumbled audibly as if in response, and she eyed the box of cupcakes. She'd bought three so she could eat one now and still have two to share when she met up with Kit. Assuming she found her phone and figured out where they were supposed to meet.

"Cupcakes!" She wheeled around, searching for the Coy Cupcakes sign. Two blocks up on the right. She'd set down her phone to take the box from the cute dancing baker. *Tara.*

As she crossed the street, the possibility that someone had already nabbed her phone ran through her mind. But Kit had joked that morning that there was so little crime in Rocky Springs, the two police officers forgot they even had a job. Hopefully, the no crime part included no cell phone theft.

She was out of breath when she pushed open the door to Coy Cupcakes. Instead of having the place to herself, it was filled with teenagers jostling to get a look at the cupcakes in the glass display cases.

"I want one of the new ones—with the pineapple flower on top," the girl at the front of the mass of teens said, having to shout over the noise.

The requested cupcake was whisked into a small box, cash was deposited in the register, and the next kid stepped up to the counter. Tara wasn't there—her sibling Shawn was. And it was organized chaos, but Shawn seemed to enjoy it, laughing and joking with each customer.

Casey tried peeking into the back to spot Tara, but the crowd made it tricky. There were at least twenty teens in a space she thought would have fit no more than half that. There was also no sign of her phone on the front counter.

Someone tapped her arm and she turned to see Tara. Her smile made Casey's breath catch, same as it had the first time she'd entered the shop.

"I'm guessing you came back for this." Tara held out the phone. "Or you tried one cupcake and decided to order five hundred more for an upcoming wedding?"

"Definitely no upcoming wedding."

"So you don't want five hundred cupcakes?"

"That would be a lot of cupcakes for just me." Casey couldn't help laughing.

"Want a phone as a consolation prize?"

"Yes, please. I'd take a phone over getting married again any day."

As soon as Tara passed her the phone, it beeped with a text. Multiple missed texts lit up the screen. Casey ignored them and met Tara's gaze. Her blue eyes were even more captivating up close—as was everything else about her. Her dark brown hair was held back in a braid like earlier, and Casey had to push away the thought of what she'd look like with her hair down. Even with the hat she wore over it and a bright pink apron dusted with what looked like flour and streaks of icing, Tara was gorgeous. She cleared her throat. "Thanks for keeping it safe."

"It would have been perfectly safe where you left it all afternoon—except today is Wednesday and the high school lets out early on Wednesdays. At exactly one thirty-five, this place turns into a zoo." She waved behind her at the scene of noisy teens waiting on cupcakes. "I didn't want anyone to knock it off the counter and have someone step on it."

"It's only a zoo 'cause Coy Cupcakes are bussin'," said one of the boys.

Several others shot back, "For real, for real."

"Bussin'?" She suddenly felt all of her forty-one-years and wondered if she was really as out of touch as her ex had claimed.

"Bussin' means delicious, or anything that's amazing." Tara motioned to the cupcake box. "What'd you think?"

"I haven't tried one yet. I'm meeting up with a friend and was going to share, but—" Casey held up her phone as it chimed with a text. "I didn't know where we were meeting."

"Looks like you do now. Hope you two like the cupcakes."

Before Casey could thank her again, Tara turned and made her way behind the counter. She disappeared through the doorway to the back, and Casey felt the happy buzz she'd been enjoying leave just as fast. "Thanks," she murmured.

"Ms. McCoy is always like that," a quieter teen with glasses said. "But no one makes better cupcakes. No one."

Casey didn't ask what he meant by "like that" but guessed it was her brusque attitude. It didn't fit with what Casey had seen earlier, but maybe Tara didn't often dance and sing into frosting bags when others could see. She looked to the back, hoping to catch another glimpse, dancing or otherwise. All she could see were stacks of empty cupcake pans and two big ovens.

Her phone buzzed with another text. Kit: *I'm at the clock tower. Are you close?*

Give me two minutes. Casey gave up on catching another glimpse of Tara and headed outside.

It didn't take long to get to the clock tower or to find Kit. She was wearing a dark green dress with tall boots and a blazer, which would have fit in LA or any other big city but looked somehow wrong in Rocky Springs. Maybe that was because Casey hadn't seen anyone else wearing anything fancier than jeans and fleeces. Of course, Kit had insisted over and over that even though she'd been born and raised in Rocky Springs, she didn't belong there.

"Thanks for waiting. I lost my phone and had to retrace my steps. Turns out I left it on the front counter of the cupcake shop. Would have been long gone if we were still in LA."

"Nothing moves fast in Rocky Springs," Kit said with an exaggerated sigh. "Ready for lunch? Or are we eating cupcakes instead? Those things are the bomb, by the way."

"I was thinking this would be dessert. And apparently, they're bussin'."

"Bussin'?"

"It's a good thing," she said with confidence. "Twenty hungry high schoolers can't be wrong."

"They could be, actually, and often are. But in this case, I agree with them. Once you try a bite of a Coy Cupcake, you'll be ruined for every other cupcake." Kit got up from the bench and waved for her to follow. "There's only one restaurant open between two and five in this town, so I hope you weren't expecting options."

"As long as the food's good, I don't need a lot of options. What's the place called?" After running from one end of the town to the other twice now, as well as the poking around she'd done earlier, Casey guessed she'd passed it.

"Don't laugh."

"Okay?"

Kit gave her a half-smile. "The Restaurant."

Casey laughed despite the promise she'd made.

"That's how you know you're in a town of three thousand people. Did you see the bar that's called the Keg? I can point it out if you missed it. It's right next to the Restaurant."

"You'd like fancier names?"

"Some imagination would be nice," Kit said dryly.

"I don't know. Maybe I've had too much fancy. I kind of like the idea of simple for a change."

Kit gave her a side-eye. "Do not tell me you're thinking of moving to Rocky Springs."

Casey shrugged. "Why not?"

"Why is the better question."

"I want to get out of LA. Do something different in a new place. Maybe Rocky Springs is what I need."

Kit held her gaze for a moment, then shook her head. "What you need is a vacation and not to think about your next step yet."

"Yeah…maybe."

Kit crossed the street at the intersection without looking to see if it was safe. No cars were in sight, fortunately. "Everything with Pavia will blow over. You know how it is in LA. People have short attention spans."

Kit was right that most people would forget. But not everyone, including all the people Casey worked with. The thought of how many connections she'd likely poisoned made Casey want to change her name. Without the last name of Stevens, she'd really have no place in the Hollywood crowd.

"I'm telling you, in two weeks the whole mess will be completely forgotten. Then you can go back and have that fresh start."

Two weeks. That was the plan. Two weeks in a town where she didn't know anyone except Kit and wouldn't be recognized. Two weeks with no obligations—and nothing to do except think of all the ways she'd screwed up. Except for the last several hours, she hadn't done that. Instead, she'd fantasized about ways she could start over in a new town.

They came to Coy Cupcakes, and Casey didn't resist peeking in through the wide glass window. Unfortunately, Tara wasn't at the counter. Probably she was in the back baking. Before Kit could notice her spying, she resumed walking. She only made it two strides before stopping again.

Right next to the cupcake shop was an empty storefront with a sign on the door that said "Space For Rent." She'd walked past it twice without giving it a second look. Now her mind spun.

"You coming?" Kit asked.

"I was just thinking…" Her idea was too ridiculous to admit, but the words came anyway. "I've always wanted to be a shopkeeper. Like as a kid I used to set up a folding table in our living room and I'd try to sell my parents old toys and things they'd bought for me. I put price tags on everything and even had my own cash register. What if that was my fresh start? I have plenty in savings to do something like that."

For a moment, Kit looked confused, but then her expression turned to a concerned frown. "Casey, you've been through a lot. I get that you want a fresh start and to do something totally new, but running a shop in a little town like this?" She shook her head. "It's feast or famine with the tourists, and things here would only be a novelty for so long. Then you'd be daydreaming about everything you were missing back in LA—including the traffic."

"Never. No way. Not the traffic." Just the idea of leaving LA and the traffic behind had her feeling giddy.

"What type of shop would you even have?"

"I don't know. Maybe a bookshop? I like it here, Kit."

"Trust me, this town's BS gets old quick."

"So does LA's BS." Here even the air felt invigorating. One day in a new place and she was considering possibilities she wouldn't have said existed a week ago. "Something about this place feels right."

"It's the altitude," Kit said. "It does things to your brain. Not enough oxygen and you start feeling delusional. And you're probably hypoglycemic now which adds to the delirium."

Casey laughed, but Kit had already started walking again. She spared one last look back at the empty storefront before following

Kit. A bookshop would be fun, but what she'd like even more would be an adult toy store. Not a traditional sex shop, exactly. Something classy. Something that took the taboo out of all the different ways people could explore and enjoy sex. The idea had been in the back of her mind for years. She'd never dreamed she'd have the freedom to go for it. But she had plenty of freedom now.

As the possibility played in her mind, she pictured a table near the front of the store with tastefully displayed vibrators. Strap-ons of every size and color would line one of the side walls. A section for the BDSM crowd toward the back. An array of lubes near the counter with the cash register. And there would be loads of books on everything from self-love to erotica.

If Rocky Springs weren't a tourist spot, there'd be no way a shop like that could stay in business. But Kit had complained that the town's population swelled to fifteen thousand or more when the summer and the winter tourists came and crowds filled the streets. *Tourists would be perfect sex shop customers.*

Could she open her own store? Could she leave LA, with everyone and everything she knew? Well, everyone except Kit.

"Hope you're hungry for a sandwich with no frills," Kit said, stopping in front of a shop with a handwritten sign that said *The Restaurant.* "The places that sell better food are only open when the tourists are here." She reached for the door handle. "Don't expect arugula or escarole. We're not in LA."

"I hate arugula." There were plenty of things she wouldn't mind leaving back in LA.

CHAPTER THREE

Tara shielded her eyes from the glare of the morning sun with her hand, convinced she was imagining things. But sure enough, Casey sat on the bench under the window of the empty storefront next door, her nose stuck in a book. "Good morning," she said.

Casey looked up and smiled. "Hi."

"I didn't think you were still in town." She'd hoped to see Casey again at the shop, but it hadn't happened, and she figured that was that.

"I wasn't supposed to be." Casey stood, revealing a rather large pile of books beside her. "Change of plans."

"Good change, I hope." Anyone sticking around Rocky Springs longer than expected—on purpose—counted as a win in her book.

"Very good, actually. Well, hopefully."

It was hard to tell whether Casey was being intentionally vague or simply awkward. It made Tara half-wish Shawn was there. She might be overly friendly with customers, but she had a knack for reading people that Tara didn't. Which was fine by her, but it sure would come in handy sometimes. "Should I be wishing you luck?"

"I could use some, so if you're offering, I'll take it." Casey hooked a thumb behind her. "I'm going to be your neighbor."

"You're renting the shop? I thought you were only visiting a friend." She'd crossed the line into nosy—at least by her standards—but told herself it was legitimate business curiosity.

"I am. I always wanted to set up shop. And some recent life changes made it feel like the perfect time." Casey gave a sheepish shrug, as though admitting it was a harebrained idea.

There might be a thousand reasons it was, but Tara didn't focus on those. She focused on the idea of a fresh new business bringing more energy and people to their little block of downtown. And, okay, she also focused on the very pleasant prospect of seeing Casey every day. "In that case, I wish you all the luck in the world. Along with a big ole welcome to the neighborhood."

Casey smiled, the kind that made her eyes crinkle at the corners and made Tara think about other ways she might put that sort of look on Casey's face. "Thanks."

"What kind of store are you—wait." She pointed to the stack of books on the bench. "Ooh, a bookstore. We need one of those. And right next door? Even better."

"I'm thinking more—"

"Aren't you supposed to be baking cupcakes, young lady?" Andrew McCoy's booming baritone cut right in, even from fifty feet away.

Casey's gaze darted away, then returned full of questions. Tara lifted a finger. "One sec."

Casey nodded but looked taken aback by the whole thing.

"I'm networking with a fellow small business owner, Grandpa. You of all people should appreciate that." He offered a salute and strode into the bakery like a man on a mission. Tara turned her attention back to Casey. "Andrew McCoy, my grandfather and the mayor of Rocky Springs thirty-two years and counting."

"Ah." Casey nodded, but the befuddled look didn't fade. "Wow."

She forgot that, for people from bigger cities, having your grandpa be the mayor would be strange. Or that a single person might be the mayor for three decades, mostly because no one bothered to run against him. "It's a small town. You're going to have to get used to stuff like that if you stick around."

"Yeah."

Tara laughed. "He's a decent guy, at least. And a great supporter of small businesses. He'll be thrilled to hear about your plans."

Casey made a face. "About that."

"Yes. I want to hear all about it." She put a hand on Casey's arm and immediately got distracted by how strong and solid it felt. She let go, having to fight the impulse to map out Casey's biceps.

"It's just that—"

A woman Tara sort of recognized strolled up before Casey could finish her sentence. She looked Casey up and down. "Morning, shopkeep. You ready to turn this wacky idea of yours into a reality?"

"So ready."

"Good. Let's do it." The woman kissed Casey on the cheek and Tara's brain did one of those instant and unpleasant reorganizations.

Casey opened her mouth then closed it, like she thought better of what she'd been about to say. She did one of those microscopic head shakes that could be read a thousand ways, leaving Tara more on edge rather than less. Casey took a deep breath, lifting her shoulders and then dropping them on the exhale. "As ready as I'll ever be. But first, do you two know each other?"

"Maybe? Tara McCoy." She pointed behind her. "Coy Cupcakes."

"Yeah, we went to school together. I was a few years behind you though. Kit Hartman. My family owns Hartman Construction."

Tara shook the extended hand. "Right. Oh my God. You were on TV. I can't believe I didn't recognize you."

Kit smiled, though it seemed regretful. "I've changed a bit since then."

Tara hadn't really watched the show, mostly because home improvement wasn't her thing. But she'd heard about it, and about it ending. Even without knowing the specifics, she understood the discomfort of coming home when the big dreams didn't work out after all. "Well, you look fantastic, and Rocky Springs is lucky to have you back."

Kit's eyes softened. "Thanks."

Casey cleared her throat. "Kit and I met in LA. She's the one who talked me into visiting Rocky Springs."

"Ah." Tara filed the detail away, not knowing whether it meant they were together but assuming so. And feeling foolish for letting her guard down enough to imagine flirting with Casey on a daily basis.

"Has this one told you her grand plan?" Kit tipped her head at Casey.

"A bookshop. So exciting. It's exactly what Rocky Springs needs." Which was true even if Casey and Kit were a couple. Her watch buzzed and she jumped on the excuse to leave. "I've got to run, but I can't wait to see it all come together."

Kit opened her mouth but closed it without speaking, much like Casey had a moment before. Only this time Tara didn't want to know what it meant. Since the pseudo flirty thing she had going with Casey was gone and no doubt Shawn and Grandpa were stirring up trouble without her, she offered a wave and booked it to the bakery. But when she got inside, Grandpa seemed to be on a rant rather than regaling Shawn with his latest mayoral exploits.

"Do I even want to know?" she asked when they both looked her way.

Grandpa shook his head and grumbled, so Shawn took over. "Apparently, someone is looking to open a sex shop in town and Gary Jenkins is all up in arms and chewing Grandpa's ear off about it."

Gary Jenkins owned the Western clothing store in town and had a reputation for being a colossal, conservative stick in the mud. Tara tolerated him at Chamber of Commerce functions, but only because picking a fight would get her a lecture on respecting her elders. "I'd be more up in arms about Gary chewing my ear off than a sex shop opening."

Shawn let out a snort but quickly covered it with a cough.

Grandpa grumbled some more. "'First it was the pot shops,' he says. 'Now we're all going to hell in a handbasket.'"

She wanted to disagree on principle, since falling on the same side of any issue as Gary felt more than a little icky. But the truth of the matter was he had a point. "I wouldn't go that far, but I wouldn't be thrilled if it was opening next door."

Shawn's eyes got huge. "What if it is opening up next door?"

Tara shook her head, happy that was one thing she didn't need to worry about. "No, that's going to be a bookshop."

"How did you find that out?" Shawn asked.

"I ran into Casey, the woman who left her phone here a couple of weeks ago. I thought she was just visiting, but she decided to stay and open up a shop. She's already meeting with a contractor." Who might also be her girlfriend? Not that it was any of Tara's business.

"Huh." Shawn shrugged. "That's kind of weird but also cool."

"It's very cool. And way better than a sex shop. Can you even imagine? Trying to sell cupcakes with a window display of dildos next door." The second the words were out of her mouth, she remembered they weren't alone. She looked to her grandfather with a cringe. "Sorry."

Grandpa jabbed a finger at her. "That's exactly the perspective we need at the zoning and planning meeting tomorrow. I have to remain neutral because of my position, but if you're there, that'll get Gary off my back."

Did she feel strongly enough to publicly protest? Probably not, but if it got her brownie points with her grandfather, she could at least show up. "I'll be there."

Shawn frowned. "Can't we all just get along?"

She went for a finger jab of her own. "Not if we want Rocky Springs to be a nice, family-friendly destination."

Grandpa clapped her on the back. "That's the spirit. Now, box me up some cupcakes that'll sustain me through the budget meeting I've got this afternoon."

Shawn snagged a box and started filling it with Grandpa's favorites. "I think all small businesses are good."

Tara rolled her eyes at Shawn's willful naiveté. "Not the seedy ones."

Grandpa nodded. "Seedy. That's a good word. We don't want anything seedy."

"Seedy is relative," Shawn said.

"Not if you're in my shoes." Grandpa took the pastel pink box. "Not one bit."

"I think that technically makes it even more relative." Shawn, not one for being obstinate, shrugged. "Just saying."

Tara straightened. "Well, fortunately for you, I'm going to put on my big girl panties and deal with it, so you don't have to go."

Grandpa bustled out, cupcakes in hand but still grumbling about seediness and the sorry state of being in his shoes.

Shawn did an impressive eye roll as the door swung closed. "He's such a dinosaur."

Tara sighed. "Yeah, but he has a point."

"What point? There's nothing wrong with sex toys."

"I like sex toys as much as the next person, but I don't want a sex shop next door." She shuddered at the possibility, then returned to the much more pleasant thought of Casey and her bookstore and how perfect that would be. For business, obviously, not for her.

"Really? You're going to play the prude card?"

"I'm not a prude. I just don't think the clientele we're trying to woo would appreciate it. I'm pretty sure the clientele we already have wouldn't, either."

Shawn seemed to weigh what she'd said. "I'll give you half a point, for the kid factor. Though I swear teenagers would be better off with vibrators than the shenanigans they get up to."

"So much no."

Shawn shrugged. "And toys should totally be a part of the wedding night and honeymoon. Even for straight people."

Tara pressed her fingers to her forehead. "Could you stop? There's not a sex shop opening next door. And hopefully, not one opening anywhere close by. I'll buy that stuff from reputable online retailers who ship in discreet packaging, thank you very much."

"Prude."

She sniffed, refusing to succumb to Shawn's goading. "I have to go. I'm notekeeper for the Christmas Market coordinating team."

Shawn offered a wave. "If the sex shop goes in next door and it's a wild success, you owe me a drink."

That warranted a groan and Tara didn't hold back. "You're such a child." She slid on her coat and grabbed her purse. "Let's hope we don't have to think about sex shops after tomorrow."

Since it was a nice enough day to walk, she headed for the front door rather than the back where her car was parked. Outside, the crisp November air and vivid blue sky chased away worries about sex shops and antagonistic siblings. She sucked in a deep breath and let it out. Glorious.

There were things she missed about New York and big city life, but being back in Rocky Springs had its perks. That included fresh air, gorgeous mountain views every day, and the luxury of building the sort of clientele she wanted without some asshole boss breathing down her neck. And the promise of cross-promotion with new businesses—the non-seedy kind—opening right next door.

She couldn't help but peek in as she walked past. Casey stood with her back to the front windows, arms spread and a commanding, wide-legged stance. Kit stood next to her, arms folded. Lovers' spat? Or maybe just a disagreement over which direction to line up the bookshelves. Either way was fine by her. She had her hands full without romantic entanglements.

Still. It was hard not to be a tiny bit disappointed. Good-looking butches were thin on the ground in Rocky Springs, and she already knew most of them. New to town and with the financial wherewithal to open a business from scratch? Well, that was practically a unicorn. She should have known better to think an available one would land in her lap.

CHAPTER FOUR

N ext agenda item. Approving business permits." The city planner cleared her throat. "As I say every month, our job as a planning commission is to determine if each business proposal is consistent with our city ordinances." She leveled her gaze on the crowd and then turned to meet eyes with the other four members of the planning board seated on either side of her. "This is not about whether we like a business or not. Understood?" Heads nodded, someone grumbled. "First up for discussion, Theo's Ice Cream."

Casey stilled her bouncing right leg and took a deep breath. She'd expected a crowd, but the room was filled to capacity. And no friendly faces in sight.

After she'd filed the business license application, she'd impulsively signed the lease on the storefront. Since it was already zoned for commercial space, and since she planned to sell books and gifts in addition to sex toys, she didn't see any reason things wouldn't go through. Kit had even told her not to sweat the planning council approval. At first. That afternoon she'd changed her tune. Apparently, someone in the planning department had leaked the information that a sex shop was opening, and Kit had overheard that some guy named Gary Jenkins was whipping up the town to protest.

"Can I squeeze in next to you?"

Casey glanced up at Tara McCoy and nodded, making room on the bench. When Tara smiled, Casey relaxed. *One friendly face.* Unless Tara had come to protest too. But she was ninety-percent certain Tara was Family and what queer person didn't like sex toys? Tara's knee bumped hers and she murmured an apology.

She shouldn't be thinking about getting romantically involved with someone, but she'd spent more than a little time imagining asking Tara out. She sensed the attraction went both ways, but if things didn't go well on a date, it would make working right next door to each other tricky. And there was the part about definitely not being ready for another relationship. Anyone with any sense would run the other direction.

"Again, this is not about whether we like the business proposal or not," the planning commissioner said, shutting down some guy in the front row. He owned an ice cream shop and didn't want another one on the same block. Reasonable, but it was a relief the commissioner wasn't letting him take over the conversation. "If there's no further comments or concerns, I'd like to call a vote. All those in favor?"

Five green lights popped, one in front of each commissioner.

"Well, that was easy." The commissioner nodded. "Theo's Ice Cream is approved. Next up, the Sweet Spot."

"I can't believe someone thought the Sweet Spot would be a good name for a sex shop," Tara murmured.

Casey glanced at her, but Tara's attention was on the hands that shot up. The commissioner pointed to a man in a cowboy hat. He stood and introduced himself. Gary Jenkins.

"Rocky Springs is a family town and we want to keep it that way." Heads nodded and murmurs of agreement followed. "Some store selling X-rated porn doesn't belong here. It's as simple as that. You want to scare away tourists and drive down business, well, then you approve this Sweet Spot. Because that's what'll happen."

Someone else called out, "Yeah, who wants to take their family on vacation to Rocky Springs and see dildos in some shop window?"

A dozen or more voices spoke at once. Gary Jenkins was still standing and helping to rile the others by calling out random sex toys, "and butt plugs and cock rings," but the others didn't need spurring. Everyone was against the idea. Casey swallowed and risked another glance at Tara.

"A sex shop really would be horrible for Rocky Springs," Tara said. "What we need are things like bookshops."

A knot of dread formed in the pit of her stomach. "For the record, I am planning on selling books. But there'll be other things like sex toys and I don't see why it's such a big deal." One look at Tara's face confirmed she'd said the wrong thing. She turned from Tara and gazed out at the crowd still shouting around them. "It's not like I'm going to put cock rings and dildos on display in the window. I want the shop to be an upscale place. Something that makes people feel good about themselves. And about sex."

Tara opened and closed her mouth. She'd clearly gotten the full picture now. "That's your proposal? You want to put a sex shop next door to my bakery, and you're calling it the Sweet Spot?"

"That was the plan. But you don't need to get mad at me—I don't think I'm getting the board's approval."

Tara held her gaze and Casey wished she didn't feel a thrum of attraction still. No way would Tara be saying yes to a date now. She was well and truly pissed.

Casey tried to shift her attention back to the town hall. Everyone was talking at once and there was no way to hear anyone clearly. The lead planning commissioner rang a little bell to call order, but no one seemed to notice. She hollered "Quiet please," but no one noticed that either. Finally, one of the other commissioners stood and put his fingers in his mouth and whistled. The piercing sound was horrible, but it worked. When most of the conversations stopped, he gruffly said, "Y'all need to shut up or leave. This is not some free-for-all."

The lead commissioner murmured, "Thank you, Bill." Addressing the hall in a louder voice, she said, "As I've said, this is not about whether we like a business proposal or not." She turned to the others on the planning commission. "I know you all have reviewed the ordinances regarding small business development and understand we must approve this business unless we feel it violates the rules in some way. Does anyone know of a rule that this proposal violates?"

The commissioner on her right said, "The problem is, Rocky Springs doesn't have a lot of rules."

"I couldn't find any rule specifically against an adult toy store," one of the other commissioners added. "This is the same problem we came up against with the pot shop."

"Just because there's no formal rule against it doesn't mean we should vote for it. We do have a moral obligation—"

"With all due respect, Jane, I disagree," another commissioner interrupted her. "No rule against it means we should approve it. The pot shop we weren't happy about—Green Solution—has brought Rocky Springs a lot of tax dollars."

"And I've seen your truck out front more than once," Jane shot back.

It was like watching a tennis match, only not as much fun. Casey's stomach twisted as the voices gained volume and the commissioners on either side of the lead commissioner started pointing fingers at each other. She forced her leg to stop bouncing and breathed through her nose, wishing her anxiety had an off button.

"What I'm saying is we were worried about approving the pot shop, but it ended up being a boon for the town."

"A boon? The only thing marijuana has brought is—"

"Folks," Bill, the whistle commissioner, spoke up, his deep voice stopping the argument. "For better or worse, we don't much like rules in this town. That's always been the way. Old west mentality means mind your own business."

"This is a porn shop, Bill." Gary Jenkins stood up again and was now waving his hands. "How the heck am I supposed to mind my own business when they're selling sex across the street from my place of business? You know the type of people those stores bring in. It'll run the tourists and families out."

The lead commissioner stood up. "Gary, I hear your concerns. However, the proposal isn't for the sale of sex."

Garry grumbled.

The commissioner pressed on, lifting a paper to read, "Items to be sold include an assortment of fiction and nonfiction books, self-care and wellness items, personal massage devices, lubricants, lotions, and…well, the proposal goes on to list a few other things but no sex." She pointedly looked over her glasses at Gary Jenkins, then at the people seated on either side of her. "If we don't like this type of business in our town, we'd have to have a law against it. Since there are no laws against it—"

Several others stood up with Gary Jenkins and they all started shouting about how morality didn't need a law. Casey watched the scene wanting to feel detached from it. But this wasn't a tennis match gone awry. Every word slammed against her chest. She hadn't planned on it being easy, but a bashing of her moral compass wasn't what she'd expected. Not before she'd even opened.

Another loud whistle from Bill broke the mayhem. "I think we need to call a vote and move on."

"Agreed." The lead commissioner looked flustered but kept her voice even as she said, "All those in favor of issuing a business license to the Sweet Spot." Three green lights popped—including Bill's and the lead commissioner. "All those against." Two red lights. "Majority is in favor so the Sweet Spot is approved to do business in Rocky Springs."

Shouting erupted, but the commissioner slammed her hand on the table in front of her. "If the town would like to change the laws, so be it. But that's not our job. Moving on to our next agenda item. Approval of proposed festivals and fairs for the coming year."

Casey didn't listen to the rest of the meeting. For all she'd weathered on social media during her divorce, everyone saying awful things about her online—most of it wildly untrue—and long-term friends picking her ex's side, she should be able to take a bruising and move on. But her hope for a fresh start with a fun new project seemed naïve now. She didn't know these people and they already hated her.

When the meeting ended, she stood and shuffled out with the rest of the crowd. Tara didn't make eye contact with her. *Fine.* She'd hoped to have an ally, and possibly even a friend, but aside from Kit, she was on her own. The more that realization settled in, the more empowered she felt. She'd wanted to be on her own. She'd wanted to prove that she could be a success at something with no one helping her. The town was simply upping the ante.

"Let them make a law," she muttered. But that would take time. Probably longer than a year. She couldn't count on that, of course. What she had to do was prove her business was good for the town. And fast. "I'm going to put this fucking town on the map."

"Did you say something?" Tara asked.

They'd come out onto the sidewalk and the crowd was filing out of the town hall behind them.

"Just talking to myself." Casey gave Tara a closed-lipped smile. "I'm sorry to hear you're against my shop. I had some ideas for how we could work together."

"Cupcakes don't really go with butt plugs," Tara said tightly.

"How about vibrators?" Casey laughed because the tension felt ridiculous. Tara's responding scowl managed to be cute even while it annoyed her. "Whatever. My shop is going to be good for this town and I know it will help yours."

"Your shop is controversial and going to offend half the tourists who keep our economy afloat. Probably more than half. On top of that, you had to go and call it something that is bound to confuse people who might be trying to find mine. Coy Cupcakes doesn't need that kind of help, thank you very much."

Casey lifted her hands. "Fine."

"I mean, really. The Sweet Spot?"

"I thought it was a good name and kind of fit with yours."

Tara scoffed. "Why would I want my bakery at all connected to your sex shop?"

If possible, Casey felt worse. Tara turned and walked up the sidewalk heading toward the mountain. She stopped after five paces or so and spun around, stomping past Casey in the other direction, and muttering, "I forgot where I parked."

Casey caught up with her in a few steps. "Look, I'm sorry. About picking the wrong name and about letting you think I was opening a regular bookshop. I tried to explain, but we kept getting interrupted and, well, there will be books."

Tara only shook her head.

"I am going to have a whole section in the front of the shop. Fiction and nonfiction. I've been researching all the titles I want to carry."

"Fiction, like erotica?"

"Well, yeah. And nonfiction like relationship guides and self-love journals. Have you read *All About Love* by bell hooks? I started that one this morning. It's really good. At first, I was thinking I'd just have how-to books, you know. But now I'm thinking books about the spirituality of lovemaking and universal love could fit in well, too."

Tara stopped, so Casey did, too. She pointed a finger right at Casey's chest. "You put erotica books on display in the front of your store along with *The Joy of Lesbian Sex* and you might as well tell all the tourists this town has the plague."

"I thought you liked the idea of a bookstore."

"Not that type of bookstore!" Tara spread her arms. "Do you know how many high schoolers come to Coy Cupcakes after school every day?"

"Yeah. They love your cupcakes."

"And how are their parents going to feel knowing there's a sex shop next door?"

"You know you can buy vibrators in drug stores now, right? And, like, Target."

Tara glowered.

"I was planning to get books about safe sex and healthy relationships. Straight and gay. Having all the information is important for teens." Casey pressed on though Tara's vibe made it clear she wasn't going to be won over. "I'll have condoms too, of course. Hadn't really thought about that part for highschoolers, but it's a good point—"

"Condoms aren't a good point." Tara made a guttural sound and threw up her hands. "Forget it. Just…forget it."

When Tara started walking again, Casey didn't try to catch up. Clearly, the conversation was over. Still, she hollered out, "You know abstinence education doesn't work, right?"

Tara raised a middle finger in the air. Despite everything, Casey laughed. Screw Tara and her cupcakes. She blew out a breath and then looked up at the dark sky. "What the hell am I doing here?"

Starting over.

As the words repeated in her mind, she realized how much she needed to. And she could do exactly that now that the shop had been approved. She might be on her own, but it was what she wanted. Sink or swim, it was all up to her now.

She started walking, pulling her jacket close around her and then stopping to button it. Obviously, she had to think about who passed her shop and, despite what Gary said, she didn't want to offend people with something obscene in the window. And Tara's point about the teens who hung out at the cupcake shop was a good one.

Some sex shops had age restrictions and she could try that. Then again, wouldn't teens be better off with sex toys and books than unplanned pregnancies and STIs? Maybe she could have an eighteen and over section behind a rope. She wondered what Tara would say to that and shook her head.

"It doesn't matter. I'm going to put this town on the map."

CHAPTER FIVE

Tara stopped dead in the middle of the sidewalk and barely resisted a groan. Casey stood in front of her soon-to-be sex shop, along with Kit and someone she didn't recognize. The prospect of Casey next door day after day—that had been so appealing only a day before—left a knot in the pit of her stomach. Assuming, of course, a knot could also gnaw, like that squirrel that got stuck in her wall that one time and chewed insulation all hours of the night.

Ugh.

She steeled herself to power walk past them, but Casey chose that exact moment to look up. "Good morning."

"For some of us, maybe." It bugged her how easy it was to be sullen and snarky, but that was an issue to dissect another day.

Kit didn't even try to hide her eye roll and the woman she didn't recognize looked from Casey to her and back, discomfort evident on her face. Casey sighed. "I'm sorry you felt blindsided last night. I hope you know that wasn't my intention."

"No? You're not in the habit of lying to get your way?" A low blow, considering she barely knew Casey, but whatever.

"Is that really called for?" Kit asked.

Casey lifted a hand. "She's entitled to be upset."

Tara scowled, unsure whether to say thank you or an indignant yeah. Or perhaps take issue, once again, with the add-insult-to-injury name Casey had chosen for the shop.

"But I hope we can get past that and work together." Casey looked at her pointedly. "Because at the end of the day, we both want the same thing."

Perhaps in the broadest sense they did, but she wasn't about to concede that point. "No, we don't."

A muscle in Casey's jaw visibly tightened. If Tara wasn't so intent on being enemies, she might have found it attractive. "We both want to bring more people to downtown," Casey said evenly.

"Yeah, but you want to bring the wrong kind of people."

Casey flinched and the woman she didn't recognize gave her a stony look.

Tara's conscience kicked in, reminding her that nothing was ever gained from simply being mean. The need to escape swelled. She averted her gaze and noticed Casey's car double-parked alongside Kit's truck. She jerked her chin in its direction. "You should move your car. They love to give tickets on this block."

Casey didn't respond. No one else did, either. She took that as her cue and walked past them as briskly as she could. Of course, her shop wasn't yet open for the day, and she'd gotten herself so worked up that her hands were shaking which meant it took her for-freaking-ever to get her key in the lock. When she eventually did, she stepped inside, relocked the door behind her, and slumped against it. "Fuck."

Shawn emerged from the stock room with a stack of the boxes they used for individual cupcake sales, in usual perky morning-person mode. "How can you be having a bad day already? It's barely started."

She could argue that most bad days got their start in the first hour of being up and about. But she needed to process, and Shawn rocked the friendly ear thing, even if they rarely agreed on how to resolve a situation. "I ran into Casey."

"Was she standing on the corner yelling 'dildos for sale' or was she minding her own business?"

Tara tried her best withering look. "She apologized for blindsiding me at the planning meeting last night."

"How dare she." Shawn went for full dramatic delivery, making Tara feel extra foolish.

"And then I made a mean comment about her lying to get what she wanted and implied her shop would bring the wrong kind of people." Which wasn't what she really thought at all. She only worried it would keep away some of the right kind of people for the bakery.

"You do know how to step in it." Shawn chuckled.

"What if she thinks I'm a prude? Or homophobic? Or…or a Republican?" She shuddered at the possibility.

"Well, you are kind of a prude," Shawn said.

"I am not." Tara stomped her foot, which didn't help the feeling like a child vibe she had going.

"Okay, you're not. I just like saying it because you're uptight and those things go so nicely together."

She didn't want to, but she laughed. Because Shawn loved to antagonize her but was smart and funny about it. "Not helping."

"Was Kit with her?" Shawn asked with a little too much eagerness.

"Why does that matter?" Smart and funny, but not subtle.

"I ran into her at the dog park. She's adopted a dog who's a wild child and I offered to help with some training." Shawn shrugged, perhaps trying for subtle but failing.

"Yeah, I'd steer clear of that whole situation." Because her half-baked crush on Casey was enough of a problem. They didn't need more entanglements on top of everything.

"Why?"

Tara sighed. "Because I'm not entirely sure she and Casey aren't together. And, more importantly, everyone in town is taking sides and you don't want to find yourself on the wrong one."

Shawn frowned.

"I know you don't like picking sides and you really don't like being told what to do, but trust me on this one." Shawn always thought the best of people. It was sweet if a bit naïve.

"What if I'm on the side of the sex shop?"

Naïve and obstinate. "I'm not going to dignify that with a response. So, if you don't need me for anything else, I'm going to get to work."

"I am, for the record," Shawn said to her back.

Tara pushed through the kitchen door and let it swing behind her. "I'd suggest keeping that to yourself, at least when Grandpa is around."

Shawn mumbled something Tara couldn't make out, but she didn't bother going out to see what it was. She had bigger things to worry about. Like making twenty dozen raspberry swirl cupcakes for the first weekend of the Christmas Market.

She got butter and sugar creaming together in the bowl of her twenty-quart mixer. While it did its thing, she weighed out flour, then added baking powder and salt before sifting it all together. Milk, egg whites, and vanilla went into the oversized measuring cup she used for wet ingredients, and she whisked them together. The whole process took less than five minutes and, honestly, she could probably do it in her sleep.

But instead of alternating the wet and dry ingredients to get a perfect batter, she slammed off the mixer's power switch. She planted her hands on her hips and huffed. Then she paced. All the while, she thought of the look on Casey's face after her wrong kind of people comment.

God, she hated apologizing.

But she was an adult. And though some might call her stubborn—or rigid—she made a point of admitting when she'd fucked up. And she made a point of making it right.

She yanked off the bandana she'd put on to cover her hair and the apron she hadn't gotten dirty yet. At least she could let cupcakes do most of the apologizing for her. She strode back to the front of the shop, making the door strain against the stop and giving Shawn a jolt.

"What the heck is wrong with you?" Shawn asked, one hand on the counter and the other up in the air like something was about to come flying.

"I'm going to go apologize."

"You are?" Shawn's expression went from startled and mildly irritated to incredulous.

"I'm a professional. I have a professional reputation to maintain. I can't be in the business of making enemies." Especially not in a town this size.

"So, you're covering your ass more than feeling genuinely sorry," Shawn said.

"You make it sound so calculating." Manipulative, even.

"Isn't it?"

Ugh. "Okay, maybe it is a little. I prefer to think of it as keeping the peace."

Shawn considered. "I can get behind that."

"Can you box me up half a dozen cupcakes to help my cause?"

"Bribery?" Shawn asked.

No point pretending otherwise. "Yep."

"I like this version of my sister."

"Whatever. Make sure you put a salted caramel in there. Oh, and a red velvet."

"You remember what she ordered." Shawn said it like it was an accusation.

"You always remember what people order," Tara countered.

"Yeah, but I'm the people person."

"And I'm the cupcake person." She wasn't sure it was a valid comeback, and she absolutely didn't make a point of remembering what random drop-in customers bought but whatever.

"If I didn't know better, I'd think you liked this woman."

If only Shawn knew. "Well, she's become my nemesis, so it's a moot point."

"Nemesis." Shawn laughed. "You kill me."

Because she had no desire to discuss her feelings—and because stubbornly denying she had feelings about Casey might backfire—she snagged the box from Shawn's hands. "I'll be back."

Casey and the other two had disappeared from the sidewalk. She had half a mind to turn around and go back the way she'd come, but that would make her a coward as well as a jerk. So she strode over and peered in the window. They huddled around what appeared to be a set of plans held by Kit, talking and nodding and occasionally pointing in one direction or another.

Tara contemplated knocking but decided to test the door instead. Open. She let herself in, but no one looked up. She waited, debating whether to draw attention to herself. But then Casey turned her way.

"Tara."

Not a hello, but not a what the hell are you doing here. So, win? "I wanted to apologize for earlier."

"Okay."

When Casey didn't expand on that sentiment, she pressed on. "When I made that comment about the wrong kind of people, I didn't mean that. There's absolutely nothing wrong with sex toys or sex positivity or stores that sell it. I only meant that I'm worried your shop being next to mine will drive away some of the right kind of people. People who may not feel the same way about sex toys but would otherwise buy cupcakes."

Kit and the other woman didn't seem terribly impressed with her explanation, but Casey's features softened. "I get it."

"I'm not saying I'm on board with all this." She made a sweeping gesture with her free hand to indicate their surroundings. "But I'm not a raging bitch, either."

No one asserted that she was, but no one asserted she wasn't.

"Anyway, I brought a peace offering." She held out the box. "I won't keep you."

Casey came over and took the box, a half-smile on her face that might have been genuine but just as easily could have been forced. "Thank you."

She thought about joking that Casey should return the favor, bring her a peace offering from the shop when she got her stock in. But the truth of the matter was that Shawn was right, she was a prude. At least when it came to dealing with virtual strangers. So she gave a brisk nod and left, feeling better about being a grownup if nothing else.

CHAPTER SIX

Warm, sugar-scented air greeted Casey when she stepped into the shop. She took a deep breath and loosened her scarf. The smell would be an easy one to get used to. Good thing she didn't have to boycott Coy Cupcakes after all.

It would have been torture walking past a bakery every day on her way to work and not stopping in for a treat at least some of the time. Especially a bakery that smelled this good. Still, she'd fully planned on giving up cupcakes after Tara's comments yesterday. Fortunately, the apology after—however flustered Tara had been while delivering it—had changed things.

Flustered Tara was adorable. And Casey hadn't done a good job pretending to be indifferent. The moment Tara had left, Natalia had raised an eyebrow at Casey and said, "Someone has a crush on her hands."

She couldn't deny it even as she wasn't sure what to do about it. Ignore it, was probably what she should do. But here she was, hoping to see Tara pop out from the back singing. "Hello?"

She waited for an answer, but none came. Dance music was playing and that, along with the clatter of pans, likely blocked out other sounds to whoever was working in the back. She stepped up to the counter, eyed the bell with the little "Ring for Service" sign and then the cupcakes lined up under the glass. Her mouth watered at the sight of one solo red velvet.

She hadn't come to buy herself a treat, though. Natalia had sent her on the errand, insisting she couldn't focus on design plans without a cupcake. Since Natalia had tried one of the cupcakes Tara had brought yesterday, she'd hardly let up about them, even joking she was ready to move to Rocky Springs. But Natalia would never leave LA. Natalia's life was LA. Then again, someone might have said the same about her as of September. A few months and one imploded marriage could change things.

She leaned as far as she could to the left, past the cash register, and peered into the back. A set of ovens, a counter with rows and rows of cupcakes, and Tara leaning over a tray of them with a bag of frosting in hand and a look of total concentration.

Casey didn't want to disturb her but didn't want to seem like a weirdo if she was caught staring. Before she'd decided to try to get Tara's attention, her phone buzzed with a text. She read the message, half surprised it wasn't an SOS from Natalia who'd been begging for cupcakes for hours. Instead, it was a text from her mother. *Have you watched Pavia's interview?*

Casey's stomach tightened. She'd gone out of her way to avoid any news about her ex, but the people in her life seemed committed to keeping her in the loop.

Everyone's already reposting it.

Casey swallowed. She didn't want to ask but she found herself typing: *Who did the interview?* Hopefully, it was some small online deal. Better yet a podcast.

Let's Get Real with Camille.

Casey cussed under her breath. She closed her eyes, picturing the fake smile Camille always plastered on for the camera. Camille hadn't liked Casey five years ago when she'd recommended Ada Lindquist over her for a big role in the miniseries her parents were directing. Probably she'd been happy to have some payback now.

Do you want to know what Pavia said?

Nope. Not even a little bit. Casey shoved her phone back in her pocket and took a deep, steadying breath. What mattered in LA didn't matter in Rocky Springs. Chances were, no one in this town had even heard of *Let's Get Real with Camille.* And she was done with people like Camille. Done worrying about old grudges. Done worrying about what her ex said about her. That part especially. She looked into the back right as Tara lifted her gaze from the cupcakes.

"Oh. Hi. Didn't realize I had a customer." Tara set down her icing bag, pulled off her bandana, and came forward, stopping at the cash register. "Everything okay next door?"

"Yeah. Everything's well…coming along." She forced a smile, but Tara still seemed to be waiting for her to say more. "And you? I mean, how are things over here in cupcake land?"

"Cupcake land is good." Tara gave a vaguely uncomfortable smile. "Hectic, but good. I'm working on a big order for a wedding and Shawn's running late because of a stray dog emergency. I swear stray dogs find Shawn from out of nowhere." She swiped back a loose strand of her dark brown hair that had fallen forward. "Anyway. How can I help you?"

"I need a cupcake for my friend."

"Only one for your friend?"

Casey considered buying Kit one as well. She'd be joining them later that afternoon to finalize all the plans. "Well, maybe two."

"One red velvet for you and what can I get you for your friend?"

Since Tara had already picked out the red velvet, Casey didn't stop her. In fact, it was sweet Tara knew what she liked. The thought that she'd made a point of knowing made Casey happier than she wanted to admit.

"You know what, make it three. The red velvet, one of those chocolate ones you brought to my shop yesterday…" she paused to find the right one. "That one on the bottom left. And Kit likes the lemon drop. I have a feeling she wouldn't forgive me if I didn't get one for her too."

Casey waited as Tara set the red velvet cupcake in a pink box and then went back to select the others.

"Natalia—my friend who's in town—said she couldn't make it through the day without another of your little demon cupcakes."

"The devil's food are especially popular with the high school crowd." Tara set the chocolate cupcake into the box. "I used to only frost these with a ganache and chocolate shavings, but one of the freshmen dared me to put little devil horns on them. It's the school mascot."

"A devil is the school mascot?"

"Yep. Rocky Devils." She turned back to the counter and reached for the next cupcake. "And one lemon drop for Kit. If you're buying cupcakes, whatever the reason, always get one for your girlfriend."

Casey nodded. "Kit's not my girlfriend, but I'll remember that rule."

The door swung open, and Natalia hurried inside. "I can't feel my toes. How can it be so cold without any snow?" She paused and took a deep breath. "Oh my God, this place smells like heaven."

Casey gestured to Tara and then Natalia. "Tara, this is my friend who never gets out of LA. Natalia. And I did tell her to bring boots."

"You know how I feel about my footwear." Natalia kicked her foot back, showing off her Jimmy Choos, before turning her attention to Tara. "So, you're the baker who ruined me forever with her demon cupcakes? Girl, what do you put in those? It's something addictive."

Tara smiled. "I feel the same way about chocolate. And sugar."

"Sugar? Let's not go there. In my mind your cupcakes are calorie free and healthy." Natalia swept forward to the glass display case with a gasp. "You didn't tell me there were so many different types." She shot a glare at Casey and then spun back to Tara. "Can you ship to LA?"

"We ship anywhere. Well, anywhere in the US." Tara reached for a card and held it out. "You can order online, and I do overnight shipping."

"Good. But I'll be ordering some right now." Natalia looked at the pink box with the three cupcakes Casey had ordered waiting on the counter. "Do you have a bigger box?"

"Give me a sec."

"Do not let me order more than a dozen," Natalia said, distractedly reading something on her phone.

"You have more than a dozen friends," Casey countered. "They're all going to want to try—"

"Oh, shit, Casey. Did you see this?" Natalia held out her phone, but Casey nodded without looking. No doubt Natalia was referencing the same post her mother had texted about earlier.

"Camile hates me. Not as much as my ex but…"

"She's a fucking wench. They both are." Natalia scrolled the comments. "I get that you stop thinking when there's a pretty girl in front of you, but why did you ever marry Pavia?"

Tara stepped out of the back with an assortment of boxes right as Natalia's question landed. Casey briefly met Tara's gaze, wondering if she had heard the name and recognized it. Pavia was unusual enough to be a name people remembered, but Tara's expression didn't change. Either she hadn't heard of Pavia Rossini or didn't realize this Pavia was the same woman everyone either hated or loved. The phone at the front counter rang and Tara glanced at it.

"You can pick up," Natalia said. "We're not in a hurry." She turned back to Casey. "You should have slept with her and moved on. Like everyone else. I get that she's hot, but that woman is pure evil. Did you watch the interview?"

"No, and I don't need to."

Fortunately, Tara was busy with the call because Natalia was hell-bent on Casey hearing Pavia's recent outburst. She read from her phone. "'Now that I'm free from the negative influences of Casey Stevens, I plan to fully commit myself to my spiritual journey of growth.' Are you kidding me? And, Casey, this was live on *Let's Get Real with Camile*."

"I don't care. I'm so over anything Pavia has to say about me."

"But you knew about the interview?"

"My mom texted me." Because no one seemed truly convinced that she was done with Pavia Rossini.

"And you're not freaking out about any of this?" Natalia scrolled on her phone. "I thought she was a piece of work before. Listen to this. 'I realized Casey was a manipulative narcissist. Now that I'm away from her, I'm going to recommit myself to my faith.' Lord have fucking mercy." Natalia clicked her tongue. "She's basically saying you made her temporarily lesbian. Oh, baby girl."

Tara looked up, briefly catching Casey's gaze but immediately returned her attention to the call. Had she overheard? Casey wanted to close her eyes and squeeze her hands over her ears. Or simply disappear. But there was no escape. The moment she let down her guard, the media circus slammed her against a wall all over again.

"You know this is going to fuel all the 'let's hate on bisexuals' crap."

Natalia was bi and Casey felt even worse about the mess realizing she was right. Someone as prominent as Pavia could do a lot of damage. "I'm sorry, Natalia."

"Oh, no. You don't apologize for her. Not anymore." She shook her head, then glanced back at the screen. "What gets me the most is that she chased you for months. Who does she think she's fooling? Temporarily lesbian my ass. And this bullshit about her spiritual journey… Is that the one where she screws everyone, including her married—with three kids—costar, and blames you for it?"

Pavia coming out as a reformed sinner and denouncing ever being a lesbian would make the news everywhere. Casey took a shaky breath, wondering at the fallout. Could she hope Rocky Springs was far enough off the main grid to avoid celebrity gossip?

"You know what really pisses me off? She got all that press coming out as a lesbian when she started dating you and then she pulls this crap. For more publicity. And yet you're the manipulative narcissist?" Natalia eyed Casey. "How do you not hate her?"

"I'm just done," Casey said. "Maybe I'm done dating forever."

Tara chose that moment to hang up the phone and look at Casey. Forever was a long time. And yet, it felt good saying it. Like a weight was lifted. Still, when she felt Tara's gaze on her, she wondered two things. One, was she really done dating forever? Two, how much of Natalia's rant had Tara heard?

"You're giving up dating when you've just—" Tara's voice stopped abruptly and she looked almost embarrassed that she'd spoken up. "Sorry. Never mind."

"It's fine. Go on." Casey wanted to know what Tara was thinking.

"Well, you're opening a store that sells sex toys and you're giving up dating?"

So she'd heard some of it. Natalia shot Casey a pitying look and said, "We need cupcakes. Lots of cupcakes."

CHAPTER SEVEN

Tara slid the last tray of the day's cupcakes out of the oven and onto a rack to cool. She flicked off the oven and swiped the back of her wrist across her forehead. Whew.

She loved the start of Rocky Springs's Christmas Markets and loved that they started the weekend before Thanksgiving so she could ease into the frenetic pace that would define her life for the month of December. The hustle reminded her of the good parts of her previous life and gave her glimpses into what Coy Cupcakes might be—more than a sleepy little shop in a sleepy little town. Oh, and Christmas. Because who didn't love Christmas?

Did Casey?

Though she'd be dead before admitting it, Casey had been invading her thoughts with increasing regularity. Like, first thing in the morning when she woke up and at random times during the day. Like, in the shower and every time she passed Casey's shop. It was beyond annoying and, if she was being honest, strayed inconveniently close to sexual frustration territory.

It didn't help that Casey had covered the windows of the shop with brown paper, preventing both Tara and random passersby from getting a glimpse of what she was up to. Of course, Tara had been angling for glimpses of Casey as much as anything. Again, not that she'd admit it.

As grumpy as she'd been about the prospect of a sex shop going in next door, she'd sort of made peace with it. If the transition of her career aspirations had taught her anything, it was that sometimes she was wrong about what she thought she wanted.

As it turned out, all the excitement that came with being part of Manhattan's culinary world hadn't made her happy. And spending every day fighting for a tiny little scrap of success was not only exhausting but unfulfilling. When she'd finally accepted she missed Rocky Springs and wanted to take over the family bakery more than she wanted to go it alone, she'd started smiling again. Not a lot— she was still naturally a cynic. But life was definitely better when she stopped fighting so hard for what she'd thought she should want. Maybe being attracted to Casey was another thing she needed to stop fighting.

"Maybe go with it and see what happens," she murmured.

"Hey, Tara. Can you pause whatever you're doing?" Shawn's voice carried through the swinging door.

"Be right there." Since she'd shut off the oven and nothing else needed immediate attention, she wiped her hands and went out. The after-school crowd milled around, along with a couple of families. Shawn had things under control, but the situation would definitely benefit from an extra pair of hands. "I'll box and you ring?"

"Perfect." Shawn slid behind the register and, as though sensing the move, the line shifted ever so slightly, clustering around the case instead of the counter.

Tara took orders and boxed one cupcake after another. She exchanged pleasantries but not much else, while Shawn asked the sort of personalized questions that came from knowing all the customers. Well, knowing and liking them. Tara didn't dislike them. It was that the one at a time game would never get them to the next level. Besides, these kids already knew what they liked and what they wanted.

She spared a little more attention for the families, especially the one in town early for the first market. She encouraged them to take a card and share it with the friends from Boulder they planned to meet up with the next day. "Oh, we'll bring them here ourselves," the mom said.

The crowd might have felt chaotic, but it thinned quickly. That wouldn't be the case over the weekend. She'd be stuck either out front or in their little booth the whole time. Well, not stuck. Just on. Extroverted. Doing the song and dance that seemed to come naturally to Shawn but left her drained. Maybe by this time next year, they could afford another staff member. She remained grateful every day they'd hired a seasonal person to cover some of the shifts at the counter and the market, but damn, it would be nice to keep them on full-time. Then she could tuck herself in the back baking and come out only for meetings with brides and corporate clients and the like.

"Hey, thanks. I know you hate leaving the kitchen when you're in a groove." Shawn bumped her shoulder. "Things were getting a little out of hand."

"You caught me at a perfect time. And you shouldn't have to handle a rush on your own." But it was nice Shawn knew she was an introvert and tried to respect it.

"How's the baking?"

"Done. Now to make all the frosting and do all the decorating." She mimed squeezing a piping bag and a sprinkle gesture. "I'm going to do the new peppermint bark first because I want you to help me nail down how much peppermint needs to be in the frosting."

Shawn offered a salute. "I accept this responsibility."

"Do you need another taste tester? I'd be happy to help."

Tara recognized Casey's voice at this point and spun around, willing herself not to be excited. "You would, huh?"

"I'm generous like that. Always wanting to help out a fellow business owner."

Shawn laughed but Tara went for a smirk. "How selfless."

"I also brought a peace offering." Casey held up a small bag.

She couldn't prevent having Shawn as an audience, but there was no need to project the conversation across the whole shop. She came from behind the counter and folded her arms. "Did you?"

"Well, since you brought me one." Casey's eyes held mischief. "And I finished stocking the shop this morning."

Okay, now she really wished they didn't have an audience. "Um."

Casey held out the bag. "Open it."

A vibrator? Lube? She racked her brain and failed to come up with something that wouldn't leave her a blushing, tongue-tied mess. What she pulled out was an orb, a little bigger than a golf ball, wrapped tightly in pink tissue paper. Not that she had the kinkiest imagination to begin with, but she had literally zero clue.

"It's not a sex toy, I promise."

She turned it over in her hand, revealing a sticker. Sensual aromatherapy bath bomb. "Oh."

"I'm going for a self-care, self-love kind of vibe. As well as stuff to help couples have more fun and be more adventurous, obviously."

"Really?" It was a pretty brilliant angle. Made the store more accessible to people who had hang-ups about going into a place that was exclusively about sex.

Casey shrugged. "I needed something I could put in the window display, right?"

A snort of laugher escaped, mostly because despite their conversation at the planning meeting, she'd had visions of dildos and butt plugs displayed like cupcakes or shoes or any of the other items the shops on their block sold. "When you put it that way."

"Anyway, we're open. Soft open for now, with more of a grand opening Black Friday. I wanted to let you know."

"That was fast." And pretty damn impressive, considering she'd gotten the permits only a couple of weeks ago.

"I want to make the most of the holiday rush. I hear that's peak retail time." Casey shrugged again, more humble than indecisive.

"Do you know about the Christmas market?" Tara asked.

"Kind of?" Casey made a face. "Kit was trying to explain them, but she's been busy on another project and most of her memories were limited to Christmas lights and hot chocolate."

Tara tilted her head back and forth. "Not a complete picture, but not inaccurate, either."

"Care to enlighten me?"

She could leave Casey to fend for herself. But the more she thought about it, the more she realized she'd rather land on Casey's side of this whole situation than Gary Jenkins's. And walking Casey through how the holiday markets worked would probably help her navigate them without any more scandal than she had on her hands already. "Sure."

"You don't sound sure." Casey raised a brow, and Tara would swear it was flirty and not just teasing.

"Do you have time now or do you need to be at your shop?" She lifted her hands to make air quotes but stopped herself in time.

"My friend Natalia is there. She offered to help me out until I can hire people." Casey blew out a breath. "And train them."

Questions and bits of business advice swirled in Tara's mind, but she shoved them squarely to the realm of none of her business. She wanted to prevent Casey from drawing negative attention—to her shop and, by extension, Tara's. That didn't mean she needed to be Casey's business coach. "Okay, let's grab a seat."

Casey angled her head toward the case. "Mind if I have a snack while we chat?"

"Go right ahead."

Casey went to the counter and Shawn boxed up a red velvet for her.

"That one's on the house," Tara called before Shawn could ring it up.

That earned her a look of suspicion from Shawn and one of surprise from Casey. She'd deal with Shawn later. For now, she gestured to one of the little café tables they'd tucked around the perimeter of the shop and took a seat.

"Thank you for this." Casey pointed to the box before opening it. "I didn't have lunch and I'm seriously running on fumes."

She'd been guilty of that a few times, though less often since moving home. "They don't pack much protein, but they'll get you through."

"I'll take it." Casey took a bite and let out a groan. "Every time. I keep thinking I'm used to how good they are, and they get me every damn time."

Hard to argue with compliments like that. "So, the market."

Casey licked frosting from her thumb. "Yes. Tell me everything."

"Well, they start tomorrow and run every weekend until New Year."

Casey nodded. "Gotcha."

"There are stalls set up in the town square. Crafts, gifts, that sort of thing. Twinkle lights and Christmas music. We have a booth where we sell cupcakes, coffee, and hot chocolate. Local businesses pass out fliers and coupons and stuff." It was great for business but managed to be a lot of fun, too.

"Wow," Casey said.

"Yeah, the whole town gets into it. And lots of people come in from out of town. They can ski during the day or visit the spa or shop. Then shop some more and pretend they're in a Hallmark movie."

Casey laughed. "Sounds like one."

"Oh, and there's a contest for the best window display."

"Contest?" Casey looked intrigued at the prospect.

"Yeah. All the businesses downtown decorate their windows. Some are super basic, just so their owners can say they participated. Others go all-out."

Casey folded her arms and leaned forward, resting them on the table and encroaching ever so slightly into Tara's personal space. "Let me guess. You go all out."

She mimicked the gesture, ignoring the way Casey's woodsy cologne crept into her senses and threatened to addle her brain. "I've been back at the shop for three Christmases and we've won the last two."

"I see. So, you want me to enter so you can beat me and then gloat about it." Casey leaned back and gave a knowing nod.

She could be indignant. But Shawn's endless commentary about her being uptight and, lately, a prude caught up with her. She lifted her chin. "Scared of a little friendly competition?"

"Not in the least. You?"

Why did it feel like they were flirting? "I told you about it, didn't I?"

Casey considered. "I guess that means it's on."

Sort of like that sense they were flirting, Tara couldn't help but feel like she'd signed herself up for way more than a battle of window displays. But she couldn't back out now. Perhaps more importantly, she didn't want to. She stuck out her hand. "May the best window win."

Casey accepted the handshake but leaned in once again. She whispered, "I'm pretty sure it's going to be you. And I'm okay with that."

"I hope you'll at least try to give me a run for my money." Tara smirked, wondering what the hell had gotten into her. Oh, and trying to ignore the jolt of electricity at the brush of Casey's palm against hers.

"Promise." Casey stood. "I really should get back. Thanks for the crash course, and the cupcake."

She stood as well. "I'll be expecting some stiff competition. It won't be satisfying to beat you otherwise."

Casey offered a friendly salute, bought two cupcakes for Natalia, and left. Tara turned her attention to Shawn, who hadn't been subtle about eavesdropping. "That was chummy," Shawn said.

"Isn't that what you wanted?" she countered.

Shawn shrugged. "I would have settled for friendly and professional, but you do you."

"I was friendly and professional." Tara pouted.

"You were almost in her lap."

"That's completely inappropriate and categorically untrue." She wanted to stomp her foot but resisted. How did Shawn always manage to bring that out in her?

"Not inappropriate after she brought you a sex present."

Tara narrowed her gaze and shook the bag. "It's not a sex present."

"Whoa, there, now. Did I walk into the wrong shop?" The voice—that sounded alarmingly like Grandpa—came from behind her.

She spun around and, sure enough, her grandfather stood there, sporting a full scowl. "No, Grandpa."

"Our new neighbor came over with a gift for Tara," Shawn offered unhelpfully.

"It's a bath bomb." Since Grandpa now looked confused as well as irritated, she added, "Like bath salts, but it's a ball you drop in and it gets fizzy."

"That's kinda cool," Shawn said.

"Damn sex shop. I've got Gary Jenkins chewing my ear off every day about how it's driving away tourists just as the Christmas market kicks off." He shook his head. "It's a nuisance."

"Are you talking about the store or Gary?" She shouldn't goad him, but she couldn't seem to help it. He sounded like a whiny boomer more than the sort of mayor looking out for the business interests of Rocky Springs.

"Both." He let out a harrumph.

"Well, we've had customers already in town for the market," Shawn said.

"And Casey's shop is open, so they must not be that scared after all."

Grandpa jabbed a finger on the counter. "I don't expect you to rally with the blowhards, but could you not rally for the other side, either? Looks bad."

Shawn looked ready to argue, but Tara could appreciate the importance of keeping up appearances. "We're Switzerland. But with cupcakes."

Grandpa grumbled but managed to pick out half a dozen cupcakes while he did it. He went on his way and Tara glanced at her watch. What should have been twenty minutes of helping Shawn with the afternoon rush had turned into more than an hour away from the kitchen. "I need to get frosting if I want to be out of here before nine."

"Hot date?"

"Jesus Christ. I was explaining how the Christmas market worked. I'm trying to be nice, not get in her pants. There's no date, hot or otherwise."

"Uh, I was talking about your bath fizz thingy. Not the woman who gave it to you. But thanks for telling me exactly where your mind is."

She huffed. "You are so annoying sometimes."

Instead of waiting for a reply, she pushed through the door into the kitchen. It didn't keep Shawn's retort from following her, though. "I learned from the best."

Chapter Eight

The flyer for the Sweet Spot had no sooner left Casey's hand than she heard the rip. It took her a moment to place the man standing in front of her. Cowboy hat, graying reddish beard, low-slung faded blue jeans paired with a faded jean jacket, and a hard look in his narrowed eyes. *Gary Jenkins.* The same asshole from the town hall meeting who'd tried to whip up a mob to close her shop before it'd even opened.

"This is not the time or the place, missy."

"I think you mean 'nor.'" The words slipped out before she could stop them. "The expression goes, 'this is neither the time, nor the place.' But I get what you were going for." Casey flashed a smile despite how her pulse raced. What was she doing engaging with him? "And I'm Casey. Definitely not Missy. You're Gary Jenkins, right?"

He didn't answer, but he seemed to try to stand taller, pulling back his shoulders and jutting his chin. He was a good two inches shorter, but the advantage of height didn't help her psyche much. She hated confrontation. Forcing herself not to turn and run, she held out her hand. He only grunted in response.

"You don't do handshakes. That's cool. Fewer germs." She pulled back her hand, hating the guy even more for making her feel like she had to win him over. She had no desire to do that—and from the sneering look on his face she'd never succeed anyway. What she needed was to diffuse the situation before the crowd around them paid him any attention. Which would be a lot easier if her anxiety hadn't kicked into high gear and every nerve wasn't screaming for her to meekly retreat.

She tried to keep her voice even as she said, "I've, uh, seen your family values flyers around town. I understand you don't like sex shops in general, but my store is different. And I think if you give it a chance, you'll see me being here will be a good thing for Rocky Springs. Honestly, I fully support family values. Love, respect—"

"You can stop your little speech." His jaw clenched as he jabbed a finger at her stack of flyers. "This filth doesn't belong in Rocky Springs."

She tried to ignore how much her hands were shaking and how his breath smelled like something had curled up and died in his mouth. When he jabbed at the flyers again, she took a step back, the retort she'd been working on in her head—about how Christmas was the perfect season for a bath bomb—floundering before the words made it past her lips.

"You have no business handing out anything at the Christmas market," he said, voice rising. He took another step toward her. "You and your sex shop have no business being here, and the sooner you get back to California with this trash—"

"Gary. Hi!"

Gary stopped mid-sentence, clearly surprised to see Tara step right up to him. She'd appeared out of nowhere with an open box of cupcakes.

"I don't mean to interrupt you two networking, but I bumped into Anna and she was telling me Bruce got a scholarship for his senior year up at CSU. That's amazing news. I'm sure you're proud. It's no surprise, of course. He always was a smart kid."

The scowl on Gary's face had morphed to a look of befuddlement, and it was several seconds later before he muttered, "Oh, yeah. Bruce. He's doing great."

"Want a cupcake to celebrate? On the house, of course." Tara made it sound like they were best friends.

How could Tara be so friendly to this asshole? Casey's pulse pounded in her ears when Tara's eyes lit on hers. She gripped her flyers tighter, willing the flood of emotions not to show on her face. She wanted to tell Tara that she sucked for taking Gary's side. But truthfully, she was the one who sucked. At any whisper of confrontation, her damn anxiety overwhelmed her. There was no chance at coming out on top in an argument when she could hardly swallow, much less manage speech.

Gary's voice punched through her thoughts. "See, this is a family town and this is exactly why—"

"Gary," Tara interrupted him, placing a hand on his arm. "I know how you feel, but I think we can all agree on not wanting a scene at the opening market."

Casey's anger flashed hot. Tara full-on siding with Gary Jenkins right in front of her was too much. She'd thought she'd nearly won over Tara. Maybe not enough to ask her out but at least to forge a friendship. And certainly she'd expected Tara to be civil and maybe even supportive in public. Apparently not. Well, screw Tara. And screw Gary Jenkins.

Without bothering to remove herself gracefully from the conversation, she simply turned and started walking. Fast, then faster. She didn't pay attention to anything more than trying not to walk straight into anyone.

What was she thinking moving to a little mountain town? Of course people here would be close-minded. Kit had warned her she was taking a risk and she'd ignored the warning, convinced she could win people over. Tara was proof that wasn't happening.

She came to the edge of the square, and the woman working the hot apple cider booth caught her gaze. Earlier that morning, the woman had offered encouragement when she'd heard it was a new business Casey was flyering for—but then she'd seen the store flyers. Now her expression was decidedly unfriendly.

At least the older lesbian couple with the table of crocheted kittens and puppies gave her a friendly wave. She'd introduced herself to them earlier and now forced herself to smile and wave back. But she couldn't handle talking to anyone now. She weaved past a family with a screaming toddler and broke into a jog as soon as she'd cleared the cordoned-off pedestrian-only zone.

Icy air stung her lungs as she covered the next block at a full run. For the past month, she'd busted her ass getting the store ready. She'd been happy to work fourteen-hour days, only taking breaks to work out or read or occasionally eat. It was a thrill opening the boxes of items she'd ordered and a fun game deciding where to place everything.

And she'd felt a flare of pride when the books on relationships and kink and self-love steadily lined the shelves alongside the erotica she'd perused each evening.

Then the first customer had walked in the door. A quiet gray-haired lady with deep lines around her eyes like she'd spent a lot of time squinting at the world. When the lady confessed to wanting a vibrator—her very first vibrator—Casey wanted to hug her. She resisted, barely, and managed to ring her up without too much fanfare. She did throw in a free bottle of personal lubricant because how could she not? The lady likely would have bolted if Casey had admitted how excited she'd been to make the sale.

More customers had filtered in throughout the day and, while she hadn't made much money, each sale felt like a promise of more to come. And the store had only been open a week. Already she'd had two customers who'd mentioned they'd been referred by friends and several times she'd overheard someone happily remark how the store wasn't at all what they'd expected of a sex shop.

She took pride in all those things, and the days at the store didn't feel long. It was exciting. Like hosting an open house party. She wanted to stand on the sidewalk waving people in and then wanted to befriend anyone courageous enough to walk through the doors. Likely the excitement wouldn't last, but every hour she'd lost herself working in the store was one more hour of distance from the dumpster fire that had been her life in LA.

She reached the store and finally slowed her steps. Since she'd yet to hire anyone, she had to close the store whenever she left, so she dug around in her pocket for the keys. *When* suddenly felt like *if* on the subject of hiring someone. Could she even make it a year in this town?

As much as she wanted to lock the door behind her and hide, she switched on the lights and flipped the sign to open. The space was warm compared to the snow-dusted sidewalk, and after all the time she'd spent getting things ready, the shop felt like home. More than the house she'd rented for sure. And she loved how she had everything arranged and how clean and professional things looked. Which did not mean she'd soon have a booming business. Especially not with Gary Jenkins and Tara McCoy plotting her downfall. She sank down on the stool behind the counter and dropped her head in her hands.

Reality was, she'd likely fail as a shopkeeper in Rocky Springs. Depressing but true. She'd read the statistics of how many businesses opened their doors and shuttered them in the same year. And yet here she was—facing down an entire town that hated her to sell flavored lube and bath bombs. Oh, and sex toys.

She pulled out her phone and tapped out a text to Natalia. *I don't think I'm tough enough to make it here.* She stared at the words for a long moment before hitting send.

Natalia texted back a screenshot of a Pavia post. *Your ex is on another rampage.* A moment later, Natalia sent another screenshot with more crap Pavia was posting about her and the following text: *You want to come back to this?*

No. She really didn't. *I could have used my savings to spend a year touring Europe. I've always wanted to check out the Louvre.*

Natalia sent an eye roll emoji. *You are literally next door to the best cupcake bakery in the entire universe. Who needs a museum in Paris?*

Natalia hadn't let up about how much she loved Coy Cupcakes. *Baker girl hates my guts.* "Baker girl" was how Natalia had referred to Tara after teasing Casey for liking her.

Ten bucks says it's foreplay. I know chemistry when I see it.

Casey might have believed Natalia earlier, but after seeing Tara with Gary Jenkins, there was no chance Tara was into her. And she wasn't all that interested herself.

The bell over the door jingled and she looked up from her phone. Tara stood in the doorway, not coming in but simply holding open the door. "Hey. I wasn't sure you'd be open."

"I'm not."

Tara glanced at the door and pointed to the "Open" sign.

"Yeah. Well. I'm not open." Casey stood but then wasn't sure what to do. She felt childish lying about something dumb, but she didn't want to talk to Tara.

"Want me to flip your sign to closed? Or are you open for anyone but me?"

Casey dropped her chin.

"Got it. Okay." Tara took a step back, as if to leave but then paused. "Gary Jenkins needed to shut the hell up. That's why I intervened. I'm sorry if it was inappropriate."

Casey came around to the front of the counter and folded her arms. "You only wanted Jenkins to shut up so there wouldn't be a scene at the market."

Tara's lips pressed together. She held Casey's gaze. "No. Not only that."

Casey shook her head. "Whatever. If you want to shop here, come on in. I guess I can be open."

Tara hung back for a moment, then sighed and walked in, letting the door close with a jingle behind her. "I've been wanting to check your place out now that you've got everything set up."

"Who's running the cupcake stand?"

"Shawn."

"What about the bakery?"

"We hire some temporary help. Plus my mom helps out for the market." Tara walked over to the shelf filled with books, turning her back to Casey.

Why was she even here? Casey wanted to ask and yet didn't. She didn't want to pretend to be nice to Tara McCoy. She'd tried to be friends already.

Tara moved from the books to the display of harnesses, biting the edge of her lip as she eyed the half mannequin suited up with the leather harness and a cock. Casey picked up the flyers she'd thrown across the counter when she'd come in earlier and tried to ignore Tara's presence. She didn't succeed, but Tara didn't need to know that. If she'd learned anything in the last six months, it was her own capacity for faking it.

Chapter Nine

Tara perused the shelves, torn between genuine curiosity about the titles Casey had chosen to stock and wanting to diffuse the tension that practically radiated from her. The latter won out, if for no other reason than being angrily ignored didn't make for an ideal shopping experience. She turned. "Gary is an asshole and a hypocrite."

She'd expected Casey to soften at the declaration, but her irritation merely took on an edge of suspicion. "And yet you couldn't wait to slather him with compliments and attention."

Tara lifted a hand. "Could we not use the word slather in any sentence that refers to Gary Jenkins? Those are mental images I do not need."

Casey cracked a smile for the briefest of moments before turning stony again. "But that's exactly what you did. And made it clear to him whose side you were on."

"Is that what you think?" she asked.

"It's what I saw."

Was she serious with that? "Jesus, Casey. I was trying to prevent a fistfight in the middle of the Christmas market. You think Gary and his crew are bad for your business? Try getting into a brawl fifty feet from photos with Santa."

Casey frowned. "I wouldn't have gotten into a fistfight."

"Could have fooled me."

"I don't fight." Casey shook her head. "I'm more of a flight or a freeze kind of person."

Shawn was like that. Tara decidedly was not. "Still. It seemed like a distraction was the way to go. And, for the record, I complimented his kid, not him."

Casey's shoulders slumped, though it felt more like a sign of defeat than letting her defenses down. "Okay."

It hit her. "You think I was taking his side."

"That's sure how it felt."

Tara jabbed a finger in her direction. "I'll have you know that not wanting to be anything like Gary is the main reason I decided to be cool about your store."

Casey made a face. "Thank you?"

"Look, we got off on the wrong foot. I'm trying really hard to make Coy Cupcakes more than the quaint little cupcake shop that caters to tourists and local high schoolers. When I heard what kind of shop you were planning to open, it felt like a threat to that, and I overreacted." She swallowed, knowing that wasn't enough. "I'm sorry."

"You don't have to apologize."

"I want to." She spread her arms. "And I was wrong. This is a nice shop. Not seedy at all."

Casey cracked a smile again, but this one held. "Thank you."

"Besides, Gary of all people has no business talking about family values." A fact he could stand to be reminded of more often.

"What do you mean?" Casey asked.

"Oh, my God. You don't know." Revelations were dropping left and right tonight.

"Know what?"

Tara glanced at her watch and did some quick calculations. "I've got to get back to the market. What are you doing after it closes?"

"Besides going home and falling face first into bed, you mean?"

Casey seemed to be joking but not, which Tara could appreciate. "Could I convince you to stay up a little longer? Maybe we could grab a drink later?" The expression on Casey's face changed and she realized she'd basically asked Casey out. Before Casey could respond, she quickly added, "Only because I think there's some things you should know about Gary if you're getting pulled into fights with him—and I don't have time to give the full story right now."

"Oh. Okay. Right." Casey nodded like she was recalibrating the drink offer. "I appreciate you wanting to help. I probably need all the inside scoop I can get. Tell me when and where and I'll be there."

❖

Tara walked into the Keg just after nine. Small groups and couples huddled at the bar or in the cozy booths along the far wall, warming up from an evening at the market or grabbing a late dinner. She scanned the room and found Casey already tucked into one of the booths with a pint of beer in front of her. She stopped at the bar long enough to snag one of her own and made her way over.

"I hope you haven't been waiting too long," she said.

Casey smiled. "Only a few minutes. But I didn't want to be one of those people drinking alone at the bar."

She slipped off her coat and slid in opposite Casey. "Are you afraid people will judge you or try to talk to you?"

Casey's chuckle had a rueful quality to it. "Yes."

"Thanks for making your day a little longer for me."

Casey nodded but didn't say anything.

"I want to tell you some stuff about Gary, but I want to clear the air between us, too." Because she wanted Casey to understand why she had so much at stake. Not to justify her behavior, exactly, but so Casey would see where she was coming from.

"You already apologized. You don't need to again."

"Not apologizing. Just..." Tara blew out a breath. "I get the feeling you coming to Rocky Springs is about wanting a fresh start."

Casey tensed.

"You don't need to explain, but I overheard enough about who your ex is to get an idea. The point is, the cupcake shop is kind of that for me."

"I thought it was the family business."

Since her throat had gone dry at the prospect of baring her soul, she took a long sip of the winter ale in front of her. "It is. And one I thought I wanted nothing to do with. But after making a big show of running off to New York to make a name for myself, I realized the idea was better than the reality."

"That doesn't sound so bad."

"It wasn't, since coming back was what I wanted. But it was humbling, too. A lot of people decided I came running home because I couldn't cut it, and they didn't hesitate to say so."

"I'm sorry." Casey reached across the table but seemed to catch herself and pulled back without making contact. "People suck."

Tara wanted to reach out and grab her hand, to assure Casey the touch would be welcome. But they were here to talk business, not get cozy. "They do. Turning the bakery into something more than a sleepy cupcake shop isn't about sticking it to them, but I'd be lying if I said that wasn't part of it. Like I said. I have big plans, and I need them to work."

"Well, if it's any consolation, I need this store to work. Going back to my old life is not an option." Casey studied her beer like it was the most fascinating thing ever.

"Can I ask why? Or is that too personal?"

Casey seemed to hesitate. "It's mostly because of my ex and I doubt you want to hear that story." She paused. "The truth is I don't want to look as pathetic as that whole saga makes me seem."

She softened at Casey's sad smile. "Part of why I ended up hating New York was falling for someone who had no interest in being there when I needed her. Probably not as devastating as your breakup, but it made me feel like a fool."

"I get the part about being made to feel like a fool." Casey regarded her with a look of understanding that felt like empathy more than pity.

"Probably I should have known better. But she was hot and knew how to stroke my ego. At least at first."

Casey let out a guffaw, but instead of reining it in, she continued to laugh. "Sorry. I just…that's exactly what happened to me, and I've never had anyone express it so succinctly. Unfortunately, she was also famous so our breakup was tabloid newsworthy."

"Who was your ex?"

Casey made a face. "Pavia Rossini. Maybe you haven't heard of her?"

She could tell Casey was hoping the answer was no. But was there anyone with internet access and even a casual social media presence who didn't know of Pavia Rossini? "I don't keep up with the tabloids, but I have heard of Pavia."

"Most everyone has—which is exactly Pavia's goal." Casey blew out a breath. "She got famous on the internet but it wasn't enough. She wanted a Hollywood career too. Based on who my parents are, she decided I was her best shot at landing a big break."

Tara might have heard of Pavia Rossini, but she didn't put a lot of stock in celebrity gossip. Which meant whatever had blown up or fallen out was squarely off her radar. Casey's last name pinged in her mind. *Stevens*. Ordinary enough not to have made her think twice about it when she'd heard it the first time. But now… "Wait. Who are your parents?"

Casey blew out a breath again, like she already regretted opening the can of worms. "Lee and Bob Stevens. The same ones you've probably heard about."

Film producers. Well, producers and directors. A Hollywood power couple if there ever was one. "Oh, wow."

"Yeah." Casey nodded slowly. "Anyway, Pavia pursued me. She was hot and heavy in the beginning. And since I was the first woman she'd ever been with publicly, it only added to the sensationalism of it all. We eloped after six months, and my parents gave her a part in one of their projects. Turns out she's a pretty terrible actress."

Tara cringed, unable to stop herself. "And then what?"

"The movie flopped and got swept under the rug before it did too much damage to the studio's reputation. Pavia was pissed. Blamed the director—who thankfully wasn't my mom. She'd given the project to one of her friends because she didn't really like the script, but she thought it would appeal to Pavia's fans and do well with that demographic." Casey paused and took a sip of her beer. "Then my dad pulled the purse strings tight midway through production. I think he realized what a disaster he had on his hands. He could have sent the movie right to a streaming service but…"

"But Pavia Rossini was starring in it."

"Exactly."

"That's really intense."

Casey nodded. "I thought so, too. And I felt bad for Pavia. Until she decided I tanked her career on purpose. She said I felt threatened and sabotaged things—like I convinced my mom not to direct the film and got my dad to cut the budget. Anyway. She decided divorcing me and turning it into a scandal would be her next starring role."

"Oh. Wow." She let the word drag, scrambling for something more meaningful to say.

"My parents don't blame me, but they've washed their hands of the whole thing, so it's Pavia Rossini and her rabid fans against the entitled daughter of the Stevens' power team who used her name and family influence to control and undermine Pavia's career." For the first time since they'd started talking, a hint of bitterness came through. Which Tara would have considered totally justified, but Casey seemed to catch herself and pull back. "So that's my sad story and why I needed to get the fuck out of LA."

Tara might not be known for being the most empathetic person, but it was impossible not to feel Casey's plight. Even if she was getting only Casey's side of the story, she'd seen and heard enough of Pavia Rossini not to doubt for a second she was an egomaniacal sociopath. "All right, then. You definitely win the sad sack game."

Casey lifted her glass. "A dubious honor but thank you."

Tara clinked hers to it and took a long drink of beer, debating whether to let it be or press on. For better or worse, letting things be wasn't her nature. "Can I ask you one thing? It's a little personal."

"I don't imagine it's any more personal than what's being said about me on social media these days," Casey said with more resignation than anything else.

"Why a sex shop?" It wasn't any of her business, but since she couldn't fathom doing that sort of thing herself, she couldn't shake the niggling curiosity.

Casey stared at the ceiling, as though having her own debate about whether to answer.

"You don't have to tell me."

"Because I've always thought sex shops were great but skewed male and hetero and, to use your word, seedy. And I wanted to do something different."

Tara nodded. From what she'd seen of the shop that evening, Casey was doing exactly that. "That's fair."

When Casey made eye contact again, the indecision had been replaced by a rueful smile. "And because Pavia was completely boring in bed and being with her was the least sexually satisfying relationship of my life. Supporting couples looking to expand their sex lives and helping people embrace taking care of their own sexual needs felt like a giant f-you to that."

It was Tara's turn to laugh. "When you put it that way, I'm sorry I was ever against it."

"Now she tells me." Casey rolled her eyes.

"Can I ask you something else?"

Casey spread her hands. "There's not much left to tell."

"Why didn't you fight back? Stick around and tell your version of the story?" She sure as hell would have had the tables been turned.

"I hate confrontation. It literally makes me feel like I'm on the cusp of a panic attack and will either pass out or puke. You know that fight-or-flight thing?"

She nodded, recalling what Casey had said about the earlier confrontation with Gary Jenkins. "Where you freeze instead?"

"Exactly. But freezing is an upgrade. I used to possum."

"Possum?"

"Play dead and hope it goes away."

Tara was officially won over to Casey's side—and Casey didn't even seem to be trying. Just opening up and being honest, something Tara realized she needed more than anything. "So. Speaking of things you hope will go away…"

"Are we going to talk about Gary Jenkins and his family values crusade now?"

She nodded. "There are things you need to know."

"Okay." Casey looked reluctantly ready to hear what she had to say. "Probably a better topic than the pathetic shambles of my life."

"Your life isn't pathetic," Tara said, perhaps more emphatically than the situation called for.

Casey rocked her head. "That's something we can argue about another time. Tell me about Gary."

"Do you want the long version or the short version?" Neither were great.

"Hmm. Let's go for short. Because a little schadenfreude is great, but a lot isn't good for me."

Tara smirked. "You're a better person than I am."

Casey mirrored the gesture. "Maybe."

A server passed with a massive plate of nachos, and Casey's eyes followed. Tara lifted a finger. "Have you eaten today?"

Casey shook her head.

"You want some of those?"

"I thought you'd never ask."

She flagged the server over and put in an order, then turned her attention back to Casey. "Gary Jenkins slept with a woman who worked at his store and was half his age. And when she turned up pregnant, he pressured her to have an abortion. Which was all well and good until one of his family values cronies spied her going into the Planned Parenthood clinic and he fired her publicly."

Casey blanched. "He didn't."

"He did. Only his wife knew about the affair and outed him. They separated for a while, but then got back together. And he's got enough pull that the super conservative crowd took him back into the fold as soon as that happened. Everyone knows about the whole thing but no one talks about it. It's gross. And, unfortunately, things like that happen a lot in Rocky Springs—people sweeping things under the rug for some folks and passing judgment on everyone else."

Casey shook her head. "That sort of thing goes down no matter where you are."

"Maybe. Only everyone acts like this town is perfect. And I have to pretend it is, too, because my grandpa is the mayor." Which made it hard to stand up for what she actually believed in.

"Well, thank you for telling me. It'll make it easier not to take his bullying to heart."

She waited a beat, but Casey didn't continue. "Or you could tell him you know what he's really like. Threaten to fight fire with fire."

"No thanks." Casey visibly shrunk in on herself. "I don't fight back. And I sure as hell don't hurl threats."

"Who said anything about hurling? You can be subtle. You can do it in a letter, even. Just a friendly reminder about people who live in glass houses." Which wouldn't be as fun as taking Gary down a few notches but would likely get him to lay off a little.

"I don't know." Casey looked at her hands, clearly uncomfortable.

Their nachos arrived, giving Tara a moment to process Casey's point of view. When the server had cleared from earshot, she gave Casey a pointed look. "What you decide to do is your business. But at the very least, don't take anything he says personally."

Casey, who'd scooped up a particularly loaded chip, set it on the little saucer in front of her. "I won't. And thank you. It helps to know the whole story."

Tara chewed her bottom lip before picking up a chip of her own. "Thanks for telling me yours."

CHAPTER TEN

The bar had mostly emptied out by eleven. Casey still wasn't used to how early the town went to sleep. Then again, as she zipped up her coat and stepped outside, ice crystals swirling in the air, she couldn't help thinking how nice it would be back at her place with a fire going and a blanket to snuggle under. Having company would make it even nicer.

Tara wrapped a scarf around her neck before joining her on the sidewalk. Streetlamps lit the street, but aside from the Keg, no other businesses were open and no cars drove past. "I'm not sure how long it will take me to get used to how quiet it is here."

"Just wait for our first real snow day. Everything shuts down and it's so quiet. Even downtown." Tara had an almost dreamy look as she gazed up at the ice crystals glinting in the halo of the streetlight.

"I take it you like those days?" Casey fought back a shiver, pulling her zipper higher to close off the exposed part of her neck.

"That coat of yours would probably be fine for a rainy day in California, but you're going to need something warmer here. And, yes, I love snow days. You know we'll have months where the temperature never gets above freezing? And plenty of days where the high is in the negatives."

"I can handle the cold. I like it actually."

"Mmhmm. California cold is not the same as Colorado cold. And this isn't cold yet." Tara winked at Casey. "We'll see how you feel about the cold in January."

"Did you mean to wink at me?" Casey grinned, enjoying the rush of color on Tara's cheeks.

"I was making a point about how your LA ass is going to be in for a rude awakening."

After swapping stories about failed relationships, they'd spent the rest of the time at the bar talking about business, with Tara offering advice on what to expect when tourist season hit. Despite the innocuous conversation, it'd been impossible not to notice how the temperature seemed to spike whenever they accidentally brushed knees or shifted closer to say something.

Casey wasn't sure what to do about the tangle of feelings in her chest. One minute she wanted to relax and flirt, but the next she reminded herself she'd barely gotten over the shock of everything with Pavia. She had to focus on why she was in Rocky Springs—to build a life for herself on her own. Latching on to the first available woman who seemed vaguely interested would only be a distraction. And she still didn't know for sure how much of Tara's interest was making sure the Sweet Spot didn't drive away customers from Coy Cupcakes.

Casey pointed to a sign in the candle shop next door. *Display coming! Hold your breath.* "About that window display contest. Want to give me some pointers, or are you worried anything you tell me could help me win?"

"I'm not worried."

Casey laughed. "I love the confidence."

"Sometimes I have a reason to be confident." Tara cleared her throat. "Anyway, it's a big thing around here. Everyone decorates their windows and then Pete from the *Bulletin* oversees the judging."

The *Bulletin* was the local paper. Casey hadn't met Pete, but she'd heard his name and figured if he was on a first-name basis with other shop owners, it meant she had no chance of winning him or any of the other judges over. "Is it required to participate?"

"No." Tara's brow bunched. "But it's fun? And I thought you liked friendly competition."

"I do but...Well, I'm realizing decorating my window will call more attention to my business and might make more locals hate me. Plus, I'm guaranteed to lose."

Tara stopped walking and faced Casey. "You probably will lose. I hate to say it but it's true."

"Because of this Pete guy from the *Bulletin*? Is he friends with Gary Jenkins?"

"No. Pete hates Gary Jenkins." Tara paused, seeming to decide how to answer. "Voting is technically open to anyone, but the women over at the Rotary Club make up most of the voters."

"And these women don't like my kind of shop?"

Tara bit the edge of her lip. "Well…"

"Got it."

"That doesn't mean you shouldn't enter the contest. Participating is good for business—for everyone's business because it's the Christmas vibe that brings the tourists in—and the decorating can be fun even if you don't win." Tara looked past Casey and motioned to the jewelry shop behind them. "Look, Bonnie and Rick have already started."

Two elves were positioned in the window, one down on his knee holding up a velvet box with a ring, the other clasping her hand to her chest. "That's kind of cute."

"Right? And it gets so much better. In a week, that window will be filled with bejeweled elves. Some of them down on their knees, some of them kissing, some of them hiding under a tree like they're trying not to get caught…"

Casey had been looking at the window, but she turned back to Tara. "So elves in compromising positions are fair game for this contest?"

Tara laughed, then clapped her hand against her mouth as she laughed harder.

"You're getting the same visual I am, aren't you?"

Tara sobered enough to swat Casey's arm. "You're terrible. No elves allowed in the sex shop window."

"Why not? They clearly can be kissing and on their knees if they have jewelry." Casey motioned to the window behind her, playing all innocence. "And I do sell some nice rings."

Tara threw up both hands. "No. Big no. If you have an elf in your store wearing a cock ring, you won't only have Gary Jenkins coming after you."

"They say there's no such thing as bad publicity. I don't think it's true, but I wouldn't mind more customers peeking in my window." Casey grinned.

"Just no." Tara shook her head, her eyes sparkling.

"Fine. No elves. I'd rather have Mrs. Claus anyway. You know she needs some quality toys for her alone time. While Santa's climbing down everyone else's chimney, you think she should be home knitting?"

"I don't know what to do with you." Tara smiled and Casey's chest tightened. She was always attractive but truly gorgeous when she smiled.

Tara continued, "Now you have me thinking about which vibrator Mrs. Claus would like."

"Maybe I can add that to the window display? A little sign with the question—"

"You better not. We'll both have trouble on our hands if I'm supporting you then."

Instead of another joking response, Casey found her gaze locked on Tara. "You on my side officially now?"

Tara gave a half shrug. "Yeah. I am. I've decided you succeeding could help both of us."

Tit for tat and nothing more? When Tara turned to start walking again, Casey fell into step, mind spinning. Had the evening been purely business for Tara? One minute she was certain they were flirting, but maybe Tara was only thinking of how her bakery could benefit. Considering how unsure she still was about her shop making it, and about how long she'd be staying in Rocky Springs, she didn't need to entertain the idea of dating anyway.

"I could help you come up with some ideas for your window," Tara said. "Coy Cupcakes has won the last two years. I know what the judges look for and like."

"You want to help me win?"

"Oh, I'm planning on winning." Tara's raised eyebrow threatened to have Casey whimpering. She had the perfect amount of sexy confidence. "It's not only about winning though. I want our whole block to look good so we draw more shoppers."

"Right." Casey recalibrated. Tara wasn't flirting. She was still thinking of her bakery. It would be extra work, but she didn't want to be the one undecorated window. And if Tara's offer was only to ensure both of their businesses looked better, she had no reason to say no. "What's your consult fee?"

"No fee. But if you want to give me a discount on something in your store, I won't say no."

Before she could ask what item Tara was thinking of, Tara stopped by a silver Subaru Outback. Everyone in Colorado seemed to have the same car.

"I could come by Monday morning if you want, after the weekend rush." Tara hit the button on her key fob and opened the door. "If you want a chance at second prize, you gotta get started early."

"Who says I'm not going for first?" Casey felt her heart jump up in her chest when Tara narrowed her eyes at her. "I mean, second place would be fine too."

"Mmhmm. That's better. I'm not helping you win, remember?"

She didn't want to outcompete Tara, but she loved ribbing Tara. And Tara wasn't rushing to leave. She leaned against the open doorway of her car as if hoping Casey would keep her longer.

"What time?" Tara asked.

It took Casey a moment to realize Tara was still thinking about the window display. "I'm usually at the store by ten. Would that work for you?"

Tara nodded, then seemed to reconsider. "I have a tasting scheduled with a bride at nine thirty. It might run late."

"Whenever you come will be fine. I have no other plans besides being at the shop." She had a feeling Tara would understand rather than find her boring because of it. After a morning workout, shower, and breakfast, she had nothing to do but to come to work. And the truth was, she'd never looked forward to work as much as she did now.

"Can I get your number? I'd feel better if I could shoot you a text if I'm running late."

Business only. Still, she couldn't help a rush of happy excitement when she gave Tara her number and felt her phone vibrate with Tara's text.

"Do you like the breakfast burritos from the Cantina?"

"You offering to pick one up for me?"

"I am." It seemed only fair to get breakfast. A store discount wasn't much in exchange for help with the display. At least, that was the excuse she used to stop her brain from asking if she knew what she was doing getting closer to Tara. No, she didn't. But she loved the zinging feeling in her body every time Tara looked at her, and her libido had officially come out of hiding.

"In that case, tell Juan I'll take my usual."

"You're on a first-name basis with the chef?"

"Juan is like a big brother," Tara said. "We went to school together and our families all know each other."

"I keep forgetting everyone knows everyone else in this place."

"Didn't know what you were getting into with a small town, did you?" Tara raised her eyebrow but laughed. "Night, Casey."

The words were simple but unexpectedly hit her square in the chest. She found herself smiling long after Tara drove off. Smiling as she walked the next block to her car, smiling as she drove home, and still smiling as she pulled into the driveway of her rental.

It wasn't until she flicked on the lights and spotted her reflection in the hall mirror that she realized how goofy she looked grinning with no one in sight. But she felt too lit up inside to care. It'd been too long since she'd had an easy fun night with a beautiful woman. No pressure, just talking and flirting. Of course it hadn't been a date. Again, she reminded herself, it had only been networking.

"But it was nice networking," she murmured, sticking out her tongue at her reflection.

Everything had been miserable and hard with Pavia for so long—months before the breakup—that she'd only felt relief when Pavia asked for a divorce. The circus that followed had been a shitstorm, and when she'd left LA vowing never to date again, she'd truly believed she wouldn't.

"Fortunately, Tara is nothing like Pavia," she said, feeling silly for having a conversation with her reflection but forging on anyway. "Which doesn't mean she'd want to date me. Or that I should date anyone anyway."

What she couldn't help thinking about, though, was that not only were Pavia and Tara completely different, she felt different around them. With Pavia, she'd always felt the need to be someone Pavia would approve of. With Tara, she didn't want to be anyone except herself. She also couldn't help smiling around Tara. She simply felt good with Tara and loved the energy that seemed to flow between their bodies.

Even when one of them pushed the other's buttons, there was this almost magnetic pull, and her heart had tripped over the way Tara had said "Night, Casey." The warmth in her voice like a precursor to a kiss.

"Except we weren't on a date." She sighed.

Maybe it was only networking, but the curtain had been officially pulled back on her past and Tara wasn't running the other direction. Tara knew who she was, knew who her parents were, knew her ex, knew about the scandal—and didn't seem to care one way or the other about any of it. For the first time, she had a chance at simply being herself with no preconceived expectations to live up to.

"All I have to do is make sure the Sweet Spot stays in business so I have an excuse to hang around town." And to hang around Tara.

CHAPTER ELEVEN

Tara hadn't planned to dive into her window display until Monday, but the Christmas market crowd had thinned by early afternoon Sunday. Not uncommon for the first weekend. More soft launch than full swing. And since she'd promised Casey help on Monday, anything she could get done would put her a step ahead of schedule.

She'd spent way too many hours coming up with the design and even more collecting and assembling the pieces. But that meant she only needed to arrange everything and boom—Cupcake Christmas Village. It would be her most intricate design to date and she had every confidence it would deliver another Rocky Springs Best Christmas Window ribbon.

She took a step back and folded her arms, tipping her head one way, then the other. She'd gotten the fleece arranged perfectly to look like a snowy mountain village and arranged a few of the buildings. A ski lift made of LEGOs and string would finish setting the scene. Then she could populate it with the felt cupcakes she'd made and decorated to look like frosted cartoon inhabitants, going about their holiday fun.

"What's wrong?" Shawn asked from behind the counter.

"Nothing." She made circles with her hands. "I'm considering."

"That sounds ominous."

Tara turned her full attention to Shawn. "You just don't like that I'm competitive about this. But if we don't do it to win, why do it at all?"

"Do you know how badly I want to psychoanalyze that statement?"

She resisted flipping her middle finger, if only because she'd given up the gesture since moving home. Well, mostly. But in the case of Shawn, it would only get her more digs and commentary on her anger issues. "There's nothing wrong with wanting to win. But I'll have you know I offered to help Casey with hers."

"Because you like her?"

"Because I'm competitive, but not heartless." And maybe a little bit of what Shawn had said. "Do you know I had to break up a confrontation between her and Gary Jenkins right in the middle of the market?" She could still see the look on Casey's face—fear and frustration mixed with something she couldn't quite put her finger on.

"Seriously? Did Casey deck him?"

"She was trying to reason with him. I stepped in and placated so he'd go away." Tara shook her head. "I'd have liked to deck him."

"I'm a legit pacifist and I'm with you on that one."

"Right? Anyway, I told her she should do her window so she could be seen as a joiner who's embracing town traditions and such. And then I offered to help because she seemed slightly terrified by the idea." Maybe not terrified, but dubious at least.

"That's very noble," Shawn said.

She shrugged. "Well, I did tell her I'd help her get second place."

"There's my sister."

Tara gave a fake laugh before hooking her thumb at the window behind her. "I'm going to go see how this looks from outside."

Shawn offered a salute in return and went back to assembling cupcake boxes. "Let me know when or if you want a second pair of eyes."

"I'll bring you in for fine-tuning," she said on her way out the door.

Outside, the weekend traffic had cleared, and the lull of Thanksgiving week was in full swing. Nearly all of the parking spaces sat empty, and the sidewalks were clear of pedestrian traffic. Mostly clear.

Standing out front of the Sweet Spot stood Casey. A Casey clad in jeans, hiking boots, and a puffer vest over plaid flannel. Like she belonged in Rocky Springs. Or maybe a queer L.L. Bean catalog. Was that redundant?

Tara ignored her own window—along with the flare of attraction—and walked over. What she found was Casey frowning at a completely empty display window. "Hi," she said.

Casey turned and the frown became a smile. "Hi."

"I was about to ask if you were getting a head start, but I see that's not the case."

Casey took a deep breath and blew it out in a huff. "I'm not sure this is a good idea."

For some reason, the comment made her feel more playful than worried. Which was weird for her but whatever. "I think you're going to have to be more specific. Are we talking about your outfit or competing against me in the window contest?"

Casey looked down at her clothes before looking at Tara, eyes wide. "What's wrong with my outfit?"

"Nothing. I was teasing you. It's great. Rugged but relaxed." *You look pretty damn hot, actually.*

Casey visibly relaxed. "Oh."

"Clearly, I didn't do it very well. The teasing, I mean." Sadly, that was more on brand for her than teasing in the first place.

"No, no. It's me."

She went for a dramatic eye roll. "If I had a dime for every time I heard the old 'it's not you, it's me' bit."

Casey scrubbed a hand over her face. "Sorry. I didn't mean—"

Tara put a hand on her arm, regretting all attempts to be clever or cute. "Hey, I was kidding. What's wrong?"

Casey's gaze went to Tara's hand and fixed there. Tara swallowed, wondering if Casey experienced the same jolt. Nothing to do with static electricity and everything to do with pheromones. The kind that had her thinking of skin on skin and her hands on places a whole lot more intimate. "Um."

As much as she didn't want to break the contact, she had a feeling something was up. And, well, they couldn't stand like that for the rest of the afternoon, could they? She reluctantly pulled her hand back and stuck both in the pockets of her chef pants. "Did something happen?"

"Oh, you know. Just another run-in with the town asshole."

Her pulse ticked up at the mere thought. And not at all in the way it had a moment before. "Seriously? Just now? What did he say?"

Casey glanced skyward. "Let's see. 'If you put a slutty Mrs. Claus in that window, so help me God, I will burn your store to the ground.'"

Forget racing pulse. Her head practically exploded with rage. "Did you tell him you'd be filing a police report for not only harassment but a physical threat?"

Casey shook her head. "I froze. Stood there like an idiot while he stared me down with his beady little eyes and breathed on me."

If it hadn't been such a serious situation, she might have laughed at the accuracy of the description. "Casey, you have to stand up to him."

"Like you did the other night?"

Tara winced. "Okay, I deserved that. But I thought you were going to send him a letter?"

"I am. It's been like a day. I haven't had a chance yet." Casey's voice took on a defensive edge.

"That's totally fair." She lifted both hands in concession. "It's just, I don't take kindly to threats. Especially the arson kind made against businesses literally attached to mine."

"You don't think he'd really…"

When Casey didn't continue, Tara shook her head. "No. He's a bully. Which means, at the end of the day, he's a coward."

Casey nodded. "Yeah."

"And for the record, I'm not only pissed because our buildings are attached. He's crossed a line that is not even a little bit okay."

That seemed to lighten the mood. "Thanks."

"For what it's worth, I think your letter will work. Especially if you allude to making his threat public, too. People might not like your shop, but they like vigilantes even less. At the very least, it'll tone things down."

"Okay." Casey seemed barely convinced at best.

"It will. I promise." Maybe a stretch, but she was all in on Team Sweet Spot at this point and prepared to go to the mat for it. "And you know what? I have an idea."

Casey's eyes narrowed. "Why does that worry me?"

She laughed, thoroughly pleased with herself. "Just trust me. Are you going to be here a while?"

"Okay and yes. And trust *me* when I say I have nowhere else to be."

She had a flash of Casey going home to an empty apartment—or house or wherever she lived—followed by one of Casey coming over to her place for dinner. And maybe more than dinner. She promptly shoved the thought aside. One thing at a time. "I'll be back in twenty."

She probably should have popped back into the shop and told Shawn where she was going. But she didn't want to waste the two minutes explaining or the ten Shawn would spend making fun of her for having a thing for Casey. Fortunately, the sun shone bright, and the temp had climbed to the mid-forties, so she jogged home and used the key she hid under the planter by the front door to let herself in. After a few minutes of rooting around, she found what she was looking for.

She jogged back to the shop with more enthusiasm than true stamina, arriving out of breath and with a stitch in her side. "Holy crap."

"Are you okay?" Casey asked, voice full of concern.

She pressed a hand to the soft spot between the bottom of her rib cage and her hip. "Not. A. Runner."

"Fair. I'm not sure if I should thank you or apologize for whatever is about to happen."

"Thank me." She straightened and handed the bag to Casey. "Victory."

Casey pulled out the dress—red velvet edged with white faux fur. "Is this a slutty Mrs. Claus outfit?"

She snatched the dress from Casey's grip and shook it out. "It's a non-frumpy and yet completely respectable Mrs. Claus outfit, thank you very much."

Casey lifted a hand. "I stand corrected."

"I was thinking you could use it for your display."

"Really?" Once again, Casey looked dubious.

"Totally. You could have a tree and stockings and maybe a little table with a cup of tea and some of your books. A cozy night, but with the promise of more to come. It could be a play on how sometimes naughty is nice. Or, like, whether you're stuffing your own stocking or waiting for Santa, we've got gifts any grownup would love."

Casey blinked at her a few times.

"Too much?"

"No, I'm wishing I had something to write on. Did you just come up with that?"

Heat rose in her cheeks, though she couldn't quite pinpoint why. "I mean, I've been thinking about it."

"You have?" Casey seemed delighted by the prospect.

"Well, no offense, but I was a little scared of what you'd come up with on your own."

Casey pouted and it was way cuter than it had any business being. "I wouldn't actually put any elves in compromising positions. Not in the public display at least."

A snort escaped. "Likely story."

"This is really great, though. Are you sure you don't mind me borrowing it?"

"Not at all." She held it out for Casey to take.

Casey did but continued to hold it up. "Do I want to know why you own this?"

She lifted one shoulder, trying to channel casual and flirty. "I may have rocked a Christmas pageant or two in my day."

Casey, to her credit, didn't look surprised. "And you don't need it this year?"

"I keep myself plenty busy with baking and our booth at the market." At least that's the excuse she used. Casey didn't need to know, but she absolutely hated anything even resembling public performance.

"That's too bad," Casey said.

"What makes you say that?"

Casey glanced from Tara to the dress and back. "I bet you look pretty damn good in red."

CHAPTER TWELVE

G ive me two seconds," Natalia said. "I have to flip someone off."

Typical Natalia. "Go right ahead. I've got to unlock the store anyway." Casey set down her phone along with the bag from the Cantina as she searched for her keys.

She stepped into the store just as Natalia came back on the line. "LA drivers. I swear. If I wasn't one of them, I could never deal. Anyway. Back to your baker girl."

"She's not my baker girl."

"Mmhmm. Sure. And you totally don't have a crush on her."

She couldn't outright deny Natalia's claim, but calling it a crush made it sound high school level. "It's more like an attraction that I'm not sure what to do with."

"That's a crush. Otherwise, you'd ask her out on a date because you clearly want to lick her cupcakes."

"Lick her cupcakes?" Casey groaned. "Can we not go there?"

"You know how much you want that frosting in your mouth. Mm. And the cake part is going to be so—"

"Don't say it." Casey laughed.

"Don't say what?" Natalia asked, all coy.

"You know the word."

"Moist? God, I love it moist."

"Stop. Please." When Natalia got going, her dirty mind surpassed all expectations.

"Fine. I'll be good and not say moist."

"I'm rolling my eyes at you." Casey flicked on the store lights and flipped the sign on the door to open. "The thing is, after everything with Pavia, I'm not sure it's a good idea for me to date anyone."

"Ever? Or are you going to give yourself a time frame?"

"I don't know." That was partly why she'd called Natalia after spending all night thinking of Tara.

"Taking some time would be good *if* you're going to work on your issues. Otherwise you're just moping."

"I'm not moping. I'm…" What was she doing? "I'm keeping myself busy so I don't have time to think."

"So your plan is to work so much you can pretend you don't have issues?" Natalia sighed. "I'm pretty sure you tried that last time. Remember how it turned out?"

"The wedding or the divorce?" Natalia knew there'd been problems from the very beginning of her relationship with Pavia. Problems she hadn't wanted to address for fear of losing Pavia. The dumpster fire she'd ended up with made that fear laughable.

"We could start with either. You fucked up royally on both accounts."

She couldn't help smiling. Only Natalia made her feel loved and accepted while pointing out her glaring failures.

"Since you aren't working on your issues," Natalia continued. "My vote is you get laid. Baker girl is hot. If she loaned you a sexy Mrs. Claus outfit—and made a point of telling you she'd worn it—she's interested."

"The Mrs. Claus outfit is for this window contest thing and I'm not sure, but she might only be helping me because it helps her store too." That thought had circled in Casey's mind along with the memory of Tara's hand on her arm. Things didn't feel one-sided, but what was Tara's goal? She half-hated that the question even occurred to her and yet everyone had something they wanted.

"Casey, do you want to get laid this year or not?"

"I'm currently surrounded by sex toys and you ask me that?" Casey chuckled.

"I'm serious. Maybe this thing with the baker is exactly what you need. A little fun with the girl next door to get you out of your head."

"That sounds like a rebound. You know that's not me." She picked up a vibrator that someone had set on the wrong shelf and put it back in its place. "I don't do casual sex."

"I know." Natalia grumbled. "Which is how you ended up married to the wrong woman. How you ended up owning a sex store is a lot more complicated. And your insistence on the whole idea of a soulmate? A therapist would have a field day with that one."

"Sometimes I think I've told you too much." But she trusted Natalia more than anyone and they'd both told each other plenty of secrets. "I like Tara." A lot. "But I'm not sure I know what I'm doing at this point. Honestly, I don't think anyone should date me right now."

"You need to let loose a little. Not every woman you fall for is supposed to be the one. Sometimes they're only the one for the moment."

"This from the person who obsessively listens to relationship podcasts and goes to weekly therapy."

Natalia snorted. "You have to have fun in life. Unless you're ready to sign up for therapy and then you have some self-work to do before any fun."

"Well, that's what I'm wondering."

"Wait, you're actually considering it?"

Casey glanced at the Mrs. Claus outfit she'd fitted on the mannequin. She wished she could have seen it on Tara. She also wished she was in a place where she could ask someone out and not feel like she'd be towing a baggage cart to their first date. "You said your therapist does online sessions?"

"She does. Oh, Casey. I'm excited."

"That makes one of us." Casey wished she felt excited. It felt more like some ominous package she'd delayed opening for far too long.

"It's hard, but in a good way. I promise."

"I know." But she hadn't wanted to rehash the mess that was that relationship. Now she knew she owed it to whoever she dated next. "I'm not sure what Tara wants. Mostly we talk about work, you know? And we're just getting to know each other… But I like her. She's serious. And focused. I mean, she can joke around too, and I feel like I can be myself with her, but I like that she's got goals. Which is why I don't want to get into something with her and then have all the stuff I haven't dealt with be a problem."

"Ah, Case." Natalia made a sound like she was looking at a sad puppy.

"Am I that pathetic?"

"No. I love hearing you like this. You're finally ready for something real."

Was that it?

"Why'd you have to move all the way to Colorado? I want to hug you right now. You and the baker are going to be so adorable together."

"What if I'm more messed up than I think? What if she shouldn't date me?"

"You're definitely messed up. But in a sweet way." A loud honk sounded on Natalia's end of the line followed by a curse. "I gotta go. I'll send you the contact info for Judy. Fifty bucks says you jump the baker girl before your first session."

Casey was still laughing when the bell over the door jingled. She looked up to see Tara with a curious look on her face.

"Am I interrupting something?"

"Oh, no. I was…" She wondered what Tara would think of the truth.

"Standing in the middle of your sex shop entertaining yourself?"

Casey laughed even as her cheeks warmed. She waved to her phone. "I was chatting with my friend Natalia."

"About good things apparently." Tara's smirk made her even sexier.

Instead of the usual baker outfit, she had on a pair of dark leggings with a red sweater and her hair was down. Was she trying to be extra sexy this morning?

"Or not?"

Belatedly, Casey realized she'd been simply staring. Now she had to say something, and her mind had no ready excuse. "We were talking about going to therapy. Me going to therapy. Natalia already goes. She loves her therapist." And now she was rambling.

"Therapy can be a good thing."

But not sexy. Casey gave herself a mental shake wishing they could start over from the beginning. "How was the tasting with the bride?"

"Great. She placed an order for two hundred cupcakes." Tara set down a bag overflowing with Christmas decorations. "Apparently, my cupcakes really are bussin'."

"They really are. And I noticed you've started your window decorations."

Tara lifted a shoulder. "I love decorating. It's hard for me to resist."

"Thanks again for helping me."

"Don't tell anyone but I've been looking forward to it." She pulled a string of lights from her bag. "You know, I went to therapy after my last relationship."

"You did?"

Tara nodded. "It helped. A lot."

"I had issues before the divorce, and I probably should have gone then." She shook her head. "I feel like I've got a handle on some things—like going for what I want with this shop—but the rest of my life is kind of a mess." She forced a smile, but when Tara only held her gaze, a look of understanding in her eyes, she dropped the guise. As unsexy as the conversation was, it felt better to have the truth out in the open.

"Don't be too hard on yourself. Most of us are messy. Although I don't know anyone else who's gone through what you went through with your ex and then decided life would be easier if they moved to a small town and opened a sex shop."

Casey chuckled. "Clearly, I wanted more people mad at me. All of LA wasn't enough. I had to get the Rocky Springs locals riled up too."

Tara rolled her eyes.

"Oh. I almost forgot. When I got us burritos, Juan made me promise to say hi."

"Juan's a sweetie. Did he give you the locals discount?"

"He did."

"Good." Tara turned her attention back to her bag of decorations. She pulled out a wreath and asked, "Did you decide whether or not you want to go with the Mrs. Claus scene?"

"Yeah, I think it's going to be perfect."

"Where is the Mrs. Claus—" Tara's voice broke off when her eyes locked on the mannequin. "Oh. Wow."

"Wow, meaning you don't like it?"

"I wasn't expecting it to look quite like that." Tara bit the edge of her lip.

The dress didn't fit perfectly, but from Tara's expression, it looked worse than she'd thought. She adjusted the bottom edge of the skirt. "Do you think it'd be better if the skirt was a little longer? Maybe tone down the sexy vibe?"

"In this case, I think it's okay if Mrs. Claus has a little sass. You do own a sex shop."

"But you don't like it?"

"It's not that. It's just…her bulge is…big. I mean, it's fine but it's definitely noticeable."

"Oh, the strap-on! I forgot to take that off. I swear I was going to." Talk about ways to scare the locals. And Tara, apparently. Casey's cheeks burned as she reached under Mrs. Claus's skirt to unhook the harness. She heard a coughing sound and looked behind her to see Tara with a hand over her mouth. "Are you laughing at me?"

"I'm trying not to. But I wish I had my phone. This would be the best video."

"With my luck, it would end up online," Casey joked, knowing she looked incompetent when the harness buckle wouldn't unclasp. She resorted to wrapping an arm around the mannequin and aggressively wiggling the strap. "It's usually not this hard to get off."

"There's so many things I could say in response to that," Tara said. "I really wish I had my phone."

Casey looked over her shoulder, and the mannequin tipped. Tara rushed forward as Mrs. Claus pitched to the side, bumping against Casey to catch the mannequin. One second later, the hook on the harness slipped and Casey tugged the strap free, the Magnum cock wiggling in the air triumphantly. Tara, her arms still latched around Mrs. Claus, took one look at Casey with the cock held high and burst out laughing.

"What the heck are two doing?" Shawn's voice broke through.

Tara sobered enough to look at Shawn and deadpan, "Decorating, obviously."

Casey couldn't help but laugh then and Tara only laughed harder. Shawn joined in, clearly not sure what was going on but rolling with it. Finally, Tara collected herself enough to right Mrs. Claus and turn to Shawn. "We had a little incident. Did you need something?"

Shawn held up Tara's phone. "You got a call. I thought it might be important."

Tara's smile faltered but only for a second. "I'll check the message later."

"Okay. Um…yeah." Shawn glanced back at the open doorway. "Casey, do you want me to put up the closed sign while you two decorate?"

"That's okay. I probably won't get many customers this time of day anyway."

"Alright. I'll be over at the bakery if you need anything." Shawn set Tara's phone on the closest counter and hurried out.

When they were alone again, Casey looked at Tara. "Sorry. That was—"

"Don't worry about Shawn. I can explain later."

Casey wanted to ask her out then and there. She cleared her throat. "Should we maybe take a break and eat those burritos before we get too much further into this?"

"Oh. Sure."

Casey set the harness down and went to the front counter where she'd left the bag from the Cantina. "Juan sent me with extra green sauce for you."

Tara made a happy groaning sound. She took the foil-wrapped package marked with her name and a little heart.

"Does Juan have a crush on you too?" Casey realized what she'd said only after the words left her mouth.

Tara's lips formed an "O" but she promptly took a bite of the burrito as she shook her head. She chewed for a moment, giving Casey way too much time to feel awkward. "Juan is married with three kids and loves his wife. I'm sure it was Jasmina who drew the heart." At Casey's questioning look she added, "She almost always works the register. Petite, dark brown hair, big smile and big boobs. Real easy on the eyes."

Casey pressed her lips together. "I feel like this might be a trick question. If I say yes—"

"I'll know you checked her out?" Tara grinned. "Everyone does. And Jasmina loves to flirt. The last time I was at the Cantina she teased Juan that she'd leave him as soon as I made her a proposal."

"I'm not surprised there's competition." Since she'd already outed herself, Casey wanted to know what Tara's response would be. A tip of her head was the only clue.

"Anyway," Tara said, going for another bite. "I recommend extra green sauce. Always."

Casey unwrapped her burrito. "I asked Juan to make mine like yours. But I didn't get a heart."

"Give Jasmina a few months. I have no doubt you'll get little hearts from her, too." Tara met Casey's gaze over the burrito. "I don't think it'll take long for you to win over this town."

The only one she wanted to win over was the baker. She nearly said as much, but the question of whether or not she should get involved with anyone stopped her. Slowing things down, though, was the last thing she wanted to do.

CHAPTER THIRTEEN

"Y ou invited her for Thanksgiving?" Shawn asked with a slow blink and incredulous look.

"Friendsgiving," Tara corrected her. "Which is why she's coming over tonight—Wednesday—instead of tomorrow." She'd technically invited Casey to both, but Casey already had virtual dinner plans with her friend Natalia.

Shawn's brow furrowed. "I think that's worse."

Tara planted her hands on her hips, exasperation taking hold. "What does that mean?"

"A Thanksgiving invite might mean you feel sorry for her. You know. All alone in a new town with no family to celebrate with. A Friendsgiving invite implies you're friends."

She frowned. "We are friends."

"Or maybe more than friends."

"Okay, now you're just being a jerk." Because even if she'd had many thoughts in that direction, she hadn't acted on them. She sure as hell wasn't going to get teased for crossing those lines if she hadn't had the pleasure of doing it.

"I'm not saying you've hooked up with her." Shawn shrugged. "I'm saying you want to."

Tara lifted her chin. "Is that why you invited Kit?"

"Well, yeah." Shawn smiled smugly. "Can you blame me?"

Any satisfaction she had from turning the tables evaporated in genuine shock. "You and Kit? For real?"

"I mean, so far we've only been hanging out doing friend stuff."

"Because you're bound and determined to stay single forever."

"I didn't say that." Shawn put the last of the cupcakes on a platter and moved it to the table. "Anyway, I don't know if she's into me. And she had to do family stuff, so she didn't even accept my invite as a friend."

"Shawn McCoy, a woman could literally fall over herself flirting with you and you'd think she was simply prone to tripping." A fact she'd given up teasing Shawn about because it had started to feel borderline mean.

Shawn looked truly surprised at the comment, but before there was time for a response the doorbell rang. "That's weird. Who rings the doorbell?"

Tara certainly didn't, and she was pretty sure Shawn's friends didn't, either. "I'm guessing the person who's never been to your house."

Shawn's eyes lit up. "Right."

"You finish in here." She gestured vaguely to the coffeepot. "I'll get it."

She hurried to the door and, sure enough, found Casey standing on the other side, clutching a bottle of wine. "Am I too early?" Casey asked.

"Perfectly on time." Without thinking, she reached for Casey's hand. She stopped herself before she'd done more than brush Casey's skin but that was enough to get her hormones racing. The situation only got worse when Casey stepped inside and they were less than a foot apart in the small entryway. She cleared her throat. "I'm so glad you came."

"Thank you for the invite. I love the idea of a dessert party before Thanksgiving. The sweets are my favorite part. But you're sure I'm not crashing?" Casey handed her the wine and slipped off her coat.

"No more than I am. Shawn started this tradition while I was away as a chance to chill and see friends before the madness of Black Friday kicks the holiday season into high gear. I won't say everyone in the Rocky Springs retail circle gets invited, but that's the basis."

Casey grinned. "I'm glad you said not everyone."

"All friends here, I promise." And maybe one she wouldn't mind turning into more than a friend.

The door opened again, and a group of Shawn's friends filed in. After introducing Casey to everyone, Shawn appeared and Tara pointed Casey to the kitchen. When they got there, she lifted the bottle of wine and hooked the thumb of her free hand at the coffee pot. "What's your pleasure?"

Casey looked at the coffee. "I don't suppose that's decaf."

Tara laughed. "It's not. Shawn's immune to caffeine and doesn't appreciate the intolerance for having it late in the day. There's herbal tea, though."

"Eh, I'll be wild. I don't expect to sleep much anyway these next few days."

"You're not nervous about Black Friday, are you?" It was hectic, sure, but she didn't even bat an eye anymore.

"Of course I am." Casey shook her head. "I've managed to stress myself out over the possibility of literally no one setting foot in the shop and the possibility of being so busy I'll regret not having any staff besides myself."

"I'm pretty sure it'll be the latter, but that'll be a good problem, right?"

"As long as I don't make anyone mad waiting to check out." Casey sighed. "Honestly I'll call the day a win as long as no angry villagers throw eggs at my window."

"I don't think they will."

Casey gave a wry smile. "It would sound more convincing if you believed what you were saying."

"Your display turned out really cute. Classy, even. I think I've got some real competition this year." Which was true by objective standards if not those of the judges.

Casey laughed. "I stand by what I said before. I don't need to win. I just don't want any more protests."

A small stab of regret poked in her chest. She couldn't take back how much of a jerk she'd been at first, but she could do her best to make up for it now. "I have a feeling you're going to find yourself pleasantly surprised."

"I'll hope you're right."

Others joined them in the kitchen and the private feel of the moment was gone. She and Casey migrated to the living room, chatting with each other but also getting pulled into different conversations. It wasn't a date by any stretch of the imagination, but she couldn't help but feel like it was nice to have both, that if she ever did bring a date to something like this, she'd want that.

Fortunately, Casey couldn't read her thoughts, and neither could Shawn. The evening passed in a blur of baked goods and laughter, and she couldn't remember the last time she'd had more fun. Well, save the cozy drinks that turned into dinner with Casey the other night after the market closed. But that was another matter.

"I should probably call it a night." Casey let out a sigh and stood. "If this next week is as busy as you all make it sound, I need to get at least one decent night's sleep before the madness."

"I should be heading home myself. I'll walk you out."

Casey nodded affably. Shawn, on the other hand, shot her a totally ridiculous and completely obvious suggestive look. Tara glared and a couple of their mutual friends snickered. Fortunately, Casey was already making her way to the front door and missed it all. She spared withering looks as she passed, but that only served to encourage them.

By the time she got there, Casey already had her coat on. Tara slid her feet into her boots and bent down to tug them the rest of the way on. Casey chose that exact moment to do the same. Their heads bumped, not hard enough to do damage but hard enough to send Tara grasping for something to steady herself. Of course, the closest thing to hand was Casey.

She grabbed Casey's arm. Casey grabbed her at the waist. They both righted themselves, and somehow the space between them had evaporated, leaving them very much in kissing proximity. The kind of proximity where she couldn't help but stare at Casey's mouth. The kind that gave her the faintest sense of Casey's cologne, which of course reminded her of that time she got to watch the sun set over the ocean next to a roaring fire.

"Sorry. I can be such a klutz sometimes."

Casey's situationally appropriate comment hit Tara like a bucket of cold water. She cleared her throat and took a step back, bumping into a bucket of dog toys. The bucket tipped and embarrassment usurped arousal. "Oh, seriously?"

"You okay?" Casey reached out to steady her and the look in Casey's eyes made it clear her thoughts had also been more on kissing than keeping her standing.

Tara's pulse tripped. "Yeah. Just clumsy too."

They both bent to pick up the assortment of toys that had spilled and once the bucket was righted, Casey said, "To be fair, I've fallen into worse things."

"That's good to know." *Really? That's the best you could come up with?*

Casey grabbed Tara's coat and held it up. Tara turned, sliding her arms into the sleeves and willing herself not to be awkward about it. Since Casey already had hers on, she busied herself with the buttons and her scarf.

Shawn appeared, somehow making things both better and worse. "You two doing okay out here? I thought I heard something crash."

"We bumped into each other. And then kicked your dog's toy bucket." Casey chuckled. "Apparently, we can't handle getting ourselves dressed."

Shawn raised a brow.

Since Casey was right there, Tara couldn't respond or even make a face without being obvious about it. "But we've managed."

Casey glanced from Tara to Shawn before looking back to Tara. Understanding seemed to dawn and she pressed her lips together. "Yes. All sorted. Too much sugar, obviously."

"Well, we'll have a mountain of it in the shop Friday if you need to pop in for an extra fix," Shawn said.

"I might take you up on that." Again, Casey glanced at Shawn, but her gaze returned squarely to Tara.

Shawn, who now stood between them, elbowed Casey lightly. "This is where you offer to return the favor. In case we need a little diversion."

Tara kicked Shawn in the shin—not hard, but it didn't stop Shawn from letting out a dramatic "ow."

Casey, to her credit, merely smiled. "Bath bomb on the house. And if you're looking for anything with a little more oomph, I'd be happy to offer some suggestions and the friends and family discount."

"Sold." Shawn elbowed Tara this time. "And I'll make sure this one takes advantage, too."

Tara closed her eyes briefly, since melting into the floor wasn't an option. "On that note, I'm going home."

Casey opened the door, letting in a gust of cold air and a swirl of snow. She winced, which managed to shift the energy of the conversation back to neutral territory. "After you."

Tara stepped out into the cold and hurried a few steps down the walk before stopping to wait for Casey. "I'm sorry. Shawn can be such a pain," she said as Casey joined her.

"Really? I think Shawn's great."

Tara planted her fists on her hips before she could stop herself.

Casey seemed to recalibrate. "But I can see how you might feel otherwise."

"Sometimes it'd be nice if everyone in my family did a better job of minding their own business."

Casey nodded, seeming to wait for her to go on.

"I know Shawn was trying to help asking you to return the favor, but I don't need that kind of help." Much like the stance, the words tumbled out before she thought them through.

Casey's brow furrowed. "Meaning you already knew you could get the friends and family discount? Or meaning you want to be sure we keep things professional?"

Any intentions of trying to feel things out slowly with Casey evaporated. Before she'd decided how to answer, however, Casey continued. "I was getting the vibe you might be interested in more, but if you're not, I'll totally back off."

"I'm not saying you should back off. At all. What I meant was I don't need Shawn's help getting a date."

"Oh." Casey opened and closed her mouth. "Yeah, I'm sure you don't. But I appreciate the effort?"

"You would." Tara shook her head but smiled. "Although really you don't need any help either."

Casey's eyes locked on hers and again her pulse rabbited. Could they skip right to the kissing part? When Casey didn't look away, desire was so obvious it seemed to spark between them. The only thing she wanted was Casey's lips pressed against hers, and exactly how much she wanted it left her wondering if she'd maybe had too much of the wine Casey brought.

"The thing is…I'm not sure me dating anyone is a good idea. I've been wanting to ask you out, but I'm kind of a mess right now." Casey dropped her gaze to her feet and kicked at the snow on the sidewalk.

There were plenty of reasons why their dating was a bad idea, and only a few of them had to do with Casey's recent divorce. Her own track record with relationships certainly wasn't impressive. And Casey might not stick around if her shop didn't make it.

But in that moment, with the snow falling all around and the glow of Christmas lights Shawn had already strung on the eaves of her house and the bushes out front, the only thing she held onto was the one reason she should. She wanted to. And when was the last time she'd done something purely because she'd wanted it?

"What if I can handle messy?" Tara tipped her chin so she could look up at Casey through her lashes.

Casey clearly got the message. "That might give me the courage to ask you out."

"Who knew that the woman who moves a thousand miles away from home and opens up a sex shop—with the whole town against her—needs courage to ask me out?"

"I didn't think the whole town was against me. In fact, I thought the baker next door was on my side."

"She's on your side now."

"I know." Casey's smile widened. "And it feels good. The thing is, I'm still not sure I'm ready for a new relationship."

"Don't get ahead of yourself." Tara lifted an eyebrow. "I never said I wanted a relationship either. We're only talking about a date here."

Casey laughed. "I did warn you I'm a mess, right?"

"You did." But a cute mess she'd really like to kiss.

Casey held her gaze for a moment and then stepped closer. "Hey, Tara, want to go on a date with me?"

"Yes."

Casey shifted forward and the emotions that had been building for weeks nearly overwhelmed Tara. Snow still swirled around them, but she didn't feel one bit cold. With the warmth of Casey's body close to hers, all other thoughts disappeared beyond how much she loved the subtle scent of Casey's cologne and how much she wanted her kiss.

"Can I—"

"Yes." She didn't feel one bit bad about not letting Casey finish her question. Especially not with the look she'd put on Casey's face. Full of sudden desire.

When Casey's lips touched hers, she didn't hesitate to move into the kiss. Casey felt perfect. Her lips were gentle, almost tentative at first, but then pressed more firmly against hers, and as she parted her lips, Casey took the kiss deeper. If she'd thought she was turned on earlier, now every part of her ignited.

Kissing had never felt quite so good and when one kiss moved to the next, she wondered if Casey would follow her home. Of course she wasn't that type but... She gripped the front of Casey's coat, pulling her closer. Casey's hand slid into her hair and a little moan slipped out. She couldn't help it. Didn't want to help it. Instead she traced Casey's bottom lip with her tongue and shivered when Casey did the same to hers.

The sound of Shawn's front door opening, and a wave of light and laughter spilling out, made Casey jolt back. They looked from the door to each other, and for a moment she felt like a teenager caught kissing after curfew. Not that she'd been cool enough for such things at the time. The laughter stopped then started up again, this time at her expense. Well, hers and Casey's. Though, really, it's not like they had anything to be embarrassed about.

"Sorry, we thought you'd already left," Juan called.

"Yeah. Don't let us interrupt," Shawn added.

Casey looked to her instead of responding, and Tara realized it was a gesture of deference. Her first instinct was to bluster and brush it off. She didn't like to be teased and she liked it even less when people didn't take her seriously. But in this moment and with these people, what did she have to prove? Maybe that she didn't have to take herself so seriously after all. She raised an arm. "We were just finishing."

Casey nodded, but there was a shadow of disappointment in her eyes.

Tara grabbed her hand. "For now."

The shadow vanished. In its place, a look of pure promise that threatened to melt her from the inside out, despite the frigid temperature. "For now."

CHAPTER FOURTEEN

"Hi Kit. Any chance you're downtown right now?" Casey desperately hoped Kit was close by. If so, there was a good chance Casey could convince her to run over to her shop for five minutes.

"No. I'm at a jobsite. What's wrong?"

"Nothing. It's just…" Casey lowered her voice when a customer looked her way. "Hold on a sec," she said to Kit, then forced a smile as she caught the customer's eye. The urge to pee was getting more insistent by the second, but she wanted the reputation of being an approachable helpful clerk—exactly as described in the first online review she'd seen. "Do you need help finding anything?"

The older woman shook her head and walked past the front counter heading to the book section. Casey returned her attention to her cell phone. "Hey. I'm back. It's been nonstop customers today—which is great—but I've gotta pee. Bad."

"I knew the holiday season in Rocky Springs was going to kick your ass," Kit said. "You need to hire some help."

"I can't hire someone in the next hour." And she really wasn't sure she could last more than another twenty minutes.

"Text Tara or Shawn. Both of them are working today and I'm sure it would be no problem for one of them to pop over. Actually, I'm surprised you called me instead of Tara—" The sound of glass shattering interrupted Kit's sentence. A string of expletives followed before Kit came back on the line. "Some days I want to throttle my brother."

"Sorry." She understood better than most the frustrations of working with family.

"Why don't you try calling Tara? You have her number, right?"

Kit's playful and encouraging tone made Casey smile. "I have her number. The thing is, we haven't talked since we kissed." It'd only been two days but still. "Wouldn't it be weird to text now for a favor without talking about…well, that?"

There was a long pause and Casey appreciated the fact that Kit seemed to be weighing the decision as heavily as she had. In fact, she'd wanted to call Tara yesterday but then decided against interrupting her Thanksgiving and coming across as overly eager or the type to take things fast. Especially after admitting she was a mess.

"You didn't talk to her yesterday? No text, nothing?"

"I thought I should wait." From Kit's tone there was no doubt that'd been a mistake. "I figured it'd be a good idea to take things slow."

"Really? Because from what you told me, you were ready to take her back to your place."

"Nothing was going to happen. It was a good night kiss."

"You're saying you don't want to shag her?" Kit's tone was incredulous.

Casey laughed. To most, Kit came across as completely serious and professional. But there was definitely another side of her. "No one says shagging. Where did you even come up with that?" She realized she'd said the word "shagging" a little too loudly when the couple discussing if they were ready to try butt plugs looked in her direction. She smiled and raised a hand, hoping the interruption meant they'd quickly decide on their purchase. "I'm not saying I'm not interested in that, but at this moment in time, I just need a pee break. There's been a constant stream of customers since eleven." She wished she could take back her words as soon as the thought of any kind of stream settled in her mind.

"So call Tara."

"You really don't think it would be weird?" She crossed her legs and tried to think of the desert. Hot dry sand as far as the eye could see.

"You need to pee. I guarantee she'll be happy to relieve you."

"Can we not use that word?"

Kit laughed. "For real though, why didn't you call her yesterday? Or at least text? After a kiss like you two had, it's pretty shitty to leave her hanging. You should have checked in with her the next day."

"It was Thanksgiving. I thought she'd be busy."

"It was a good kiss, right? I mean, the kind of kiss you'd like to repeat."

"Yeah." No denying it. Tara was an amazing kisser. And the memory of how Tara had moaned and pulled her in deeper had kept her awake for hours after. "I just don't want to rush things. You know I've got baggage."

"We all do. And the holidays are the best time for unpacking all the baggage."

Maybe Kit was right, but did Tara deserve that?

"It's not too late. Shawn told me Tara was so distracted thinking about you that she put the stuffing in the fridge and the cranberry sauce in the oven."

"Shawn said Tara was thinking of me?"

Kit groaned. "You've got zero game, Casey. How is it you grew up in Hollywood with two famous parents, hung out with gorgeous actresses and actors all the time—who you had no problem working with or marrying—and still don't know what to do when a woman is into you?"

She nearly admitted that was the problem. For most of her life she'd battled feeling not as good-looking or as talented as anyone around her. And after everything with Pavia, it was hard to pretend to be suave or debonair with someone she liked and not worry she wasn't going to mess everything up. "I have a few issues."

"A few?" Kit scoffed. "I'm mostly teasing. It's just that Shawn and I were talking yesterday about how cute you and Tara would be together."

"What's happening between you two anyway? Last we talked, you weren't interested in dating anyone in Rocky Springs."

Kit made a long mmm sound before saying, "I thought you had to pee. And weren't you going to text Tara?"

Casey lowered the phone and quickly tapped out a text to Tara. She tried not to second-guess the favor request and kept the message simple. "Done."

"After the pee break, ask her what she's doing later tonight. Ten bucks says you two end up shagging this weekend."

"No one says shagging," Casey repeated, laughing this time.

"Sure. Have fun shagging."

Casey tried to collect herself when the woman who'd been in the book section came to the front counter with two books—one on the benefits of masturbation and one erotica book. "I gotta go. Thanks for your advice." She ended the call and scanned the barcode of the first book. "Good choices. Anything else you needed today?"

"Well, I could probably use some shagging advice too." She held out a credit card. "Maybe you can offer that in the future."

"I'd need to hire someone more qualified than me." Casey bagged the books and slipped in a free bookmark. "Thanks for coming in today."

The woman with the books had no sooner left than the bell over the door jingled and someone else came in. Casey pictured the desert again and tried to convince her bladder it could handle waiting a bit longer. When she glanced up, the person who'd come in still stood in the entryway, looking a bit like a clichéd deer caught in the headlights. Except this particular deer was a twenty-something queer whose gender she guessed was fluid. Black hair with an undercut, olive complexion, a red flannel under an old-school leather motorcycle jacket and rainbow Converse. The rainbow Converse weren't really necessary—the queer vibe came across loud and clear—but made the look all that much more adorable.

"Nice shoes," Casey said, offering what she hoped was an encouraging smile. A lot of people hesitated at the entryway, and rainbow Converse was clearly following this trend. "Feel free to look around. If you have any questions, I love talking about all this stuff."

Rainbow Converse nodded and took a tentative step forward, gaze roaming from the lotions and lubes display to the front row of books. At least half the customers had to be prompted to walk beyond the front mat, as if they'd used all their energy psyching themselves up simply to walk into a sex shop and didn't have any courage left once they were inside.

The couple who'd been analyzing the butt plug options for nearly fifteen minutes came to the register finally, each holding a box. They'd picked two different styles, both good for beginners.

"Can I recommend some lube, or do you have that at home?"

The man looked at the woman and after a brief nod from her, he turned to Casey and said, "Yes, please."

She convinced them to get not only lube but a book on how to enjoy anal sex. They were so excited by it all that by the time she'd rung up the sale, she'd almost forgotten how much she needed to pee. Almost. Still no text from Tara, unfortunately, and rainbow Converse wasn't heading for the door. Instead, they were stopped in front of the packing gear. Casey approached, using the excuse of straightening a few of the butt plugs the earlier customers had considered and discarded on the wrong shelf.

"I can give you some feedback on the different styles of packers if you're interested."

"Um, yeah. I am." Rainbow Converse's cheeks colored with a blush.

"Have you ever packed before?"

Head shake.

"Okay." She reached for the display packer on the bottom shelf. "This is the one most folks try first. It gives you some weight and a bulge in the right spot. I know it looks a little small, but I think it's a nice place to start. You'll want to wear boxer briefs to keep everything in place."

"Um. Yeah. I wear those." Rainbow Converse didn't reach for the packer however. "I was, uh, hoping to find one that I could use to pee with? So I could stand, you know?"

"Ah. Yeah, this one won't work for that." Casey set the first packer back and reached for the next one on the shelf. "This one does. There's less bulge in your shorts but gets the STP."

"Stand to pee?"

Casey nodded.

"I was wondering if that's what those initials meant on the box... What about sex?"

"Honestly, I haven't tried it, but I've read the reviews and everyone says this model isn't great for that purpose."

"Which one do you recommend for that?"

"Okay, so you're asking a lot," Casey admitted. She set down the second packer down and reached for a third. "I've been told that this one works for all three. Packing, STP, and sex. But it's more expensive. And honestly, I recommend a harness if you plan on any serious action."

Rainbow Converse laughed. "I'm hoping?"

"Aren't we all?" Casey returned with a grin. A flash of pink caught her eye and she looked past rainbow Converse and spotted Tara in her baker's apron. "Take your time with the decision," Casey continued. "Unfortunately, I can't do returns on any of these items."

"Right. I wouldn't want someone's returned cock either."

"Exactly. Can you excuse me for a minute?"

Casey hurried over to Tara. "You don't know how happy I am to see you."

"I could say the same, but I think for different reasons."

"Probably the same reasons but I've got one more." Which for some reason seemed less urgent now.

"We could argue that, or you could go to the bathroom."

Casey grinned. Arguing with Tara wasn't what she wanted to do, but she loved the fact that they could banter. "I'll be right back. And thank you."

In the time Casey peed and washed her hands, Tara had rainbow Converse at the register with one of the packers. She bagged it up and sent them on their way. "I'm impressed you figured out how to check them out that fast. Did you get the printer to work for a receipt? It can be a little punky."

Tara held up a credit card. "I'm paying for it. I know Aspen. They're a good kid but they've got crummy parents. Good friends of Gary Jenkins."

"Oh. Shit."

"Yeah." Tara sighed. "Parents kicked them out of the house last year—for the trans thing. They bounced between living out of a car to finally moving in with one of Shawn's friends. They sleep on a couch."

"Damn."

Tara nodded. "But Aspen finished their GED and got started at the community college. Once they finish there, they'll probably blow this town and never look back. And I wouldn't blame them. It's not an easy place to be trans." She paused. "Thanks for taking the time to explain everything—and for making Aspen feel like it isn't weird to want a packer."

"It isn't weird."

"I agree, but most people in this town don't feel the same. Aspen told me they've been wanting one for years but talking to you gave them the confidence to finally go for it. What you did might not have felt like a big deal to you, but it was huge for them."

Tara's praise was sincere and Casey wasn't sure what to say in response. She thought what she did was important but hearing someone else echo that?

"Anyway," Tara continued. "Can you charge me out for the purchase of my very first packer?"

Casey shook her head. "That one's on the house."

Tara folded her arms. "I don't want you to give things away. Please let me buy it?"

"It was free. Special only today. I promise I won't make it a habit to give things away."

Tara narrowed her eyes and let out an exasperated huff. "Fine. But just so you know, I won't make it a habit of letting you win either."

Casey laughed and the look Tara gave her in response only made her heart bump higher in her chest. "It's really good seeing you."

"Yeah, I could tell how much you needed that break," Tara teased her. "You know, you could hire someone so you'd have backup." She hooked her thumb toward the front door. "I bet Aspen could use a job."

"That's not a bad idea." Casey wanted to hire someone at least part-time, but she'd hoped to have more consistent income first and know how much she could pay. Still. If today repeated itself, she wouldn't be able to wait. "But, for the record, I'm happy seeing you for other reasons, too."

The doorbell rang again, and Casey barely held in a grumble.

"Welcome to the holiday season," Tara murmured. "I should get back to work too."

"Any chance you'd be up for dinner tonight? I wanted to thank you for all the help with the window display. I've gotten so many compliments on it."

Tara tipped her head. "You already offered a store discount."

Casey shook her head. "That's not enough."

"I feel like I should argue, but my fridge is empty, and I was already dreading a trip to the grocery store. So, sure." She tapped a finger to her lips. "The restaurants in town are going to be swarmed tonight though."

"I can pick up takeout. Thai at my place?"

Tara hesitated for only a moment. "Green curry is my favorite. Extra spice."

"Of course you get extra heat." Casey grinned.

"Always. Text me your address?"

Tara left, leaving Casey to wish she could follow. She wanted another five minutes together. An hour would be even better. Or all day. But at least she only had to wait until dinnertime and sharing take-out and a quiet evening together sounded perfect.

Chapter Fifteen

Tara pulled up to the address Casey had given her and frowned. The Craftsman duplex was fully decked out for Christmas—lights, garland, oversize shiny balls. There was even an inflatable snowman in the front yard, flanked by two inflatable penguins. Not that she had anything against inflatable snowmen. Or penguins.

It struck her was all. She'd barely managed to pull her decorations from storage. Getting a tree up and a few lights strung would be about as much as she could muster with how busy things were at work. The fact that Casey had managed all this and was running her shop solo was enough to make Tara feel like a lump of coal. She shook off the sensation and got out of the car, scurrying up the walk and knocking briskly on the door Casey had indicated was hers.

It opened in a matter of seconds and Casey stood on the other side, bathed in the light and warmth spilling out around her. "You made it."

She stomped the snow from her boots and hurried inside. "You say that like you were expecting me to bail."

Casey shrugged. "If you're half as tired as I am, I wouldn't have blamed you."

"And let you eat all the curry?" She lifted her chin. "Seriously, though. If you're beat, we don't have to hang out."

"No, no." Casey shook her head with enough vigor to make Tara smile. "I mean, we both have to eat, right?"

"I'm not going to lie, the prospect of Thai food instead of warmed up soup has given me a second wind." Especially since the soup would have involved sitting on her sofa alone.

"Good to know what your priorities are." Casey grinned. "Come on, it's in the kitchen."

She followed Casey down a short hall, past a sparsely furnished living room and to the kitchen. It had the look of total renovation done in the last decade—clean white cabinets and butcher block counters. A trio of stools flanked the breakfast bar, though the eating area held nothing more than the fourth stool and several piles of boxes.

"It's cute that you went all out for Christmas before you've fully unpacked."

"Oh, that's my neighbor. Neighbor slash landlady. She asked if I'd mind her decorating both sides instead of just hers." Casey winced. "I should have warned you I'm still in the settling in phase."

"No warning needed," Tara said. "And if it helps, knowing that makes me feel better."

Casey's expression turned inquisitive. "What do you mean?"

"Well, it took me months to unpack, so there's that. But mostly I meant the decorations." She lifted a hand to start ticking things off. "One, you just moved here. Two, you're the only one working at your shop. Three—"

"Oh hey, speaking of. Do you have Aspen's contact info? I loved your idea of offering them a job."

She loved that Casey planned to take her advice. "I do. Want me to reach out with a soft ask first?"

"Would you? That would be great. I don't want it to be creepy that I suddenly have their number."

"I'm pretty sure all you'd need to say is you're the person from the Sweet Spot, but yeah."

"Thanks. And sorry." Casey lifted both hands. "Didn't mean to interrupt."

She blinked a few times, the day clearly catching up with her. "Where was I?"

"You were explaining why my neighbor's holiday cheer makes you feel better?" Casey made a face, clearly at a loss over the logic.

"Right." Tara laughed. "I thought you'd put it all up and it made me feel like a slacker and a Scrooge."

Casey narrowed her eyes. "I thought you loved Christmas."

"I do. It's just…" How could she explain without sounding pathetic?

"It's a lot and you work a ridiculous number of hours at this time of year?"

"There is that. It's also, I don't know, hard to go all out when you live alone. I've always loved Christmas—especially in Rocky Springs. I love how the whole town goes all out. But decorating solo when you live in a little apartment…"

Casey's features softened. "I get that."

She didn't mind her place, but the fact that she was renting a generic one-bedroom apartment with almost nothing on the walls two plus years after she'd moved in did bother her. "I think I put all my energy into the bakery. Including my decorating energy."

"Your window display is amazing." Casey, who'd started pulling cartons and containers out of a paper bag, paused to look at her. "Do you think you'll stay in Rocky Springs?"

"Forever?" She hesitated. "At this point, that's the plan. Which sounds weird to admit. I'm only in my mid-thirties and I already know where I'm retiring."

"I love that."

"Really?"

"I wish I had something I was so sure would last." Casey got out plates and utensils. "Was coming home hard for you? After being in New York, I could see this would be a big transition."

"I was excited to come back and take the bakery to the next level. Coming home alone…well, I won't bore you with that part."

"I don't think any part of you would bore me."

It could have been a throwaway line, the kind of thing meant to make her feel better and keep the conversation going. Only it didn't feel like that. It felt like Casey genuinely liked her and wanted to know everything she was willing to share. "Well, I'm bored of it. And starving."

Casey took the hint like a champ, pulling cans of seltzer from the fridge and gesturing for Tara to serve herself first. She'd ordered a smattering of things and teasingly offered to share if Tara would. She would have on principle, but Casey's tastes perfectly matched her own. In addition to the green curry, there was pad see ew and cashew chicken, along with a pair of crispy fried spring rolls. They filled their plates, and Casey offered either the breakfast bar or the sofa.

"Oh, definitely the sofa," Tara said. "Did you even have to ask?"

"I didn't want you to think of me as a slovenly bachelor."

She tipped her head. "Hard to look slovenly when you're rocking such a Spartan aesthetic."

Casey winced but grinned at the same time. "I'm working on it. I've been a little busy."

"Fair."

"And décor isn't exactly my strong suit."

"I could help," Tara said before she could stop herself. "If you wanted."

"Depends. Do you like decorating, or do you feel sorry for me?"

"Yes." A cheeky answer for her, but Casey seemed to bring that out in her.

"I'll take that. Shall we?" Casey angled her head toward the living room.

"Absolutely."

They settled in and spent a moment haggling over the best Christmas movies, unexpectedly agreeing on *White Christmas* as an underrated gem. Casey queued it up and they ate, letting the song and dance numbers fill the silence. When their plates were empty, Casey set them on the coffee table and pulled the blanket from the back of the sofa. She held it up in invitation. "Yes?"

Tara nodded even as her mind raced to all the things she'd like to get up to with Casey under a blanket.

Casey shook it out and spread it over both of them. Casey leaned her way; she leaned Casey's. Not a full-on cuddle, but their shoulders touched. Not enough to satisfy the sexual cravings she'd developed in the last few weeks but it felt too good to complain. She let the familiarity of the movie and the coziness of the whole setup relax her. Between that and the big dinner and the long day, it wasn't long before her lids started to droop. And though her instinct was to stay alert and present and put together, something about being next to Casey made her feel safe, and she let herself drift.

Tara woke to the swell of orchestral music and the credits rolling slowly up the screen. How had that happened? And more importantly, where was she?

The details of the room came into focus. The fire that had almost gone out. The extra deep navy-blue sofa.

Oh, and Casey.

Casey's chest under her head. Casey's arm draped ever so perfectly around her. Casey's whole body strong and warm and sure and impossibly close. And Casey softly snoring.

Tara barely caught herself from jolting upright. Casey didn't stir, giving her a minute to plan her next move. She could move around slowly until Casey woke up, and they could have a chuckle over both being tired enough to pass out in the middle of a movie. She could try to slip away without waking Casey, prepared to pretend it had never happened. Or maybe…

Maybe she could chill the fuck out and enjoy it. Cuddling counted as taking things slow, right? And damn if being cuddled up against Casey wasn't the best feeling she'd had in longer than she cared to admit. What was the harm in taking some comfort, getting a little turned on, and generally being reminded that she was a woman with sexual desires and the need for physical touch?

"I can literally hear your brain turning." Casey's voice slurred slightly from sleep, but she was one hundred percent awake.

Tara lifted her head enough to make eye contact. "Does that surprise you?"

Casey chuckled. "Not even a little."

"Are you freaking out right now?" *Please say no.*

"Why would I be freaking out? Are you freaking out?"

"Well, I had a moment right when I woke up, but I talked myself out of it." Which was both true and way more than she would normally disclose to someone she'd only maybe started dating.

"That seems legit. I'm glad you talked yourself out of it." Casey's arm came a little more tightly around her. "It's kind of nice."

"I think so too."

"Do you want to stay?" Casey asked.

"No. I mean, yes. But no." Not the best answer to channel her general coolness with the situation.

Casey smiled. "I understand."

Tara sat up, suddenly aware of how Casey might be interpreting things. "It's not because I don't want to. If anything, it's because I want to a little too much."

Casey gave her a slow, sexy once-over. "Yeah."

"Could we get together again soon? They're officially opening the ice rink on Sunday. Of course it will be a zoo opening day. It's usually less busy midweek—if you'd be up for something like that." She didn't know if skating would be Casey's thing, but hanging out in public might be safer than either of their places until they decided whether they were going to wind up in bed together.

"That's sounds perfect. I'll try to get Aspen hired and at least minimally trained. And if not, I can close the shop for a few hours midday."

The significance wasn't lost on her. "I'm pretty sure Aspen will say yes. And they're really smart."

Casey nodded. "I'm glad. Because I'd be tempted to hire them even if they weren't based on what you've told me."

She thought about the rough start she and Casey had, how wrong she'd been. "You're a good egg, Casey Stevens."

"Thanks." Casey dropped her head and Tara was pretty sure she blushed. "And since you've gone and said that, I should probably send you home. We've both got early mornings tomorrow."

Tara didn't resist the urge to groan. "So early."

Casey stood, though she seemed reluctant about it. "I'll still be solo, but let me know if there's anything I can do to help. I owe you one."

She pointed to the empty plates still sitting on the coffee table. "You bought me dinner."

"That was me repaying a favor."

It was silly for her to get butterflies over the way Casey looked at her, but she did anyway. "I see."

"So, I still get to do something nice for you. And we get to hang out again." Casey ticked the items off on her finger.

Forget silly, Casey had her feeling downright smitten. Maybe it wasn't the smartest thing to do, but she'd done much dumber stuff so that had to count for something. And much like waking up in Casey's arms, damn, it felt good. "Deal."

Chapter Sixteen

At least ice skating was something Casey was good at. Since she'd had to reschedule from Tuesday to Wednesday to give Aspen more time to get up to speed in the shop, then had to push back the time they'd set to meet in order to figure out why the credit card machine had suddenly stopped working, she didn't want to let Tara down more. But all the worries about leaving Aspen alone disappeared the moment she saw Tara.

"Hi, stranger." Tara's smile was warm and conveyed more than basic pleasantries.

"Hey. Sorry I had to reschedule and then change the time and—"

"You don't have to apologize." Tara reached out and caught Casey's arm. She gave it a squeeze. "These things happen. Especially during the holiday rush. How's it going at the shop?"

"Good. And it's good to see you." It had only been a handful of days since Tara had been at her house, but it was too long for her. "You'd think working right next to each other we'd see each other more."

"The busy season doesn't last forever. Things will calm down before you know it and then we can pop over for social calls."

"Social calls? Is that what they call it around here?"

"That's what my grandma calls it so don't get any ideas." Tara laughed.

Tara looked amazing in a pair of tight jeans and ankle boots, and Casey wanted to pull her close for a kiss. The fact that they were in the middle of downtown Rocky Springs stopped her. Life in a small town was different for sure. She wouldn't have hesitated in LA.

Tara's gaze zeroed in on Casey's bag. "Did you bring your own skates?"

"I've got these narrow long toes and most skates don't fit right." Casey tried to play it off, hoping she wouldn't come across as snobby by not renting a pair. But Tara was squinting at her feet now. "It's not weird bringing my own skates, is it?"

"No. Not at all. Shawn hates renting skates and always brings a pair."

"But? You had kind of a skeptical look there for a minute."

"Well…" Tara shook her head. "Now I'm wondering what your feet look like and was trying to picture toes too long to fit in normal shoes."

Casey laughed. "Maybe don't think about it too hard."

"How long are they, though?"

"My dad used to call them monkey toes. On the plus side, I can pick up almost anything."

"With your toes?" Tara looked at Casey's feet. "Hidden talents, huh?"

"I usually don't talk about it," Casey said.

"Why hold that back?"

"You'd be surprised how many people don't want to think about long toes."

"Those people are boring." Tara waved her hand like she was dismissing all the long toe-haters. "Is it hard to find shoes that fit?"

"You have no idea." The fact that she'd even mentioned her toes was notable. Usually, she hid her feet from girlfriends, wearing socks and shoes whenever possible. Now she'd brought it up without even thinking and instead of feeling the usual embarrassment, it seemed ridiculous that it ever mattered. "Do you want to see?"

"No. Well, yes, but not now. It's freezing and I'm not making you strip off your socks to show me your monkey feet." Tara stepped forward and lightly kissed Casey's cheek. "But it's adorable you're willing to."

Casey's cheeks grew hot, even as she wished the kiss had been on the lips.

Tara seemed to notice, tilting her head to the side and narrowing her eyes on Casey. "Was that not okay? I should have asked." She shook her head a moment later. "I'm sorry. But no one's around and I wanted to kiss you."

"It's definitely okay. It surprised me a little because, you know, small town and all."

"Don't worry. No one's looking at us." Tara stepped back and gestured to the nearly empty ice rink where only a mother and a preschooler were skating. There were a few people in line to rent skates, but everyone had their backs to them.

Tara's demure kiss had Casey longing for more. But she needed the next one on the lips. And some privacy would be even better.

"How long do you feel comfortable leaving Aspen?" Tara asked.

Casey snapped back to the moment. It was only two in the afternoon, and Aspen had been nervous about being alone with the credit card machine acting punky. Plus it was only their second day. "Probably only a couple of hours."

"Then we better make the most of it."

Tara's suggestive tone had Casey struggling even to nod in response. They could skip the ice rink altogether and go back to her house...

"Get your skates on and I'll meet you out there."

It was hard not to stare at Tara's backside when she spun and headed for the skate rental line. She didn't want to hold back where Tara was concerned, even if rationally she knew she should take things slow. The problem was her hormones. The way Tara's hips swung as she walked, the way she brushed her hair back, the way she glanced at Casey with a flirty look—all of it short-circuited logic and left her with a pulsing clit. She let herself have one more look at Tara's backside, and then focused on her skates.

Once she was laced up, she paid the fee for her and Tara and went out onto the ice to warm up. It'd been almost ten years since she'd done any regular skating and at least twice as long since she'd been on an outdoor rink. Still, it all came flooding back. When Tara joined her, the smile on her lips looked almost suspicious.

"What?"

"You could have told me you were a professional. Now I'm going to feel like a huge dork when I fall on my butt while you're doing spins and those other tricks."

"I'm not a professional." She took Tara's hand, steadying her when she wobbled. "But my dad was. Before he met my mom, and before he ever got into making movies, he was a professional figure skater."

"Was he the one who taught you to skate?"

"He did. But as soon as I got the basics, he signed me up for lessons with the same coach he'd had. I liked it better when it was only me and my dad having fun on the ice."

"Are you and your dad close?"

"Not exactly. He's always been focused on work." Casey had let go of Tara's hand but took it again when Tara seemed about to lose her balance.

"What about you and your mom?"

"We've always been close though lately… We aren't talking much. I know she's disappointed." She gave a half shrug. "But she's always disappointed in me so that's not really new." She laughed but Tara seemed to study her more closely, as if knowing the laughter was a cover. "Anyway, at some point you stop trying to make your parents happy and do your own thing."

They skated together the length of the rink. When Tara didn't say anything, Casey decided it was safe to shift gears. "How's your relationship with your parents?"

"My mom is amazing. She's always supported me." Tara's lips pressed together. "My dad died my first year of college."

"Oh, I'm sorry. That must have been hard."

"It was. I miss him still." Tara exhaled. "I love my mom and my grandparents and Shawn, of course, but my dad was always the one who smoothed out all the problems." She paused. "Anyway, I get that family dynamics can be hard. So, are you going to show me some more tricks?"

"What would you like to see?" Casey let go of Tara's hand to skate backwards.

"Even skating backward is a trick compared to what I can do."

Which didn't mean Casey didn't want to pull out all the stops. "My old coach probably won't be impressed but here goes nothing."

Tara clapped her hands together when Casey bowed, her smile widening. Only a handful of other skaters were on the ice and she had plenty of space to open up. She picked up speed quickly, feeling the tension flow out of her body. When she skated around a mother and a kid, doing a little spin for fun, the kid cheered. Tara did too.

She leapt off the ice and the wind whipped her cheeks. For a moment, the sun blinded her and her heart lurched. She worried she was too out of practice and wouldn't stick the landing on the salchow. In the next second, though, her blade caught the ice. As soon as she had her balance, she did a toe loop and then went into another spin. She skated backward, passing the mother and kid who had now stopped to watch. She waved, then did a few waltz jumps, before passing a group of teens who clapped too.

She considered doing more tricks, enjoying the adrenaline and the rush of being back on the ice, but when her eyes met Tara's, she was done showing off. She simply wanted to skate with Tara. The look on Tara's face brightened more as she came closer and the delight in her eyes was everything Casey wanted.

"Impressed?"

"So much."

Casey reached out a hand and Tara clasped it tightly. "Don't be too impressed. I've still got monkey toes."

"Monkey toes, she tells me," Tara said, shaking her head. "You wanted me to feel sorry for you but then you pull out Fred Astaire on ice moves."

Casey skated in front of Tara and took both of her hands, one in each of her own. She skated backward, picking up speed as Tara gave her a wary look.

"What are you doing?"

"You scared?" Casey slowed the pace a bit.

Tara hesitated a moment before shaking her head. "No, but I don't usually skate with a partner."

"First time for everything, right?"

"I guess?" Tara glanced down at the ice. "I don't want to fall."

"If you go down, I go too."

"Not helpful."

Casey grinned, picking up the pace again and pulling Tara toward her. "Do you trust me?"

Tara's sharp intake of breath and the way her eyes darted up to Casey's said all that needed to be said.

"Not yet. Okay." She slowed again and started to let go of Tara's hands. Tara clasped tighter though and shook her head.

"I didn't say no."

Casey smiled. "You didn't."

"What are you thinking?"

Tara's tone was serious and Casey wasn't sure if the question was about skating or something more. "I was thinking that you've been showing me how to do so many things around this town. I'd kind of like to return the favor. If you'll let me." She waited a beat and then another.

Finally, Tara tipped her head. "Be careful with me."

Not simply be careful. Be careful *with me*. "I'll catch you if you start to fall." She spun to Tara's left side. "If I can't, I promise to fall too."

Tara laughed. An easy warm sound Casey had quickly come to love. "You could have left it at the first part."

Casey had to again fight the impulse to kiss Tara. Instead, she widened the distance between them and held out her hand.

For the next half hour, Tara's eyes didn't seem to leave hers. The world spun around them and Casey hardly noticed anything or anyone besides Tara. She taught Tara a few simple partner dance moves, and before long, Tara was perfectly following her lead. When one turn ended with Tara in her arms, their lips only inches apart, Casey felt herself shift closer and it was only Tara's finger landing on her lips that stopped her from a kiss. She hardly breathed, the space between her and Tara charged.

"People are looking," Tara said. There was no doubt Tara knew what she wanted. "You had to show off and get everyone's attention which means you missed your chance for that sort of thing." Her tone was firm but her eyes shined.

Casey sighed and pulled back, missing Tara's finger on her lips the moment it slipped off. "That'll teach me not to show off."

"Poor you." Tara tutted. "Making women swoon but having to wait for the kiss."

"Does that mean I get it later?"

"Maybe. You haven't let me fall yet."

Casey skated alongside Tara, wanting to reach for her hand but holding back. "Thanks for suggesting this. It feels amazing to be out on the ice again. I think I might come here every day until it closes. How long do they keep the rink open?"

"Until New Year's. But it's usually busier than this." Tara looked over at the group of teens who had gotten off the ice and were heading to return their rented skates. "You moved here with skates. Why?"

"I moved my whole life. Didn't leave anything behind." Except drama and bad memories, she added to herself. "And when I was thinking of visiting the first time, Kit told me about an indoor rink in one of the towns near Rocky Springs. But I haven't made time to look up where that rink is."

"You've been busy."

Casey's phone chirping seemed to confirm Tara's words. She reached into the front pocket of her jacket and tugged it out. "Aspen. Okay if I take this?"

"Of course."

She wasn't surprised that the credit card machine was on the fritz again, but disappointment washed over her all the same. As she told Aspen that she'd head back to the shop, she saw her feelings mirrored in Tara's expression. When she ended the call, Tara said, "So I guess this means I can't convince you to come back to my place."

Casey opened her mouth and then closed it, laughing. "I love that you don't hold back."

"The funny thing is, I usually do." Tara skated closer to Casey, then glanced around. The next instant she shifted forward and met Casey's lips with her own. The kiss was over as fast as it had started, but it sent a rush of arousal through Casey. Arousal, but something more too. Never before had she felt so comfortable with any woman she was simultaneously impressed by, attracted to, and worried she might let down. That last part she wished she could let go of, but she was still the same mess who had gotten married and divorced in the space of six short months.

Tara pushed back from her. "Hey, look at me. I'm skating backward like a pro." Her left skate wobbled over a ridge in the ice and her arms shot out as she suddenly lost her balance.

Casey rushed forward, catching Tara's hand. She managed to stop Tara's fall and keep her own balance, and a moment later Tara was laughing and leaning against Casey's chest.

"That was a close one."

"Yeah, I thought we talked about no falling today," Casey said.

Tara met her gaze. "I like knowing you can catch me."

CHAPTER SEVENTEEN

Tara almost didn't invite Casey back to her place after closing the shop for the night. She hadn't wanted to come across as clingy or desperate or any of those other dreadful words that could be the kiss of death when starting to date someone. But Casey had seemed genuinely disappointed about having to cut their time together short. Plus, she'd had to go back to work, and Tara didn't. It seemed wrong not to invite her over for dinner. So here she was, making coq au vin blanc for the first time in God knew how long and wondering if tonight was the night she'd finally get laid.

It probably wasn't fair to say finally. She and Casey had only gone on one official date, after all. And they'd agreed to take things slow. Still.

She'd wanted to go to bed with Casey the first day they met. That sizzle of attraction—one she hadn't experienced since moving back—had taken her by surprise and reminded her what it felt like to want someone, pure and simple. Yes, there'd been a few weeks of antagonism thrown in, but that had more to do with her ambitions for the shop than genuine animosity. If anything, trying to convince herself she disliked Casey only intensified how attracted she was. And then they'd become friends and the flirting got going in earnest and here they were.

It wasn't a bad place to be, even if she had no idea how long it would take them to actually get to the sex part. She might not be the most patient person, but she believed strongly some things were worth waiting for. Casey fell into that category. As did this coq au vin.

She dipped a spoon into the sauce and brought it to her lips, blowing a couple of times before giving it a taste. Not bad, but not entirely good, either. She chuckled to herself. Like sleeping with someone for the first time. Lots of potential, but the pieces didn't all click yet.

Tara chewed her bottom lip and frowned. It was missing something. She dropped the spoon into the sink, then returned to stare at the pot. Acid, for sure. She splashed in some white wine vinegar and grabbed a good pinch of flaky salt from the ceramic dish she kept next to the stove. She stirred gently, making sure not to disturb the perfectly browned chicken, and gave it another taste. There. Perfect.

Her good mood only got better with the knock at the door. She hurried to answer it and, even though she knew Casey would be on the other side, the sight of her standing there in her puffer jacket and jeans gave Tara a jolt of pleasure. And arousal. Definitely arousal. "Hi."

Casey returned the smile. "Hi."

She grabbed Casey's hand and pulled her inside. "I'm glad you're here."

"I'm glad I'm here, too." Casey sniffed the air. "Why does your apartment smell like my favorite French restaurant back in LA?"

"Because I made you a French dinner."

Casey paused, jacket halfway off. "You did?"

"Why do you sound surprised?"

"Because I don't know anyone who cooks fancy French food, especially after a morning of work and an afternoon of exercise."

Tara shrugged. "My workout was pretty tame compared to yours. You put on quite a show."

Casey winced. "Too much?"

"Just enough. Now, take off your coat and boots and stay a while."

Casey did and followed her into the kitchen. She pointed to the pot. "May I?"

She didn't know if Casey was after a deeper sniff or a taste, but she was fine with either. Especially now that she'd gotten the sauce how she wanted it.

Casey lifted the lid and peered in. "What is it?"

"Coq au vin, but with white wine. It's a little lighter but still cozy." Aka, a perfect pre-fuck dinner.

Casey narrowed her eyes slightly, as though she'd heard the part Tara hadn't said out loud. Or maybe she happened to be thinking it, too. But instead of giving herself away one way or the other, she simply smiled. "It looks, and smells, fantastic."

She canted her head, feeling bashful all of a sudden. "It's peasant food, really."

Casey set the lid back in place. "A lot of the best food is, don't you think?"

She thought about Juan's burritos, about having a baguette and a wedge of brie with a bottle of wine on her one trip to Paris. "Yeah."

"There's a story there, I can tell. Will you tell me?"

How did Casey know the exact right thing to say? And how had she managed to date so few women who did? Things to ponder alone, that's for sure. "I was just remembering my one time in France."

"I want to hear more." The look in Casey's eyes said she meant it.

"Let's get settled and we can trade travel stories. I'm sure you've been more exotic places that I have."

Casey shrugged, but Tara got the sense it was to downplay her experiences more than deny them. She invited Casey to pour wine while she dished up the chicken. She grabbed the salad from the fridge and the bread she'd set to warm in the oven and it wasn't long before they sat at the little table in her breakfast nook with steaming bowls between them.

True to her word, Casey peppered her with questions about the places she'd been. She did the same, realizing quickly that while she might have done a lot and seen a lot by Rocky Springs standards, Casey's life made hers seem downright provincial. Of course, with movie directors for parents, she probably should have expected it.

They finished eating and cleared the dishes. Tara waffled between suggesting another Christmas movie and trying for at least a make out session on the couch. But the second they walked into her tiny living room, Casey's eye went right to the naked spruce standing rather sadly in the corner. "You haven't decorated your tree yet," Casey said.

She flicked her wrist, more at Casey than the tree. "I've been a little busy."

Casey looked the tree up and down. "Would you like help or are you one of those people who's super particular and has to do it themselves?"

She raised an eyebrow. "I have no idea what you're talking about."

"No, of course not." Casey was clearly teasing her but added, "I think we all have a few perfectionist tendencies."

"Honestly, I'm not as bad with ornaments as I am with other things, and I'd love company to do it as much as help, but I don't want it to feel like I'm putting you to work."

"After all your help with my shop window, it's the least I could do."

She lifted a finger. "Yeah, but you paid me for that in breakfast burrito."

Casey mirrored the gesture. "Yeah, but you made me an incredible dinner."

Tara shook her head. "You're easy."

"Yep. Anyway, tree. As long as you don't move every single ornament the minute I hang it, I'd love to help."

Even at her fussiest and most fastidious, she couldn't imagine. "Who does that?"

"People," Casey said without missing a beat.

"Not this person." Tara poked her thumb into her chest. "I mean, unless you're really bad at it."

Casey laughed. "Fortunately for you, my mother is one of those people, so I come already trained."

She wanted to know more but sensed asking would be more can of worms than casual curiosity. So, she put a pin in it and turned her attention to the tangle of lights she'd regrettably stuffed into a bin the first week of January and not looked at since. Casey ribbed her for secretly not always being organized but switched to compliments when Tara quickly untangled the strands. They worked the strings around the tree, making a surprisingly good team.

Tara plugged them in, and they took a moment to admire their work. Then it was Casey who clapped her hands and asked where the ornaments were. "Gotta keep moving. We're on a roll."

Casey seemed to delight in her mismatched collection. She confessed Christmas ornaments were her souvenir of choice. "You get to enjoy them, but then put them away. Magnets, shot glasses, those little spoons. Those babies have to be out. And dusted."

Casey laughed. "I love that you're somehow a sentimental softie and yet painfully practical at the same time."

"I resemble that remark." She shook her head. "But please don't say it in front of Shawn. It's pithy enough that I'd probably end up with it embroidered on an apron or something."

"Now I know what I'm getting you for Christmas."

She'd been joking, but it got Tara wondering what she should get Casey. Because she should, right? They weren't girlfriends, but they'd agreed to date. That was Christmas present territory. Something for her house, maybe. Or the shop.

Her mind wandered and she continued to hang ornaments. She let her gaze land on Casey and linger. It was shockingly easy to imagine a cozy Christmas morning together. Inviting Casey to the big family dinner at her mom's house. Was it weird to imagine that as easily as what it would be like to tumble into bed together? Or to imagine it even before they'd done the tumbling?

Casey hung a crocheted snowman and tipped her head. Then, as though sensing Tara was watching, looked her way. "This is nice."

Tara added the sparkly penguin she'd been holding and pulled her mind back to the moment. "Nicer than passing out on your couch, you mean?"

"I don't know. That wasn't all bad."

Her stomach did a flip at the memory of waking up in Casey's arms. "This is safer, though."

"Safer?"

Should she admit exactly where her thoughts were? "If we were on the couch and not sound asleep, I'd be worried about keeping my hands to myself. This at least keeps them busy."

"Is that so?" Casey seemed surprised but maybe also a little delighted by the prospect.

"We agreed we'd go slow. I'm trying to respect that." Even if it was getting harder with each passing minute.

Casey frowned. "Right."

Disappointment deflated the swell in her chest like the air rushing out of an untied balloon. "Or maybe you're rethinking that altogether. I'd respect that, too."

"Tara."

The way Casey said her name, the intensity of her stare—it was enough to fill her right back up. With desire. With confidence. With certainty that Casey wanted her as much as she wanted Casey, whether or not they acted on it. "I've been known to be bossy in relationships. I don't want to be like that with you."

Casey narrowed her eyes. "Not even a little?"

She was pretty sure Casey was teasing her, but she'd been burned enough times that she couldn't back down or tease back. Instead, she shook her head.

"Hmm."

"I mean, I'm not a wallflower. I couldn't even pretend to be that convincingly."

Casey smiled. "That's a relief."

"I guess, at least for now, it feels like I should defer to you." Which was ironic given how they'd met and how free she'd been with her opinions about everything up to this point.

"Because I'm the sadder and more recently brokenhearted?"

"No. I mean yes." She pursed her lips. "Only the recent part. My track record isn't any better in the grand scheme of things."

Casey came around to her side of the tree and took her hand. "Is it wrong to say I like that you're not entirely and perfectly put together?"

"No, because it's mutual. I feel like I can be real with you. That's…" She searched for the right word. "Refreshing."

"I told Natalia that spending time with you was like a breath of fresh air."

"Thanks." Definitely the first time anyone had said that about her.

"I mean it. You are who you are. No pretense, no agenda."

"Well, I do have the one agenda." She looked Casey up and down. "But I'm being respectful."

"Right, right." Casey nodded slowly. "Deferring to me."

"Letting you decide when you're ready," she said, more as a clarification than a correction. Making it clear she sat squarely in the camp of when and not if.

"What if I was ready tonight?"

The other emotions of the night—good and bad—faded to the background. What remained was desire, pure and simple. The kind of desire that was laced with arousal. With anticipation. "I'd ask you what you were waiting for."

Chapter Eighteen

Therapy could wait. Casey had never been more sure of that. No, she didn't have a clear plan. And, yes, she still had issues she needed to work on. She also didn't know what Tara wanted in the long run. But tonight none of that mattered. What mattered was that when she kissed Tara, she knew the strum of desire was the same in her too. There was no guessing, no uncertainty.

When she closed the distance between them, Tara's lips parted, tongue darting to hers, and she stopped thinking. Their bodies pressed together, and Tara's sharp inhale confirmed everything she felt. Finally, she could let her libido lead.

Between kisses, Tara said, "I don't know why I wasted time being mad at you."

"It had something to do with dildos. Apparently, you don't like them near your cupcakes."

Tara laughed, pulling away before Casey could kiss her again. "For the record, I have no problem with sex toys." She moved her hands up Casey's arms and settled at her shoulders. "I was maybe a little nervous about what you were going to put next to my cupcakes but—"

"A little?" Casey teased her.

"Yes, only a little. And I do hate the D word but I love how they—" Tara stopped short and her cheeks reddened.

"You love how they what?" Casey wanted Tara's answer. The air between them had gotten hotter with simply the mention of sex toys.

"Weren't we busy kissing?"

Tara moved to kiss her again, but Casey turned so she'd only get her cheek. Tara's eyeroll managed to ride the line between sexy and playful and only increased the temperature between them. "Embarrassed to tell me what you think about dildos?"

"Do you have to keep saying that word?"

When Casey started to say the word again, Tara pressed a finger to her lips. The move was so hot Casey's breath caught. Now she was the one wishing they could stop talking and go back to kissing.

"I'm not embarrassed." Tara's chin jutted up. "But it is a ridiculous word and plenty of women agree with me on this. Plus, I feel a little silly talking about sex toys with you."

"Why?"

Tara's breath came out in a huff. "You own a shop that sells them."

"Which makes me a little worried if even the word dildo has you feeling uncomfortable."

"Fine. I'll tell you the truth. I hate the word, but I love how they feel. It has been a hot minute since I've had someone want to wear one for me, though, and I'm a little out of practice. There. I said it."

"You do? Love how they feel I mean."

Tara nodded, her eyes locked on Casey's. "One of my favorite things. I love the sensation. I love...all of it."

"That's fucking hot."

"You're welcome. Want to know more?" She didn't wait for Casey's answer before continuing. "Hearing you talk to customers and seeing you be all confident handling the strap-ons and everything else in your store makes me so turned on I can hardly think." Tara's hand moved down Casey's arm. "Can we go back to kissing now?"

"What if I want to hear more about how turned on you get thinking about dil—"

Tara interrupted Casey with a kiss. One long deep kiss that took her breath away. When they parted, she opened her eyes. Tara's eyes stayed closed a second longer before meeting hers.

"You're good at changing the subject."

"I wasn't trying to change the subject," Tara returned. "I was helping you refocus."

"So your kisses won't always be that good?"

"Oh, I make a point of being good at kissing. And other things."

Casey started to laugh but was stopped with a look from Tara. Pure desire. Tara touched Casey's throat and drew a slow line downward, pausing at the hollow at the base of her neck and then with Casey's nod, continuing lower. She traced down the line of buttons and only stopped again when she reached the belt. She hooked the buckle with her index finger, pulling Casey toward her subtly as her tongue slipped over her lips.

Casey felt a throb between her legs. "Fuck."

"Good. We're on the same page." Tara arched an eyebrow, her lips curving in a smile. "I don't mind keeping you focused, you know, when you look at me that way."

Casey couldn't return the playful banter. Her thoughts were consumed with how much she wanted Tara. She threaded her fingers through Tara's hair, loving that she wore it down tonight. Silky locks slipped through her fingers and caught the light from the Christmas tree. "Everything about you drives me a little wild."

Tara's eyes caught the sparkling lights. "Then why are we still talking?"

Casey shifted forward and kissed Tara again. She slid her hands down Tara's sides. When she slipped under the sweater, the feel of Tara's warm soft skin against her fingertips sent a jolt through her. "I have a feeling I'm in trouble with you."

"Don't worry. It's good trouble."

And maybe that's what she needed. She didn't slow to overthink as she pushed the sweater up or unhooked Tara's bra and tossed it to the couch. When she turned back, Tara moved into her hands, full breasts filling her palms. "Damn. You feel good."

"Then warm me up a little," Tara said, shivering and shifting closer.

"I can do that." She thought of taking Tara to the bedroom where they'd be plenty warm under the blankets, but she didn't want to wait. She needed Tara now. And she didn't stop herself from going for what she needed.

Tara's body was everything she wanted and so responsive it made her heady. And Tara didn't hold back, her teeth grazing Casey's neck as her hands roamed freely. Their moans and low hungry sounds filled the room, turning Casey on more.

She wanted Tara naked—wanted to slide her hand between Tara's legs, wanted to feel Tara arch against her, wanted to know how Tara tasted and how she sounded when she came. She pushed Tara back a step and then another until she was pressed against the wall.

"Did you want a bed?" she asked, pulling back from a kiss to catch Tara's response. "I want to do this the right way."

"Who says this isn't the right way?"

Tara's words were all she needed. They moved together again, Tara working shirt buttons loose as Casey explored every inch of Tara she had access to. She wanted more. When she dipped her head to take a nipple between her lips, Tara responded with a sharp gasp. Tara pulled back for a second but then pushed her breasts toward Casey in the next breath.

Casey sucked until the nipple was a hard bud with Tara moaning and urging her on. She tried to ignore the desire to bite Tara's breast. Just a nip on the rounded soft flesh that pressed against her mouth. It was something she'd never done. Something she'd never felt permission to do. But when she glanced up, Tara looked as if she knew exactly what Casey wanted.

"You can go harder."

Casey hesitated. "You sure?"

Tara's nod let her give into her desire. She grazed her teeth over the soft breast and then bit. Tara gasped but pushed herself more into Casey's mouth.

"Fuck, I like that," Tara said. "More where that came from."

She wasn't sure exactly why she wanted to bite. Or what made her want to be more aggressive with Tara. All she wanted to know was that Tara wanted it too. When she moved to Tara's other breast, she didn't hold back. Tara's nails sank into her arms, followed by a low groan of satisfaction.

Casey tugged at Tara's leggings, needing her naked. She pulled away from Tara's breast and asked, "How do you feel about pants?"

Tara let out a short laugh. "Is that how you ask a woman to strip?"

"Not usually."

"Usually you don't have to ask?" Tara seemed to be baiting Casey, but her look was playful.

Casey shook her head, touching Tara's leggings again. "May I please take these off?"

"It's cute that you're the one saying please after getting me all wet." Tara kissed her lips, then her cheek, then her neck before whispering into her ear, "You tell me you want to take it slow, make me wait while I get all hot and bothered over here thinking all I get is your help decorating my damn tree, and then you jump me in my living room."

"I—"

Casey didn't get to apologize or ask if Tara wanted to go to her bedroom. In the next moment, her mouth was taken up with Tara's hard kiss. Tara pulled back and said, "I like pants, but I don't want to be wearing them at the moment. I'm wet and want other things besides pants."

"How wet?"

"It's almost indecent." Tara's teeth traced along Casey's collarbone. She pushed Casey's open shirt off. "You got to bite me. Can I bite you back?"

Casey nodded, a thrill of anticipation zipping through her. The thrill merged into a moment of sharp pain when Tara bit down on her shoulder. Pleasure flooded through her when Tara pulled back with a guilty smile.

"You liked that, didn't you?" Casey asked.

Tara touched the already reddening spot. "I can't believe I did that." She covered her mouth. "It's going to leave a mark."

Casey caught Tara's hand and pulled it away from her mouth. "I've never had someone bite me."

"I'm sorry—"

"I like it. You can do it anytime." Casey pushed Tara back against the wall. "Now about your pants."

Tara looked down at Casey's hands, index fingers hooked under the waistband of her leggings. "You want me to take them off?"

"I don't want you to have to do anything by yourself tonight." She pushed Tara's pants down an inch, running her hands along Tara's waist like she intended to go slow. "Do you know how much I want to feel how wet I've made you?"

Tara shifted forward, kissing her. "See for yourself."

She pulled away from the kiss, dropped to her knees and stripped off Tara's pants along with her underwear. The scent of Tara's arousal filled her senses. It was everything she wanted. When she kissed Tara's thigh, Tara tensed.

"Stop me if this isn't okay." She kissed Tara's other thigh, trying to slow herself down, trying to wait for Tara's signal. She glanced up and Tara was waiting for her eyes. She ran her hand through Casey's hair, lips parted in anticipation. When Casey put a hand on each of her thighs, Tara shifted her legs apart.

Tara wasn't joking about how wet she was. Dripping. Casey touched her tongue to the wetness, tasting what her body had been anticipating and finding it even better than she'd imagined. She slid between the folds, pressed Tara open more and then circled her opening.

"Oh, damn." Tara fell back against the wall, fingers tangling in Casey's short hair. She gripped Casey's shoulders and parted her legs further. Casey dipped her head and found Tara's swollen clit. She lashed and stroked until Tara was panting between her moans. Then Casey sucked down hard.

Tara came fast, crying out as a sudden orgasm claimed her. She sank into Casey's mouth in one moment, then pulled away, only to push herself firmly back on Casey's lips. She trembled and cussed, squeezing her legs together as the wave of her climax rolled through her.

When she finally shivered and then relaxed, Casey stood and wrapped her in an embrace.

"Sorry, that was—"

"Don't apologize for anything." Casey kissed her cheek and then her lips.

"I came faster than I thought I would," she admitted, her expression sheepish.

"It was fucking hot. The only hard part about you coming fast is it makes me want you all over again." Casey kissed her again, gently this time.

"Who says you can't have me again?"

Casey's eyes darted to Tara's. "Are you serious? You'd let me have more?"

She was more turned on than ever. Tara wanted her. No question. And wanted more. She slid her hand down Tara's front, between her breasts and over her belly. She hesitated at her center, searching Tara's eyes for permission. It seemed too good to be true. When Tara only held her gaze, making her burn all the more with longing, she had to ask. "Can I touch you again?"

"You've been doing lots of touching," Tara returned.

"I want you to come on my hand."

Tara stroked down Casey's arm. She gripped Casey's wrist and then pushed her hips forward. As soon as Casey felt the wetness on her fingers, she pushed inside. Tara gasped and let go of Casey's wrist. She shifted her grip to Casey's arms, rocking her hips forward and back, and letting Casey's finger glide in and out of her opening.

"You feel so good," Casey murmured.

"I was going to say the same thing." Tara moved away from the wall and wrapped her arms around Casey's back. "More?"

In the next stroke, Casey slid another finger inside and Tara moaned her pleasure. Tara wrapped her arms around Casey, and murmured, "That's what I want."

They fell into a rhythm. Each time Casey stroked, Tara arched into her. She was perfect. Tight and slick and responsive.

Casey didn't think she could ever get enough. Her own clit pulsed as her thumb strummed against Tara's between thrusts. She realized she was panting as much as Tara and her back was wet with sweat. But she had no intention of stopping. Every time she rocked back, Tara murmured, "More."

Tara had been wet before but now she was soaking. Her wetness dripped between Casey's fingers and down her thighs. Still she asked for more. When her breath hitched, Casey pushed deeper. She worked Tara's clit and a responding quiver in her own made her knees weak.

"Don't stop," Tara pleaded.

Tara was close. Casey loved that she could get her there. It'd been too long since she'd had sex that felt this easy and right. This good. Her fingers simply fit in Tara. And she knew her thumb landed on exactly the right spot because of the sounds Tara made and how her walls clenched.

As Tara's climax built, she wished she could slow things down. She wanted to keep doing exactly what they were doing for the rest of the night. She could hold Tara up when she got too tired to stand…

That thought zipped out of her head when Tara cried out. She came hard, again cussing even while tremors took over. Her center rhythmically clenched Casey's fingers until she pressed herself hard into Casey's hand.

"Fuck, you feel good."

"Ditto," Tara murmured. She sagged into Casey's arms saying, "Don't pull away yet."

Casey kissed Tara's cheek. "You're amazing."

"You haven't even gotten me in bed yet," Tara said, her words slurring as an aftershock had her clenching Casey's fingers again.

Casey smiled.

When Tara opened her eyes, she smiled too. "What's got you looking all cocky?"

"This hot baker." She pulled her fingers out and Tara shifted her legs together with an adorable moan. "So how soon can I do that again?"

"Are you saying you didn't get enough?"

"Not nearly enough."

"I don't know what to do with you." Tara shook her head, but her eyes betrayed her. Casey's words had definitely made her happy.

"You could let me have more."

"I'm not saying no but I want a bed next time."

Casey wanted to suggest that now would be good for a *next time*. Her body was begging for a release. Still, she didn't want to assume Tara wanted anything more. She stepped back from Tara, trying to tamp down her desire, and glanced around the room. For a moment she was disoriented. Like she'd been pulled from a dream. Christmas tree on her right, window on the left with the curtains half drawn and the streetlights illuminating flakes of snow falling soundlessly on the sidewalk. Tara's gaze tracked to the window.

"It's snowing again."

"I feel like that happens a lot around here." It was a ridiculous thing to say and she couldn't help adding, "Is that a Colorado thing?"

Tara laughed, making her tingly and warm, and then kissed her cheek. Considering all the kisses they'd already shared, it was funny that a cheek kiss along with Tara snuggling up to her made her chest feel tight. But that's what happened.

She was still processing her emotions when Tara said, "I could show you some other Colorado things."

"Like what?"

"My bed." Tara winked and added, "I don't want to send you out in the cold. It wouldn't be polite."

"I like that people in Colorado are polite and offer you their bed when it snows."

"Not everyone in Colorado is that polite. You got lucky." Tara reached for Casey's hand. She brought it to her lips, then opened her mouth and slid her tongue over Casey's fingertips. "Still deciding on if you want to stay?"

"No. I mean, yes." She shook her head. "You've got me distracted."

"Because I'm naked?"

Casey swallowed. "I think that's part of it." She let her gaze drop to Tara's breasts, then lower past her midsection and down her thighs. When she met Tara's eyes again, Tara smiled.

"Like what you see, Casey Stevens?"

"So much."

"Then come to bed with me."

There wasn't one thing that Casey wanted more.

Chapter Nineteen

Tara woke, arm trapped under her and completely numb. The rest of her wasn't much better. How could a body feel stiff and sore while being so loose and limber at the same time? Oh, right. A marathon sex session that lasted half the night. She rolled from her stomach to her back and let out a groan.

"Huh? What?" Casey's head jerked up and her gaze darted around before landing on Tara. "Are you okay?"

God, she wished she could be subtle sometimes. "Yes. Sorry. I didn't mean to wake you."

"Don't apologize. I wake with a start sometimes. I'd swear I heard something. Like an animal in distress." Casey narrowed her eyes. "Was that you?"

Tara winced. "Yeah. I, um, my arm was asleep."

"Oh." Casey smiled, like that was a perfectly logical explanation. "I take it that means you slept well."

Like the freaking dead. "I did. You?"

Casey let out a happy sigh. "So good. I swear orgasms are the best sleep aid on the planet."

She chuckled. "They do seem to have that effect."

Casey's gaze drifted down, taking in Tara's naked torso. "Especially when they're as good as they were last night."

"And plentiful." She honestly couldn't remember the last time she'd come so many times in one night.

Casey's left hand cupped Tara's breast. "So plentiful."

Slightly self-conscious in the light of day, Tara cleared her throat. "How early do you need to be at the shop?"

"Depends. Do I get to talk you into having sex with me again?"

She crossed her arms. "You can't possibly still be horny."

Casey didn't miss a beat. "Now that I know how good sex with you is, I'm hornier than ever."

She laughed because it was ridiculous, but also sweet. And, if she was being honest, hot. How delightful.

Casey's face scrunched up. "I take it I'm alone in that feeling."

Realizing she'd given Casey the absolute wrong impression, Tara grabbed her hand. "I definitely want more of you but this time I think I need a twenty-four-hour recovery window."

Casey's expression remained serious. "Was I too rough? I didn't mean to get so carried away. I—"

"You were exactly the right amount of rough. I practically begged for it." She'd loved every minute. "But I might be a tiny bit out of practice."

"Oh." Understanding dawned in Casey's eyes, mixed with appreciation and quickly followed by arousal.

"Which isn't to say I don't want to get back in practice." Though was it even fair to compare the sex in her last couple of relationships with what she and Casey got up to last night?

"Well, you know what they say."

She narrowed her eyes, more instinct than true suspicion. "What?"

"Practice makes perfect."

Tara let out a graceless snort, but then she laughed. Because of course Casey could turn some terrible motivational cliché and make it sexy. "Are you offering yourself up for the task?"

Casey seemed to genuinely consider. "I do think continuous education and exploration are essential to a robust and satisfying sex life."

"Wow, you should own a sex shop or something."

It was Casey's turn to snort, and Tara found it more adorable than was probably reasonable. "Or something."

"Speaking of…"

"Practice making perfect or my shop?" Casey asked.

"Yes." Tara went for a mischievous grin. "I was hoping we might pick something out to, you know, enjoy together."

"Yeah?" Casey sounded excited, if slightly surprised, by the idea.

She'd broached the subject, but shyness creeped in and stole any trace of swagger she might have had. "It's important to support my fellow businesswoman."

Casey nodded slowly. Surprise or not, she definitely saw through Tara now. "You did mention a fondness for dildos."

"Along with my discomfort with the word, if you recall."

"Oh, I recall." Casey leaned in. "Is there something you prefer to call them? Cock, perhaps? Strap-on?"

Tara's breath caught at Casey's almost whispered suggestions. "If you're offering to use one on me, you can call it anything you want."

Casey visibly swallowed. "Is that so?"

She nodded.

"Well, then, I think you should come by the shop on your way into work and pick one out."

The mere thought—holding them in her hand, imagining how the different sizes and shapes would feel—had her clenching her thighs together. "If I pick it out before work, I won't be able to think about anything else all day."

"That's the point."

"You've got a naughty streak, Casey Stevens." And she liked it far more than she'd thought possible.

Casey ran a finger along her jaw and down her neck. "So do you, Tara McCoy. And I'm so glad you're letting me see it."

Her stomach did a flip that had more to do with feelings than simple arousal. She was already naked, but the sensation left her feeling exposed and antsy. "Well, even naughty people need to eat, so we should talk breakfast before we both have to hustle off to work."

"I'm definitely ready for food. I can't remember the last time I've woke up this hungry."

She liked that she'd given Casey an appetite. "I can make basic eggs and toast with what I have on hand, or we can go out."

"We should go out. You cooked for me last night. You shouldn't have to, again."

Tara studied Casey's upbeat expression, searched for the words she hadn't said. "You have a hard time letting people do nice things for you, don't you?"

Casey's head fell forward for a second, but her smile didn't falter. "Whatever gave you that impression?"

"Maybe because it takes one to know one?"

"I guess that makes us good company."

They took turns in the shower. Tara threw on jeans and a sweater and tucked her bakery clothes in a bag. Casey pulled on her clothes from the night before and said she'd change when she got to work. "You keep extra clothes at work?" Tara asked.

"After an incident with an exploding bottle of lube the week I opened, yes. Yes, I do."

She laughed at the image. "I'm sorry I missed it."

"Let me assure you, it was not a good look. And fake strawberries and cream is not a scent I need following me around all day."

A more woodsy earthy smell fit Casey better. "Sometimes I wonder if I smell like cupcakes all the time."

"You smell perfect," Casey said. "Which is partly why I didn't want to stop last night."

Tara knew she couldn't handle more but Casey's comment made her think of it. She pushed away thoughts of sex and tried to focus on breakfast. "I'll get a ride home from Shawn later if you want to drive us both?"

Casey parked in her usual spot near the shop so they could stroll together the few blocks through downtown to the diner and enjoy all the finished window displays. They'd had a couple inches of snow overnight that only added to the holiday feel.

They stepped into the diner and were enveloped by warm air and the aroma of bacon. The poppy beat of classic Christmas music vied to be heard over the hum of conversations and the clatter of utensils on plates and spatulas against the flat top. Colored lights blinked from where they'd been hung over the register and around the display case of pies, reflecting off the old school silver tinsel garland wound around them. Casey stopped, as though she'd run into a physical wall instead of one made up of sights and smells and sounds.

"Too much?" Tara asked.

Casey shook her head, grin wide. "I love it."

The before work crowd was clearing out, so in under a minute, they were seated at a booth overlooking the snowy sidewalk. Barb, a fixture of the place for as long as Tara remembered, came over with menus and a pot of coffee in hand. Casey's nod of enthusiasm rivaled her own feelings about the first cup of the day. Barb filled their mugs and left them to contemplate their orders.

"You're sure it's not too much? Even I get a little sensory overload in here sometimes."

Casey shook her head. "I feel like I'm in a movie."

"It's not the first time you've said that. I can't decide if Rocky Springs is that picturesque or if movies are that much in your blood." Or maybe it was her own jaded eye that kept her from appreciating all that this tiny town had to offer.

"A little of both, maybe. I mean it in a good way. It's such a refreshing break from LA."

For some reason, Casey's use of the word break gave her pause. "I guess that's why more people visit than stay."

"And those of us that do stay get to enjoy it all the time."

She couldn't tell whether Casey meant that as a passing observation or a personal declaration, but today wasn't the day to tease it out. They only had a couple of hours before their respective shops opened and, between the workout she got last night and the day she had in front of her, she had every intention of spending it carb loading. "Do you have the same thing every time you go to a diner, or do you mix it up?"

Casey didn't hesitate or bother looking at the menu. "Western omelet with cheddar. Hash browns. Whole wheat toast."

"Okay, then."

"I take it that's not your approach?" Casey asked.

"As a pastry chef, I'm always looking for new takes on sweet stuff. And I need protein, but I'm not big on eggs." Saying it out loud made her feel like a picky third grader.

"So…" Casey's gaze dropped to the menu for a moment. "You'd go with the Fruity Pebbles French toast and a side of bacon?"

She twitched her lips one way, then the other. "Are you ordering for me or making fun of me?"

"I don't see those needing to be mutually exclusive." Casey's eyes were playful but held challenge—a surprisingly enticing combination.

"For the record, I've had it and it's insanely sweet, even by my 'I make cupcakes for a living' standards." Though she secretly loved that's what Casey picked for her.

"Hmm." Another perusal of the menu. "What about the cinnamon chip Belgian waffle with bananas?"

"Sold." She'd had that, too, and it was one of her standbys.

Barb returned and Casey, to her credit, made deferential eye contact and waited for her nod before ordering for both of them. "You got it, sweet cheeks," Barb said, slipping her pencil behind her ear after she'd scribbled on her pad.

"Are you ready for the big window display winner announcement this weekend?" Tara asked after Barb left to put in their order.

"Ready to clap and be gracious when you win, you mean?"

"Hey, you could take home the ribbon." She hadn't said anything to Casey—mostly because she didn't know how much sway she actually had—but she'd been quietly campaigning for votes for Casey's window to win. At first it had been about sticking it to Gary without having to be public about it and put her grandfather in an awkward position. But now that she and Casey were dating, she wanted Casey to have that boost. The personal one as much as the one to her business.

"I absolutely won't, but I appreciate that you helped me make a good showing. I think it's helped my 'just one more small business in town' vibe."

She quirked a brow. "As opposed to the vibrators for every occasion vibe?"

It was a terrible joke, but Casey still laughed. "Exactly."

"For what it's worth, I like your vibe." And pretty much every other aspect of Casey she'd seen so far. Including that stubborn determination to make it when the cards seemed stacked against her.

Casey's expression somehow softened and intensified at the same time. "For what it's worth, the feeling is mutual."

"Maybe you'll have to recommend one to me. Along with, you know." She tipped her head back and forth, torn between brazen and blushing.

Casey sipped her coffee and set the mug down like they were discussing the day's forecast. "The cock you're going to pick for me to fuck you with you mean?"

Tara coughed and looked around, certain someone had heard. But the tables around them had cleared and Brenda Lee was rockin' around the Christmas tree rather loudly. No one had heard but her. And on the other side of her embarrassment sat an intense desire—for Casey, for that cock, and for all the things they'd get up to with it. So she might as well sit back and enjoy it. She took a sip of her own coffee, then said, "Yes. The cock I'm going to pick out for you to fuck me with."

CHAPTER TWENTY

Tara slipped her hand in Casey's as they left the diner. She mumbled something about never leaving home without gloves in December, and then a bit louder added, "Must have been distracted."

"Huh. Why?" Casey guessed but wanted to ask—wanted the answer—anyway.

"I woke up with some hottie in my bed."

"I could see that happening often to someone as sexy as you. Must be a real hardship."

"Sadly, it doesn't happen nearly often enough." Tara sighed like that was a real disappointment though her look was playful.

"It could happen more if you say the word."

"And if I play my cards right?"

When Tara simply held her gaze, Casey couldn't come up with a bantering return. Everything felt perfect. Not only Tara's hand in hers but everything else about the morning. Sunlight glinted off the newly fallen snow, capping the cars parked along the street and frosting the nearby mountains. The air was crisp but with an expectant edge, like the wind had paused to enjoy the day but might bring a storm later. Something to push everyone indoors to enjoy a cozy evening when the Christmas lights flickered on the garland-lined street posts and the bare-branched mulberry trees. The sidewalk trees were all dotted with ornaments and the decorations could have been too much, too overdone to push the Christmas spirit, but like the diner with the waitress singing carols, all of it fit.

And all of it made Casey happy. Ridiculously happy.

She couldn't ignore the feeling of being right where she was supposed to be, holding the hand of the person she was supposed to be with. Happiness zipped through her even as she tried to ignore a whisper of foreboding. Reality was, she had no plan where Tara was concerned. She had no clue what the next step should look like or if there would even be a next step.

Stop. Things can simply feel good.

There wasn't always a piano about to drop. She glanced up again, squinting in the blindingly bright Colorado sunshine and taking in the cloudless sky above the mountains. The sky was a shade of blue that didn't exist in LA. Gorgeous deep blue. She took a deep breath, reminding herself it was okay to take things slow and not have a plan. It was dumb to expect everything to implode simply because things felt so good.

"I like you," she said.

Tara gave her a side-eye and then laughed. "I like you, too."

Casey felt her smile strain her cheeks and then noticed how others passing by all smiled back—if they happened to look up from their feet or their phones. No one seemed to care that two women were holding hands. Casey wouldn't have let go even if someone had said something though. Tara's hand felt too good, warm and soft and fitting perfectly with hers.

"Also, I'm kind of glad you forgot your gloves."

"You like an excuse to keep me warm?" Tara's tone was light, but she seemed to know the truth and shifted closer to Casey as they neared the intersection.

A car slowed for them to cross and then the window rolled down and a Black man inside waved to Tara. Tara waved back, saying, "Hi, Clyde." As he drove past, she turned to Casey and added, "Clyde owns the auto shop over on Oak Drive if your car ever needs anything. He's the best mechanic around."

"Good to know."

Another car slowed before they'd gone far, and a younger guy lowered his window and called to Tara. She said hello, waving back, and then turned to Casey. "That's Clyde's son Luke."

"Does he work with his dad?" Both cars had turned the same direction.

"No. Luke's an IT guy. I can't remember which big tech company he works for but he's all remote now. He went to school with Shawn and was big into computers even back then. Cool guy but his sister is even cooler. And queer. She designs websites if you ever want to overhaul yours."

"I love that you know everyone. I don't need Google. I can just call you and say—so I need an electrician."

"Miguel. He's the best."

"And a plumber?"

"Bailey's Plumbing. They're a little pricey but always honest." Tara steepled her fingers and tapped them together. "What else?"

Casey grinned. "You know the best part? Since I know Tara McCoy, I don't need to get to know anyone else. She can hook me up with anything I need."

"It'd probably be good for you to get to know other people here too."

"Why?"

"Well…" Tara's brow furrowed. "What if we get in a fight? Who are you going to complain to?"

Natalia, probably. Or maybe Kit. Aside from her parents, Natalia and Kit were the only ones from her previous life who even knew where she was now. But Casey said, "I don't want to fight with you about anything. I'm not really a fighter, remember?"

"Not dealing with issues can be as much of a problem as having a fight and getting it all out." Tara bumped against Casey. "But we don't have to talk about that today."

Casey met her gaze and smiled. "Thanks?"

"Not talking about it today doesn't mean I'm letting you off the hook entirely. But I'm enjoying our post-sex high too much at the moment to start that conversation."

Casey had been too, though now her earlier anxiety pushed up and she wondered again about going to therapy. It wasn't like the opportunity had passed. She could still start even if she'd already slept with Tara.

They stopped at the next intersection for a delivery truck and then a handful of other cars. Rocky Springs was officially waking up for another busy day of the Christmas season. Yet, for the first time in months, the business of being busy seemed to swirl past Casey. She didn't stress about getting to her shop early or worry about how much money she had to make that day to keep the doors open. The reality of needing to make a profit was more pressing now that she also had to pay Aspen, but today everything felt doable.

She didn't think anything could bring her down from the high she felt with Tara. Not until they were halfway down the next block and Tara's steps slowed. "Something wrong?"

Tara didn't answer, her gaze narrowing on two women standing in front of Casey's store. The women had their backs to Casey and Tara, talking to each other with heads bent together. Then one turned to the side, gazing between Coy Cupcakes and the Sweet Spot. Casey spotted an envelope in the older woman's hand. Some kind of notice for her shop?

"Mom?" Tara asked, her steps picking up again as she let go of Casey's hand. "What are you doing here? I thought you were taking Grandpa in for his physical."

Casey's stomach clenched like a fist, but she forced herself to keep up with Tara. She'd seen Tara's mom a few times, but they'd only had a cursory introduction. From the look on Tara's mom's face now, her gaze darting between Tara and Casey, she knew something was going on between them. How much had Tara told her? And did she approve? What if Tara's whole family hated her? Casey pushed those questions away as she struggled to recall Tara's mom's name. Debbie?

"Oh good. You're both here." Debbie's cheery tone made Casey glance at Tara.

"Is everything okay?" Tara asked, clearly still in the dark as much as Casey was. "Did Grandpa's doctor have news about the tests?"

"Yes, but that's not why we're here." Debbie seemed to read Tara's continued look of concern because she added, "He has to increase his blood pressure medication and they want him back next week to check a few other things. Nothing serious."

Tara exhaled, visibly relieved.

"We're on serious business, here, however," the woman next to Debbie said, a slight huff in her voice. "It's a good thing you came when you did. Neither of us brought tape."

"Uh, Casey, this is Patricia," Tara said, still seeming not to know why the elderly woman was with her mom or why both of them were outside Casey's shop. "And, Patricia, this is—"

"Oh, I know who she is." Patricia's coifed gray bob was several shades lighter than her gray coat and her deep wrinkles made Casey guess she was pushing ninety. Still, she seemed plenty full of vigor as she waved the envelope. "We were bringing her this. It's too big to slip under the door. We already tried."

Casey squinted at the envelope. Next to the name of her shop was the number one circled in blue. She looked between Patricia and Debbie but didn't have time to ask whether it was good news or bad before Tara clapped her hands together and let out a cheer.

"Oh my God," Tara said. "You won!"

"I won?"

Debbie nodded, seemingly as excited as her daughter. "And Coy Cupcakes came in second."

Patricia handed Tara a similar envelope but with a circled two on the front. "You've gotten one of these envelopes before, so you know what's inside." She turned to Casey as she added, "Since you're the newbie, and the big winner, you better read everything. Hang your ribbon in your window and then brag all over the web about it. That's what you young people do, right?"

"What Patricia means," Debbie said, giving Casey an apologetic look, "Is the committee would appreciate it if you could post a picture on social media. All the downtown businesses benefit when people see posts about Rocky Springs. More posts mean more visitors."

"You are on social media, aren't you?" Patricia gave Casey a hard look.

Casey's mouth had dropped open with the realization that her window display had taken first place and only now did she close it. "Uh, yeah. Sure."

"Good. Then post all about this."

Technically, she didn't have any social media accounts. She'd deleted everything before the move and hadn't bothered setting up anything new. But that didn't mean she couldn't set up something for the shop that morning. And by now, the Casey Stevens who lived in Rocky Springs and owned a sex shop wouldn't likely be found by any of the "online friends" who'd known the old Casey Stevens.

"And congratulations, my dear. I thought the Mrs. Claus taking a night to pamper herself was brilliant."

"Thanks." Casey glanced at Tara. "Honestly, that was Tara's idea."

"I'm not surprised." Patricia patted Tara's arm. "I knew you'd come around to see this," she hooked her thumb behind her to gesture at Casey's shop, "was exactly what Rocky Springs needed. Fresh and sexy."

Now Casey was fully floored. She'd never have guessed that a woman like Patricia would have been on her side. Tara hurried to say that it hadn't taken her long to see the value in the new business next door while Debbie heartily agreed.

"We all know sex sells and this town could use more shoppers," Patricia said. "More tourists in general and more fresh arrivals wanting to stay, too, if you ask me."

"As long as we stick to calling everyone fresh arrivals," Debbie said, shaking her head.

Patricia gave a half-shrug and turned to Casey. "I may have called you fresh meat during the social committee meeting."

This time it was Tara's mouth that dropped open. Casey stifled a laugh and Debbie interrupted with, "Maybe you could open your shop early? Patricia wanted to look around and I have to admit I do too."

More surprising news.

"I'm ninety-one. I doubt there's anything in there I haven't already seen, but you never know."

Casey pulled out her keys. She held the door for everyone to file past and Tara brought up the rear, stopping right in front of her with a wide smile.

"You seem surprised you won. Your window really did come out great."

"It did but... Did you have something to do with it?" Casey couldn't help thinking that Tara might have swayed some votes. She'd overheard a few customers in the past week mention someone in the cupcake shop had insisted they check out the window display next door.

Tara clasped her hand to her chest. "Why would I help the competition?"

"You did, didn't you?"

"Did what? Catch the hottest newbie to show up in Rocky Springs?" She went up on her toes and placed a quick kiss on Casey's lips. When she pulled back, her eyes seemed to dance with happiness. She glanced in the direction of her mother and Patricia. "I was hoping to pick out that special item we were talking about earlier, but now I'm thinking I might need to ask for a rain check. I have to open up the bakery and there's no telling how long Patricia and my mom will be here."

Casey couldn't hide her disappointment, though they did both have to work. "What are you doing tonight? I'm open til seven. You could come by around closing time."

"Sounds perfect."

Another quick kiss, then Tara went to tell her mother and Patricia she had to open the bakery, and in the next breath she was gone. Out the door so fast Casey didn't have a chance to tell her how amazing the night and morning had been.

Fortunately, thoughts of what they'd done and what they might do later kept Casey's mind spinning for the rest of the morning and the afternoon as well. Aspen showed up for a four-hour shift, giving her time to slip home for a workout and a shower before getting back to the store for rush hour shoppers. The last customer left at seven with a bag full of bondage equipment and a big smile.

It had been a big sales day and Casey couldn't help a ripple of pride as she closed out the register. Sure, the holiday shoppers wouldn't last, but every time she caught a look at the ribbon hanging in the window, she felt like the shop might really have a chance of making it.

She checked the time and scanned to see if Tara had texted. Nothing. She eyed the row of strap-ons, wondering for at least the tenth time that day which one Tara might pick. Then she fell to tidying the shelves and restocking the massage lotions. She could have gone in the back and put up her feet for a minute—the storage room now doubled as the breakroom since she'd bought a settee from the antique store two doors down. And it really was quite comfortable. But her mind was too focused on Tara to relax.

She may have been sniffing lotions, trying to choose one Tara might like, when the bell jingled and Tara herself came in.

"The sign says closed but the door's unlocked and since I know the owner…"

Casey set the coconut vanilla lotion down. "Hey."

"Hey yourself." Tara paused. "Judging from the look you're giving me, I'm thinking it's okay with you if I do a little late night secret shopping?"

"Secret shopping?" Casey crossed the distance to Tara. "I don't know if my shop is ready for that." She wrapped her arms around Tara and added, "But I sure like seeing you. Is that the look I gave you? Or was the look more along the lines of…I've missed you all day even though we saw each other this morning? Or, damn, I can't wait to get my hands on you."

"A little bit of all of those looks, actually." Tara smiled. "I missed you all day too."

"Best news ever." Casey pulled her closer and into a deep kiss. They'd shared plenty of kisses last night, but she was hungry for more. Having Tara in her arms made her want more than kissing though, and it took Herculean effort to break off the kiss. Still, she pushed back and cleared her throat, reminding her libido that the end goal would be even better if she gave Tara a chance to find what she'd come for. And even if the closed sign was up, the lights were all on and the door was unlocked.

"This is the first time I've had a secret shopper. Do you mind if I lock up before you look around?"

"Good idea. Once I find what I want, I'm not sure how long I'll be able to wait to try it out."

Tara's words, along with her searing gaze, sent Casey's arousal through the roof. "I can't wait to see what you pick."

Chapter Twenty-one

Tara didn't wait for Casey, heading right over to the corner of the store that held the toys. She'd noticed the wall of cocks before—pretty hard to miss—but she hadn't paid particular attention. Probably because looking would have reminded her of the sex she wasn't getting. But that had changed.

As far-fetched as it would have seemed only a month ago, it felt so obvious now. Like one of those things destined to happen, just waiting for her to catch the hint. And not only had she'd come around and gone to bed with Casey Stevens, here they were about to up the ante at her suggestion.

She'd bristled when Shawn teased her about being a prude, when Casey had implied as much. Because she wasn't. She believed consenting adults could, and should, do whatever they wanted. She believed toys and lubes and all the other stuff Casey sold were all about helping people enjoy sex more, on their own or with a partner. Or multiple partners. The culture of shame and judgment—the culture that gave people like Gary Jenkins a soapbox to stand on—was bullshit.

Of course, none of that philosophical or feminist conviction meant she had the luxury of expertise in that department. Sure, she'd had a couple of girlfriends who liked playing with dildos, and she'd had the same trusty vibrator since college. Not literally the same one but the same style. It got the job done and kept her sane during her increasing disillusionment with New York and implosion of the relationship she'd thought would get her through. But that was pretty much the extent of it.

This, what Casey was offering now, exceeded her experience about tenfold. It was beyond hot. But also, maybe, a bit intimidating.

"You look so serious right now." Casey's voice, though quiet, just about sent Tara out of her skin.

She squared her shoulders in an attempt to look stern rather than startled. "It's serious business, picking out the right thing. There are a lot of choices."

Casey angled her head, seemingly willing to play along. "There are. But if you can pin down your basic preferences on size and shape, we can narrow things down before tackling texture and color."

Tara cleared her throat, oddly at ease with Casey's spiel. "So, what you're saying is, substance over style."

"Absolutely. Though, at the end of the day, you should be able to have both."

She nodded slowly. "Okay, so, any parameters you want to give me on your side of things?"

Casey cocked her head, her cool salesclerk demeanor giving way to an air of confidence. "I can work with whatever you give me."

Tara swallowed, any lingering traces of insecurity swallowed up by desire. "Good to know."

Casey reached around Tara and picked up a modestly-sized, pink-and-purple-swirled number. "This is a nice entry-level model. People starting out, or those with smaller anatomies, tend to find it really accessible."

"I think I'd prefer a bit more length." Tara couldn't believe she was admitting it, but something pushed her to go for what she'd always wanted. "And girth."

Casey's demeanor remained calm, but arousal flashed in her eyes. "Certainly." She returned the item to the shelf and picked up one a few sizes bigger. "I find the heft of this one quite nice."

The flesh-toned silicone felt heavy in her hand. Solid. Sexy. "That's very pleasing."

"It gets excellent reviews."

The casual comment left Tara wondering whether Casey meant customers at her shop or women she'd fucked with it.

"Online, I mean," Casey said, as though reading her thoughts.

She laughed. "Thanks for the clarification."

"Of course." Casey selected an even bigger one from the shelf, a rigid looking thing in electric blue. "If you're really focused on size, this one is quite popular."

Tara shook her head, trying to focus on Casey's words more than the cock in her hand. She held it up. "I think I like this one."

"I thought you might."

As important as open communication was, she loved that Casey intuited her preferences. Excellent reviews notwithstanding. "So, we're done?"

"Well, that model comes both straight and with a curve. Do you have a preference?"

She wrinkled her nose. "I really want to make a joke about straight never being my preference."

"For what it's worth, I'd go with the curved one anyway. It's better at hitting…certain spots."

"Is it weird that I'm super turned on and also finding it hard not to giggle?" Or was it even weirder to admit?

Casey didn't hesitate. "Not weird at all. I think sex is best when it's a little playful."

God, when was the last time she'd been playful about sex? College? Better not to do the math on that one. Especially when she had more important matters to attend to. She picked up the box holding the curved model. "Will you model it for me?"

Casey's eyes narrowed slightly. "Here?"

Tara nodded.

"Now?"

She smiled. "Pretty please?"

"Hard to resist when you ask so nicely."

"Oh, wait. You need a harness, though." Damn logistics.

"Actually, I need a new one. I did a purge after, you know." Casey shrugged, as though slightly embarrassed.

"I totally respect that." She followed Casey over to the display of harnesses and Casey wasted no time grabbing a brown leather one with burnished brass rivets and buckles. She couldn't help but smile. "Someone knows what they like."

"I've been eyeing these since I first unpacked them. They're handmade by this queer couple in Boulder. I just didn't have a reason to buy one for myself."

Tara imagined the dark leather against Casey's skin. The feel of it under her fingers and the way it would smell. "Until now."

"Until now."

"Can I come back there with you?" she asked.

"Will you give me a couple minutes head start? Wiggling into and adjusting a new harness isn't the sexiest of moves." Casey grinned that sexy grin she had.

"I'm pretty sure I'd find it sexy, but of course."

"Thanks." Casey pointed to the wall behind the register. "How about you flip the main lights off. Don't want anyone to think we might still be open."

The mere thought of being interrupted—or caught—ratcheted her anticipation up a few notches. "On it."

Casey slipped into the back and Tara took care of the lights. She double-checked the sign on the door and the lock while she was at it, then gave Casey another minute before joining her.

Tara walked into the back room and stopped short. She didn't know what she'd been expecting, but Casey—naked save the strap-on and a sports bra—wasn't it. On top of that, Casey was rocking what Tara could only describe as an underwear model pose. One hand on her hip, one behind her head. And a slightly unnatural curve in her torso that made it look like she was doing crunches standing up but highlighted a legit six-pack of abs.

Casey dropped the hand over her head and straightened. "Too much?"

Tara crossed the small space, unable to resist the urge to touch. She traced the line of muscle on Casey's stomach. "The exact right amount."

Casey sucked in a breath and seemed to hold it. She locked eyes with Tara. "I have to admit, I almost forgot how good it feels."

"Wearing a cock, you mean?"

Casey nodded.

"But you're not even fucking me yet." The only downside to their current situation from where she stood.

"I could fix that." Casey's head tipped a few degrees.

Tara's gaze followed, landing on an antique settee upholstered in navy velvet. Curiosity warred with wanting Casey to push her down on it and fuck her right then and there. "Should I even ask why you have that here?"

"I wanted something comfy to sit on when I'm able to snag breaks here and there." Casey paused. "And I saw it in the store down the block and liked it, but it doesn't go with anything else in my house." Another pause. "And it seemed kind of sexy."

Tara didn't try to hide her smile. "Perfectly logical reasons."

"I'd be lying if I said I haven't fantasized about putting it to good use."

As hard as it was to give up the proximity of Casey's body, Tara stepped over to the settee and ran a hand along the fabric. It felt even more luxurious than it looked. "For a nice cozy nap?"

Casey chuckled, but it had a ragged quality to it that had Tara pressing her thighs together. "Not exactly."

"Maybe you should give me a demonstration."

Casey looked her up and down. "Maybe you should take your clothes off."

As unsexy as she might have felt in the chef pants and Coy Cupcakes T-shirt she wore, Casey's suggestion—command?—threatened to ignite her from the inside. She lifted the shirt over her head, grateful at least to be in a reasonably sexy bra. Then she toed off the Danskos that were as much a part of her uniform as the Coy Cupcakes apron and hat. She pushed the pants down over her hips and kicked them away. Left in that bra and a pair of matching hip-hugger panties, she struck a pose of her own. "Better?"

"Much." Casey wasted no time coming over to where she stood. "Though I do think there's still room for improvement."

Tara gasped when Casey reached behind her and flicked her bra open in a single, fluid motion. Then she giggled at being so cliché.

"Was that not okay?" Casey asked.

"So okay. Better than okay. Maybe a little surprised."

"I like surprising you."

"I like it, too." Tara frowned. "It makes me feel a little boring."

"Trust me, there's nothing boring about you."

That definitely wasn't true. But it didn't mean she couldn't bring a little boldness to the table. Surprise Casey. Maybe even surprise herself. She gave Casey a nudge toward the settee. "You look tired. You should sit down. Oh, and get rid of that bra."

Casey didn't argue, simply tugging off the sports bra.

Tara looked around until her gaze landed on a shelving unit stacked to the top with boxes and a few loose bottles of lube. She flicked her head. "Mind if I open one of those?"

Casey nodded. "Help yourself."

She picked one at random and, after a minute of fighting with the safety seal, sauntered over to where Casey sat. "Sit back. Make yourself comfortable."

Again, Casey obliged.

Something about the move made Tara feel powerful. As bossy and uptight as she could be in her day-to-day life, sex had never been one of those places where she had the confidence to really take control. Somehow, Casey gave her that, without losing a drop of her butch swagger or toppy energy. It was as much of a turn-on as what she was about to do.

"You look incredibly sexy standing there like that," Casey said.

"I'm glad you think so." She squirted some lube onto her hand. "Though I don't plan on standing for long."

Tara leaned in and worked the lube all over the cock, taking particular pleasure when she pressed the base into Casey's clit and Casey groaned. She continued the motion for longer than was necessary, arousing herself in the process.

"There. That's better." She straightened long enough to work her underwear down her legs, swaying her hips back and forth to give Casey a little show. It worked. By the time she crawled into Casey's lap and straddled her thighs, Casey's eyes flashed with pure lust.

Tara reached between them, guiding the cock to her opening. Between the lube and her own wetness, it slipped in with ease. But that did nothing to detract from the exquisite fullness of having Casey buried completely inside her. She closed her eyes and let out a groan of her own.

"Do you have any idea how gorgeous you are right now?" Casey asked.

Tara blinked her eyes open. "If it's half as gorgeous as you, I'm a complete sex goddess."

Casey smiled. "You are."

"Just you wait."

Tara placed her hands on the back of the low sofa, one on either side of Casey's head. She used the purchase to rock forward and back, sliding the cock most of the way out before pushing against it, sending it as deep as it would go. Casey's hands came to her hips, holding firm without stopping her from setting the pace.

"Fuck, you feel good." Tara practically panted out the words, feeling her orgasm start to build.

"So good." Casey's hips thrust into her, matching her rhythm perfectly and adding just the right amount of pressure against her clit.

"You keep that up and I'm going to come."

Casey's movements didn't let up. "That's the point."

Tara continued to rock, not even trying to hold herself back. A droplet of sweat ran between her breasts. Casey's breathing shifted, ragged between her moans and mumbled encouragements. Sensing Casey might come with her pushed Tara over the edge. She squeezed Casey's thighs between her own and rode the orgasm. Like a raft carried along a whitewater torrent, she gave herself over to the thrill and held on for dear life.

When the crashing waves finally calmed, she realized that Casey's body had slowed and eventually stilled. Tara lifted her head. "You didn't have to stop."

"It's okay."

"Do you not come like that? I know some people don't. I want to get you off. Tell me how."

Casey kissed her. "You're sweet."

She shook her head. "I don't want to be sweet. I want to fulfill your sexual fantasies."

"In that case…"

"What?" Tara poked her lightly in the ribs. "Tell me."

"I'd like you to catch your breath and then let me bend you over the back of this lovely piece of furniture."

And just like that, she wanted Casey all over again. She extricated herself from Casey's lap and stood, stretching her hips this way and that. "Damn."

"Are you okay? Did I hurt you?"

Tara laughed. "A little stiff. Haven't been straddling much these days."

Casey's lips twitched with a mischievous smile. "Is that your way of saying you want to do that less? Or more?"

"Let's go with more. But later. Right now, I think you had a request." She sashayed around the sofa, putting an extra sway in her hips. "Where exactly did you want me?"

Casey stood and followed. "Wherever you're most comfortable."

Since the back of the settee was low, she settled herself there, bending over it and bracing her hands on the cushion. "How's this?"

"So unbelievably perfect. I have half a mind to simply stand here and enjoy."

She gave her butt a wiggle. "What about the other half?"

"It's reminding me that doing is way better than watching."

"Oh, good."

Tara spread her legs a bit wider and closed her eyes. Casey wasted no time coming up behind her, caressing her low back. "Shall I get a little more lube?"

She laughed. "I don't think that will be necessary."

Casey positioned the cock.

"You don't need to be gentle," Tara said. "Or slow."

Casey thrust into her, deeper than Tara had managed on Casey's lap. "Fuck. Yes."

That seemed to be all the permission Casey needed. She gripped Tara's hips once again, but this time there was no doubt she was the one in control. Long, slow strokes at first, but they quickly gave way to a more insistent pumping. Tara pressed into the settee, afraid her legs alone might not be enough to hold her steady.

She had no real thoughts of coming again. At least not until Casey reached around her and pressed a small vibrator to her clit. And then she barely lasted thirty seconds before the orgasm crashed over her like a wave. That seemed to send Casey over the edge. She dropped the vibrator and her fingers dug into Tara's hips. Her whole body tensed, and she called Tara's name in a way that sent shivers of pleasure through Tara's still quaking body.

Tara let her arms go and her body slumped. Casey didn't collapse on her, but she kept her body close. Tara matched her ragged breaths to Casey's and enjoyed the process of coming down together. Casey eventually stood. "That might be the hottest thing I've ever done."

Tara hefted herself upright and considered. "Yeah. Same."

"Thanks for coming over."

"Thanks for that." She pointed to the cock, then to the vibrator on the floor, still buzzing. "And that."

"My pleasure," Casey murmured.

"And mine."

"Will you come home with me?" Casey asked.

Tara looked her up and down, wheels already spinning. "Depends."

"On?" Casey seemed more amused than concerned.

"On whether I can convince you to leave here exactly like that."

Casey looked down before making a face. "It's a little cold."

Understanding dawned and Tara laughed. "You can put clothes on. But I don't want you to take anything off."

"I see." Casey made a show of stroking the cock a few times. "You want more of this."

She might not be able to walk tomorrow, but that seemed like a trifling detail at the moment. "I most certainly do."

Chapter Twenty-two

Casey had been floating all day. The evening with Tara, the morning together, all of it was the best dream she'd had in months. Years. But it wasn't a dream. It'd all been real. She'd been thinking about Tara nonstop since. And about feelings she couldn't deny anymore. She was falling hard. She wanted a relationship with Tara. Committed and serious. She wanted to plan a future together and although she was nervous about bringing it up, she thought Tara was on the same wavelength. After last night how could she not be?

"Did you hear what I said?"

"I'm sorry—I'm at the shop and doing ten different things." But mostly daydreaming. It was late and the shop was empty, and she'd already closed the register for the night. Casey gave herself a mental shake, recalling what her mother had started the conversation with. Something that had been posted about her online.

Most mothers probably started conversations with "hi, how are you?" but Lee Stevens had zero patience for small talk. And since Casey had become her employee fourteen years ago, every phone call was a business meeting. Apparently, this was true even when Casey was no longer her employee.

"I know you've insisted on not responding—"

"Mom, I don't care what the internet trolls say about me." They'd been raking her name through the mud for months now.

"This isn't only about you." Her mother exhaled, leaving no doubt about her frustration level. "If you'd had someone handle the PR from the beginning, I wouldn't have this headache now."

Casey ignored her mom's condescending tone and asked the question she didn't want answered. "What are they saying?"

"You really haven't read the comments on your post? You shouldn't have put anything online if you truly wanted to hide. Now you've stepped on Pavia's turf."

"What are you talking about?" Casey's mind spun when her mother didn't answer. She seemed to be giving Casey time to come to the realization herself, but nothing made sense.

Since ending things with Pavia, she'd stayed off social media. Her mom was right—that was Pavia's playground—and she had no interest in a dodgeball game with Pavia or her rabid fans. In fact, she'd only posted one thing online in the last six months. The picture of her holding the first-place ribbon for the window display contest.

But there was no way Pavia could have seen the post. She'd set up a new account for the Sweet Spot and her name wasn't even linked to it. At least not publicly. Plus, the picture barely showed her face. She was wearing a beanie and had pulled it down low over her ears because the wind had been gusting snow when Tara offered to take the picture. And the post was less than twenty-four hours old.

"It can't be about my store. How could anyone even link that to…" It didn't make sense unless someone in Rocky Springs had been trying to oust her.

Gary Jenkins' face popped into her mind. One quick online search and he'd have realized who she was connected to and the boon from posting something negative about her and her shop. But was he committed enough to do that or only a blowhard wanting local attention?

"You want to keep hiding out, pretending this mess will simply go away, and meanwhile Pavia is only becoming a bigger problem. You need to deal with her."

"We're divorced, Mom. That means I don't have to deal with her."

"Oh, is that how divorce works? Maybe I should try it."

Casey felt her mom's words cut like a blade. It was no secret her parents were in a loveless marriage, but this felt like a personal attack. Sarcastic and uncharacteristically mean. Despite how the media portrayed her mom as cold and calculating, she'd never been a bad mother. Sure, she hadn't been the parent to bring homemade cupcakes to school or chaperone field trips, but she'd read bedtime stories, patched up skinned knees, and called the school when Casey got bullied.

Casey had looked up to her mom. Lee Stevens was the woman who could make anyone, from famous actors to governors, stumble over their words. She accomplished big things and didn't waste time worrying over others' opinions. Even if she wasn't the type to break out with hugs, Casey always felt her mom loved her—in her own way—and wanted her to succeed. And Casey had felt close enough to trust her advice on colleges as well as on the jobs she'd gotten before taking a position with Stevens Productions. Unfortunately, any maternalistic leanings vanished the moment she'd started working for the family business. Now she'd disappointed her mom by quitting and moving to Colorado, and the criticism had gotten harsher.

"I'm not hiding out." Maybe there'd been a little hiding initially, but not now. "I moved here for a fresh start and that's exactly what I've gotten. Things are going well. The shop is already doing better than I expected and I met someone who—"

"I hoped you warned the new girl."

"About what?" Casey's building anxiety bumped up a notch.

"Hold on. Apparently, when I ask for no interruptions, that's not what it means."

The line went silent and Casey imagined her mother in the office across from the studio chewing out some poor fool. Maybe her new secretary. Or Ted, the bumbling assistant director. She tried to recall all the names and faces at Stevens Productions even as she wished she could simply hang up and go back to pretending her life only existed in Rocky Springs. No Pavia, no drama.

Her mother cleared her throat, as if announcing she'd returned to the call. "I know you'd hoped Pavia would move on. We all did. And maybe eventually she would have, but you've kicked a hornet's nest now."

"Mom, I don't even know what hornet's nest you're talking about." Casey tried a slow deep breath as her mind whipped from one Pavia scenario to another. "Pavia said she didn't want to hear from me ever again so I've gone out of my way to not be in her life. And after she cheated—"

"Who cheated on who, who left who, who divorced who...none of that matters. What's important at the moment is public perception."

"At the moment or always?"

Her mother didn't bother with a response. Facts never seemed to be as important as public perception to either of her parents. Lee and Bob Stevens were legally married despite not having spent any time under the same roof in over two decades simply because the perception of them running Stevens Productions as a team was more important than their happiness.

"Pavia was a loose cannon from the beginning. But you decided to get involved and you got the studio involved."

Casey debated pointing out that giving Pavia the lead role in *Sunset Summer* hadn't been her decision. It was true she'd suggested Pavia for the role, but when it came to the final call, she hadn't been asked. "This is something about the movie?"

"No. This is about that lovely picture of you and Mrs. Claus."

Casey's stomach turned. So it was the picture with her winning display. It still didn't seem possible that Pavia had found it. Unless Gary Jenkins had figured out who she was and ignited a fire. She glanced at the store computer wondering if she should pull up the account now. She hadn't been online since she'd posted it.

"PR people exist for a reason, Casey."

Casey didn't bother with a response. She stared at the computer, knowing the right thing to do was check the account, but it was the last thing she wanted to do. "I don't want to think about how Pavia even found that post."

"I'm sure she had help from her fans."

Fans. The word was much too nice to describe the assholes who'd jumped on the Pavia bandwagon and ripped Casey's reputation into pieces. Pavia's fans, together with Gary Jenkins, was the stuff of nightmares. "I don't understand why anyone cares. So what if I've opened a sex shop in the middle of nowhere Colorado?"

"They care about taking you down. You've given them the perfect opportunity. And they're ready to take the studio down too. This isn't only about you."

Casey clenched her jaw, thinking of all the times her mother had told her not to be selfish. It was the same line she used whenever Casey had to pretend to be happy about some sacrifice that had to be made and it always came down to Stevens Productions. No one doubted Lee Stevens's first priority was her studio.

"I'll take down the picture and close the account."

"You're going to need to do more than that. Read what she posted about your father and the studio."

"Why is she bringing Dad into this?"

"What does Pavia want? What has always been her goal?"

To be loved? Casey knew this was true. Pavia considered herself unlovable, but it was the one thing she wanted most even if she never said it. Still, her mom probably wasn't thinking that Pavia craved acceptance and love.

"She wants attention, Casey. That's all. But this is unacceptable. Close the account and figure out a way to stop her from making good on her threat to sue."

"Is there something you're not telling me? Something in Pavia's contract?" She really didn't want to think about her parents engaging in shady business dealings on top of everything.

"What I'm telling you is a lawsuit—even unfounded—would be messy and public and expensive."

Of course being in the right didn't even make the top three. "Mom, Pavia won't talk to me. I literally can't even call her. She blocked me. And even if I could, I don't think it's worth the risk. You know she threatened to get a restraining order."

"She has no grounds for a restraining order."

"That doesn't matter with Pavia." Casey sank down on the stool by the register. Fortunately, the shop was empty and she didn't have to hide the wave of exhaustion when it hit. She hadn't gotten much sleep with Tara last night, and she'd decided to fit in a workout that afternoon instead of taking a nap, but adrenaline from a good sales day and looking forward to an evening with Tara had kept her from feeling tired. Now less than two minutes on the phone with her mother and she was completely spent.

"You've never stood up to her. Never shown her that you're not someone to mess with."

"That's not a thing you're supposed to need to do in a relationship." Casey said, the press of tears more from frustration than anything else. She pushed them away, hoping her voice wouldn't betray her. "She thinks I've destroyed her life. I honestly think it'd be best if I just take down the post and didn't respond."

"She's drinking again. And using."

The words hit like an unexpected right hook. "What?" Casey fought back the words "that can't be" as her mother restated what Casey had already heard. The truth settled over her. Pavia wasn't sober anymore. But being sober was what made her who she was—in so many ways. "Are you sure?"

"Confirmed by multiple sources."

"Shit."

"That's an understatement," her mother deadpanned.

As a teen, Pavia had been so enmeshed in drugs and alcohol she'd nearly killed herself. Her parents had both been actors and she'd had some bit parts as a kid but never gotten famous the way she wanted. Then she'd fallen in with the wrong crowd. Life had unraveled quickly. At nineteen she was living on the street, trading sex for booze. And other things. Her parents washed their hands of her and she'd seemed to have no future. Ten years later, she made her way out of that world.

When Casey met her, Pavia Rossini was famous on the internet because of how she'd gotten back on her feet. She'd recorded everything—starting from the rock-bottom place she'd been when she'd decided to get clean. The world had watched as she climbed a ladder she'd built herself. And her fans loved her not in spite of being a once-addict but because of it. She took all the bad parts of her past and laid everything out for anyone who wanted to pick through the mess. It was risky, but it had paid off.

Pavia Rossini had made recovery sexy. That's what everyone said and it was true. It was the one thing Casey admired her for even after all the other chips had fallen.

"I've made some calls. It's been a busy morning." Her mother sighed heavily. "Stevens Productions can pay for a rehab program. Quietly, of course. All you have to do is convince her to go."

"So you want me to tell her to stop posting about Stevens Productions and then say, oh and by the way, if you do that we'll pay for you to get sober? Do you know how that's going to sound? And how do I even get in touch with her at this point? She'd probably blow up a computer if I emailed her. I wish I knew why she hated me so much."

"You were there when her life went to hell. And instead of staying and letting her verbally attack you, you left. You walked out and didn't look back."

"Are you saying I should have stayed?" Casey felt shaky even asking the question.

"Of course not. Her life didn't go to hell because of you. You were collateral damage."

Casey looked at the ceiling as tears welled. So much for keeping emotion out of the conversation.

Her mother continued, "Look, Pavia is going to implode, but I'm not willing to let her damage the studio any more than she already has. You need to talk to her. Convince her to go to rehab—quietly and quickly."

After her mother ended the call, Casey stared at the phone. Reeling, she turned to the computer, wondering if she could hold down the rising bile long enough to get online and delete the store's social media account.

Before she'd pushed herself into action, the bell jingled and Tara walked in.

"Hey." Tara's smile was bright. Almost too bright.

Casey blinked a few times and then scrubbed her face with her hand.

"Everything okay?"

"Um, yeah. Yeah." Casey straightened as Tara headed for the front counter. She leaned to one side of the register and pecked a quick kiss on Casey's lips. She smelled like sugar and vanilla and everything good in the world, and Casey was torn between wanting her to leave because everything felt too overwhelming and desperately wanting Tara to be the only person who existed.

"You sure you're okay?" She tipped her head, studying Casey.

"Yeah." She swallowed. How was it that when they'd kissed that morning everything had felt easy? "Long day."

"Tell me about it." Tara exhaled. "But my car's chock full of gingerbread waiting to be assembled into houses and all the decorating supplies you'd ever want. Ready for an evening with the Rocky Springs seniors? I'm sure the Christmas music's already playing."

"Sounds like a party." Casey forced a smile. It had sounded fun that morning, but now decorating gingerbread and pretending everything was fine seemed like an impossible task. She stood, glancing again at the computer. Would waiting two hours matter?

Tara's brow bunched. "Did you change your mind about wanting to go? You look beat. I mean, still sexy, but in that I've-been-working-my-ass-off sort of sexy." She reached out to run a hand through Casey's hair, no doubt pushing some strands back into place. "If you want to beg out, that's completely okay. I was planning on doing this solo before you volunteered."

"I know. And I'm sure you can do everything alone but…I'd like to try decorating a gingerbread house." Maybe not right now, but backing out wouldn't be cool. She took a deep breath. "I'm tired but I can push through—I'd be even better with some caffeine."

"The seniors always keep coffee on hand."

"Then I'm good to go."

Tara nodded, seeming to weigh Casey's words over whatever she was feeling. "This time of year most of us are trying hard to be merry while pretending we aren't running on fumes."

"That's what the holidays are all about, right?"

Tara smiled. "Yes, but it doesn't mean you can't back out of plans to take care of yourself."

"I don't want to back out." Casey wasn't lying now. "I want to hang out with you. And, you know, a dozen or two seniors." If only she could simply forget about everything else.

"Alright." Tara studied her for a moment longer, then said, "I had two customers picking up cupcake orders mention how surprised they were by the number of people coming in and out of your shop. 'Since it's new,' they said. But I don't think that's what they meant."

"Honestly, part of me is surprised too. I keep telling myself it's good to be busy."

"Definitely."

Even if it made for a long day. Maybe the exhaustion was what made it harder to process everything her mother had said. Taking a few hours to think before calling Pavia was probably a good idea. Then she'd delete all traces of the Sweet Spot's social media presence. Maybe the situation wasn't as awful as her mom had made it seem.

"It's not hard decorating a gingerbread house, is it?"

"Wait, are you telling me this is your first time?" Tara's eyes lit up at Casey's nod and without missing a beat, she said, "As long as you know the difference between a candy cane and a gumdrop—and don't mind following my orders—you'll be fine."

If only that was all she needed to think about.

Chapter Twenty-three

Tara held the two squares of gingerbread that made up the roof and counted to thirty. She did a visual check-in on the residents who had the dexterity to assemble their own. Mrs. Brown was a pro, who'd probably been making gingerbread houses since before Tara was born. Mr. Lopez looked less confident, but he had Ms. Chapel on one side and Mrs. Tran on the other, and both seemed more interested in his progress than their own structures. Or perhaps they were more interested in him.

She released that roof and moved to the next. Six residents sat waiting, ready and happy to decorate but not in it for the building phase. Casey chatted with two of them and had taken it upon herself to attempt construction. Her tongue stuck out to one side, making Tara wonder if it was a genuine display of concentration or for show. Either way, the residents ate it up, cackling when Casey tried to attach two of the taller pieces to each other rather than placing them opposite.

"Good thing someone is supervising around here," Casey said, loud enough to be certain Tara would hear.

She'd lost count for the current roof but was pretty sure she'd held it longer than needed rather than less, so she went over to investigate more closely. "Well, it's hard to keep tabs on such a rowdy bunch. Nobody told me it was going to be gingerbread decorating for party animals."

The whole group laughed. Even the notoriously grumpy Mrs. Richardson cracked a smile.

Casey made a confused face. "Didn't you get the memo? That's the only reason I came."

Tara tucked her tongue in her cheek and pursed her lips. "Because that's what you are? A party animal?"

"You know it." Casey put her hands in the air, still holding the piping bag. When she attempted to—Tara imagined—wave them like she just didn't care, a blob of royal icing went flying. It landed with a splat on the right lens of Mrs. Richardson's glasses.

Casey looked horrified, everyone else at the table froze, and Tara braced herself for the stern talking-to that was sure to ensue. But instead of launching into a lecture on appropriate behavior or a tirade on the problems with young people these days, Mrs. Richardson reached into one of the bowls of decorations, plucked out a purple gumdrop, and stuck it to the errant icing.

"Do you like my look?" she asked.

Casey, unburdened with the knowledge of Mrs. Richardson's usual demeanor, laughed first. One by one, the residents around the table joined in. Tara did, too. It didn't take long for Mrs. Tran to hold up a pair over her own eyes. Ms. Chapel, always looking to one-up her, picked up a couple of red ones. Tara thought she might go with a Rudolph impersonation, but no. She placed them right where her nipples would be. Or, perhaps more accurately, where her nipples would have been a few decades ago. She gave her shoulders a little shimmy, much to the delight of Mr. Lopez and the consternation of Mrs. Tran.

"I thought this party was PG," Casey said over the laughter.

"PG-thirteen," Mr. Lopez said.

"More like PG-one-hundred-thirteen." Mrs. Brown shook her head and resumed the intricate frosting icicles she'd begun adding to the eaves of her house.

Casey appeared moderately cowed, but no one else paid much heed. Low-grade bickering came with the territory. Tara imagined she'd feel the same if she were cooped up all day with the same bunch of people and didn't have the freedom to come and go as she pleased. It was one of the main reasons she'd reached out to the facility. Baking was her superpower and she liked to use it for good, not only for profit. No matter how much Shawn might tease her to the contrary.

There was also the matter of not having much of a life outside the bakery. She'd been back in Rocky Springs more than two years now and really didn't have a lot to show in the friend department—not new ones and not rekindled connections from high school, either. As much as she and Shawn weren't the closest, that's who she spent the majority of her time with. Casey had been such a nice departure from that. Even more than the sex, it was so great to enjoy someone else's company. And to have her company enjoyed in return. Despite their initial rocky start, she didn't seem to be too intense for Casey, too much. It was a critique she'd heard more than once from friends and girlfriends alike. But Casey seemed to like her exactly as she was.

Of course, the sex was pretty fucking fantastic. All she had to do was close her eyes and her mind was back at Casey's shop. The feeling of velvet under her fingers, under her cheek, as Casey bent her over the back of the settee and fucked her from behind. The powerful thrust of the cock and the tight grip Casey had on her hips. That gloriously primal sound Casey made when she came.

"Tara?"

Her fantasy evaporated in a cloud of powdered sugar. In its place, the Rocky Springs Retirement Community activities room and Mrs. Brown's quizzical expression. "I'm sorry. What did you say?" Tara asked.

"I asked if you had a number seven tip. My poor arthritis is struggling with this number four."

"Oh. Yes. Of course." Tara rooted around in her box of piping supplies, attempting to will the flush from her cheeks. "Sorry about that."

Mrs. Brown tutted. "Back in my day, I could do string work with a double zero."

She made a show of bowing. "Beyond my skills on my best day."

"Wait, there's something you can't do?" Casey appeared seemingly out of nowhere. "I don't believe it."

For all her sternness a moment before, Mrs. Brown let out a peal of laughter. She put a frail hand on Tara's arm. "You've got a good one there. You should hold onto her."

What was weirder: the insinuation she and Casey were a couple or the fact that Mrs. Brown had picked up on her queerness in the first place? She smiled, trying not to look as awkward as she felt. A glance at Casey made it clear the feeling was mutual.

"Don't mind me, I've only come for more peppermints." Casey grabbed a handful from the bag and escaped back to her spot at the table now in full decorating mode.

Tara opened her mouth but closed it again, not quite sure what to say.

Mrs. Brown gave her a knowing smile. "I've been watching her, and she's even more of a smitten kitten than you are."

Tara chuckled—at the phrase more than the sentiment behind it—and swapped out the piping tip on the bag with the slightly bigger one. "If you say so, Mrs. B."

"Trust me. I've been around. I know these things."

Mrs. Brown returned her attention to the gingerbread house in front of her, leaving Tara in a scramble to find something to do with herself. Fortunately, she had the final house to deliver to its patiently waiting decorator, which she did, with perhaps more flourish than necessary. She then turned her attention to the rest of the group, checking in on progress and doling out plenty of "oohs" and "ahs."

Casey kept up a steady stream of banter with the residents, but behind the back and forth, her eyes looked tired. At one point, she got up to replenish the frosted mini wheats being used as roof tiles, and Tara seized the chance to have a few seconds to themselves. "How you holding up?" she asked.

"Great," Casey replied with more speed than conviction.

"I can handle this crew if you want to go hide in a corner." She tipped her head. "Or the car."

"No, no. I'm good."

"I don't want to say I don't believe you, but I really don't believe you." She was going for playful but worried she sounded like a nag.

"Like I said earlier, long day."

She could appreciate that, especially at this time of year. Still. "What if I said I'd like to take you home when we're done here. Feed you dinner then put some of this frosting to good, and yet very naughty, use?"

Casey's expression didn't change.

She'd either misread how exhausted Casey was, or there was something else going on. "Are you sure you're okay?"

Casey nodded, but it was far from convincing. If anything, she seemed almost annoyed by the question. "Yeah, I'm tired. That's all."

"We could go back to my place and crash. I wouldn't say no to a hot shower and crawling into bed with you."

Casey's smile was weak at best. "That does sound nice, but I need to go back to the shop for a bit. I've got piles of inventory to wade through."

Having been at the shop the day before, she knew that was a lie. But how much to press? And more importantly, was Casey's not wanting to spend the night together about the two of them or something else entirely? "Do you want some help? I'm very organized and, I've been told, good with my hands."

That got her a chuckle even weaker than the smile. "I appreciate the offer, but I think I could use some alone time. All this time with people is starting to catch up with me."

She got that—probably more than the next person, even. But something about it didn't sit right. Casey lumping her in with people, maybe. Or the fact that Casey seemed reluctant to look her in the eye. "I get it."

"Thanks," Casey said, sounding genuinely relieved. "Do you mind dropping me back off at the shop since that's where my car is?"

"Sure. I mean, of course not."

Casey nodded, but it looked a little like she was doing the head bob part of the chicken dance. "Cool."

Tara stole glances at Casey as they finished cleaning up. She kept pausing and staring off at nothing. Under normal circumstances, she'd tease Casey about where her mind was. But given Casey's reaction to her frosting comment, Tara knew better than to attempt anything resembling innuendo.

They loaded up the car and Tara drove them in the direction of the shop. Casey stared out the window, and she may as well have been a thousand miles away. Worry about whatever was bothering Casey warred with irritation that Casey didn't want to tell her whatever was going on. Irritation with herself piled on top—both that she let herself be so invested and that she was chasing someone who clearly didn't want to be chased. Ugh.

When she pulled up out front of the Sweet Spot, Casey got out without even a cursory kiss good-bye. Tara seethed and hated herself for it. "See you tomorrow?" she asked as Casey got out, also hating herself for being passive-aggressive.

"Um, yeah. I think. I may need to go to California for a few days, but I haven't arranged it yet. I'll let you know."

Tara opened her mouth to ask some variation of "are you serious" and "are your parents okay," but Casey was already closing the door behind her.

Before the door slammed shut, Casey caught it. She opened it enough to duck her head back in. "Thanks for inviting me tonight. I had fun."

And with that, she was gone. She disappeared into the shop before Tara could utter her new question: what the fuck?

She put her car back in drive and headed home, emotions even more of a tangled mess than before. Maybe she'd been misreading Casey all along. Maybe they were casual friends who'd become fuck buddies and nothing more. Or maybe Casey's mature, working on her issues facade was just that, and Tara had been gullible enough to fall for it.

Whatever it was, she didn't like it. And she really didn't like the sinking dread it left in the pit of her stomach. If Casey wasn't willing to be real with her, there was no point even attempting to hold on to whatever they had, and no way in hell would she humiliate herself trying. No matter what Mrs. Brown—or Shawn or anyone else for that matter—insisted.

Chapter Twenty-four

Casey screwed up, and she knew it. Going to the gingerbread party when she ought to have canceled and dealt with the Pavia situation had definitely been a mistake. At the time, she'd thought she could pull off pretending nothing was wrong. In fact, she had pulled it off for the first hour. She'd held everything together, even joked around with the seniors and mostly not thought about the dumpster fire on social media or the conversation she needed to have with Pavia. Then she'd gotten the text from her dad. He rarely texted and it'd been months since they'd spoken.

While Tara was distracted helping one of the seniors frost a chimney, she read her father's one line text: *we need to talk*. One line and all the anxious misgivings she'd bottled up after her mother's phone call burst out like a shaken can of Pepsi. That's when she made her second mistake of the night. Instead of telling Tara she needed to leave early to deal with a problem at the shop, she'd pushed through.

Before they'd even left the senior center, she'd formulated a handful of worst-case scenarios, each one making her feel more anxious than the one before. Her mind was so caught up in the Pavia situation and all the what-ifs, she had no recollection of the drive from the senior center to her shop. She couldn't even recall if she'd said good-bye to Tara. She knew she hadn't offered to help unload the decorating supplies from Tara's car and she knew there'd been no good night kiss. Unfortunately, she didn't think of those things until hours later when she was lying awake fighting with the bedsheets.

Everything felt impossible. Even sleep. She'd tried calling her dad, but he didn't answer. Pavia had her number blocked and didn't respond to the email or instant message she sent. Even Natalia didn't respond to her text. Which wasn't a huge surprise because nearly once a week she went on a technology cleanse—powering off her phone and vowing to give up one platform or another.

Natalia's tech cleanse wouldn't last long, but without her advice, Casey had no option except facing the comments on the Sweet Spot's social media post alone. The trolls ranged from funny to crass to legitimately scary. And Gary Jenkins had in fact led the whole crusade, commenting on her post with link after link of every article and interview with a negative mention of her parents or herself. The Pavia fans, and then Pavia herself, had taken over from there.

She got several screenshots before closing the account, conflicted between never wanting to step foot in social media floodwaters again and wondering if she should save everything so she could report the half-dozen online death threats she and her dad had received.

She'd passed the night sleeplessly and was in no better condition when the sun rose. The only good news was that lying awake all night allowed plenty of time to set a plan. After booking the last seat on a direct flight to Burbank out of Denver for that afternoon, she went for a run, hardly noticing the icy air cutting into her lungs and greedy for any endorphins she could drum up. She showered and changed, texted Aspen, and then packed for a two-day trip.

Aspen met her at the shop an hour later, clearly nervous. "You sure leaving me in charge is a good idea?"

"It's either that or the store stays closed the whole time I'm gone." On an ordinary week, it wouldn't be an issue, but missing even a day of the holiday season would be a problem. "We'll post the limited hours—you won't have to work longer than your usual shift. And if you have any issues, you can call me. I'll have my phone on me the whole time I'm gone."

Aspen nodded. The cautious "okay" they gave did not project confidence, but Casey repeated the promise to always have her phone on. What problem could come up that she couldn't talk Aspen through? She stopped herself from answering the question and instead asked Aspen if they were hungry. Buying breakfast was the least she could do.

After burritos from the Cantina, Casey left Aspen at the shop with detailed instructions on how to open and close for the day. With an hour before she had to leave for the airport, she had one last thing on her to-do list. Last, but most important.

The sugary scent of maple hit her nose when she pushed open the bakery door and Shawn gave her a wide smile, glancing up from the cupcakes going into the display case. "Howdy."

"You know I never thought anyone besides my dad said howdy—until I moved to Colorado." Casey watched Shawn shift the last cupcake into place, trying not to be too obvious when she leaned in for a look into the back.

"I love old Westerns. My grandpa and I used to watch them together and I always pretended to be a cowboy." Shawn set down the emptied tray. "I'm guessing you're looking for my sister?"

"Is she here?"

"Nope. You missed her by about five minutes. She came in earlier than usual and whipped up this new maple cupcake. Smells amazing, doesn't it?" Shawn paused long enough for Casey to agree. "Honestly, she wasn't in the best mood. She mentioned you... She tends to bake like a madwoman when she's upset and she was clearly on fire when I got here so I asked what was wrong." Another pause. "You might want to call her."

A swell of emotion pushed up. Shawn was on her side, she could tell, but now she knew without a doubt Tara was upset. She'd guessed that'd be the case, but part of her hoped she'd made the problem bigger than it was. Really, all she'd done was be distracted for an hour or so of their evening and then forget to kiss her good night. But even as she tried to rationalize the whole thing as a minor fixable mistake, she worried about what Tara would say when she found out why she'd been distracted.

"I was hoping to talk to her in person before I left town." She should have called first thing. But should she tell Tara the whole truth? Would that only make things worse?

Shawn came out from behind the counter. "Where are you going?"

"Back home. Something...came up. I'll only be gone for a few days." Hopefully, she could get through to Pavia in that time. At least start the process of getting her into a rehab program. "Aspen's covering for me at the shop. I should be back Friday." In time for the last weekend of shopping before Christmas. If she missed that, the store might as well close for the month.

"Home as in Hollywood?" Shawn's voice was wary.

"My folks live in Burbank. But yeah."

"Everything okay with your folks?"

"No." Casey took a deep breath. "I mean, health-wise, yes, but… it's a long story."

The lines in Shawn's forehead softened. "If they need your help, you gotta go. Family's important. You want me to keep an eye on your shop? I can be backup for Aspen."

"That would be amazing. I'm sure you have plenty to do here, and I know you're spending lots of time with Kit—"

Shawn held up a hand. "I can do lots of things all at once. Helping is what I'm good at. But I think you should try talking to Tara before you leave. Maybe tell her what came up with your family."

Casey nodded. "Do you know where she went?"

"No. She was mad at me, too, and wasn't saying much."

That definitely didn't bode well. "I'm sorry if I made things harder for you."

"Don't worry about it." Shawn's smile was sympathetic. "She said she'd be back but didn't say when. I can send her next door as soon as I see her."

"Could you text me instead? I'd rather come here to talk." Casey was half-tempted to wait at the bakery, but she had less than an hour before she had to leave for the airport and plenty she could do in the meantime.

"No problem. And good luck with whatever's going on with your folks."

"Thanks." She waved and stepped outside, bracing as an icy wind gusted down the street. Since her run that morning, the temperature had dropped noticeably. Now all she wanted was to be cozy and warm inside with no plans to go anywhere.

Unfortunately, she was stuck dealing with Pavia. She did feel bad that Pavia was drinking again. But no part of her wanted to be sucked back into Pavia's world. She glanced back at the bakery wondering if she was going to regret telling Shawn a half-truth. With any luck, Shawn and everyone else in Rocky Springs would never know she hadn't simply gone home to take care of a family thing.

Her phone rang as she stepped into her shop. Aspen looked up from the counter, eyes wide. "Oh good. It's you. I thought it was going to be my first solo customer."

"You've held down the fort alone before." She pulled her phone out of her back pocket when it rang a second time. Natalia.

"I know." Aspen's brow creased. "But you've always been close in case I needed you. Like that time the credit card machine went down."

Casey hooked a thumb to the back room. "I have to take this call real quick, but, Aspen, I know you can handle being the one in charge. I wouldn't have asked if I didn't think you could do it."

When Aspen nodded, still seeming reluctant, Casey answered her phone. "Hi."

"Holy Fuck. Your mom called me. I can't believe this shit."

"Can you hold on a minute?" Casey reached the back room, closed the door behind her, and dropped onto the settee. "The thing is, I can believe it. I spent all night thinking...why didn't I see this coming?"

"Casey, she's going after your dad."

"I know. Because in her head, he screwed her over and she wants him to hurt too."

"But he never screwed her over," Natalia said. "He never did anything to her."

"He halved the budget midway through filming and didn't tell her directly that a bunch of her scenes were being cut."

"Okay, but her acting sucked. Your dad made the right call."

Did he? Even at the time, Casey wasn't sure. And that was before Pavia turned into a cannonball.

"Remember how pissed she was when he said he didn't have time in his schedule to meet with her?" Natalia continued. "She's calling him a sexual predator. Have those two ever even been in the same room together?"

The question gave Casey pause. She ran through all the times Pavia and her mother had been in the same space. Her father was never there. "I don't think so. He was doing that project in Brazil when I met Pavia and then he went up to Canada right after to finish filming *Roulette*." Which had been the studio's box office win for the year.

After he'd finished *Roulette*, he'd had time to look over the expenses and some of the scene cuts for Pavia's film. He'd called Casey to tell her the bad news—that he was disappointed at what he'd seen and was tightening the purse strings. She'd been the one who had to deliver the news to Pavia.

"Pavia's completely lost it," Natalia continued. "I listened to your message this morning and then went online but the post was taken down. Your mom called before I could call you back. Newsflash, my crush on your mom hasn't gone anywhere. I had to remind myself to breathe the whole time she was talking to me."

Despite everything, Casey smiled. "I really don't get what you see in her but—"

"Are you kidding me? She's a powerhouse, hot as fuck, and brilliant."

"Also, she's straight."

"And married. But we know at least one of those things is only for show."

Casey shook her head. "Natalia, my mom loves one thing. Her job."

Natalia sighed. "Yeah. So, what are we going to do? How can I help?"

For all the other things Natalia could be at times—dramatic, overbearing, too loud—Casey had never once questioned their friendship. The fact Natalia was in her corner meant more than she could know. "Can you pick me up at the airport? I was planning on going to my mom's place, but I'd rather stay at yours. I'll only be in town for two nights."

"We could both go to your mom's. Have a little sleepover."

Casey had never understood Natalia's infatuation with Lee Stevens. Bob Stevens was a different story. Plenty of women had been attracted to him over the years and made no secret of it. But what about on his side of things? Had something happened between him and Pavia back when the movie was in production? And was there any truth to the article Gary Jenkins had reposted about her father's connections to the Hollywood producers who'd been charged with sexual assault?

Truth or not, it was enough to get the wolves circling for blood. As much as she wanted to avoid it, she needed to talk to Pavia. For that to happen, she needed to set aside everything that had happened between them. And then Pavia had to get sober.

"Do you know anyone who's still friends with Pavia? I mean, any of our friends. One who played Switzerland in this whole mess."

"Why?" Natalia's disdainful tone made it clear it wouldn't be easy.

"I have to talk to Pavia."

"Are you sure you want to?"

"No." Casey pinched the bridge of her nose. "And yes. Both at the same time."

"That sounds like you and Pavia. How are things going with your baker?"

"One minute I think things are amazing." Casey glanced down at the velvet fabric under her arm. She could still picture Tara there, thighs spread and gaze locked on Casey. That night had only been sex. Hot as hell, but only sex. Were they building something more or only keeping each other company? "The next minute, I'm wondering if I'm fooling myself all over again thinking I could do a real relationship."

"Tara McCoy is nothing like Pavia."

"Thought you didn't know her name. You only ever call her my baker."

Natalia clicked her tongue. "When you talk about Tara, I have to tease you a little. I can tell how much you like her. It's real, you know? Nothing like how you were with Pavia."

"How was I with Pavia?"

"A doormat." Natalia chuffed. "She was chaos, and you were the one trying to fix everything after she stormed out of every room. I never understood why you even liked her."

"I think mostly I wanted to help. Things have always been harder for her, you know? She had to deal with so much pressure her whole life." Casey paused. "I guess I wanted to be the hero who made things easier. Someone who came in and paved roads so she could become a big star."

"And then she drove off without you."

"Honestly, I always knew that risk was there." It was one of the reasons she'd never let herself get completely attached. "And I wasn't ever really happy, but I wanted things to work out for her. For her sake more than my own."

"You were a very sweet doormat." Natalia chuckled when Casey groaned. "At least tell me you learned something from all of that."

"Oh, I learned plenty."

"Enough to think about your own happiness with things with your baker?"

"Yeah. Her happiness too, but…I feel good when I'm with Tara. I'm happier than I've ever been. Not just with Tara but here in Rocky Springs. Running my shop. All of it. And especially when I'm with Tara. The thing is, being with her seems almost too easy." Or at least it had seemed easy until last night. Still, Casey figured an apology and explanation could fix things. Tara was understanding and reasonable. Two things Pavia never was.

"Too easy. Gah. You know, for once, I want someone to pick the sweet easy choice who's clearly right for them. Not the firecracker who only wants to use them. Honestly, Casey, I don't see why you're trying to get in touch with Pavia now. Who cares what she said about you online?"

"My mom cares. It's not about me. It's about Stevens Productions. And something might have happened with Pavia and my dad. I need to know."

"I'm sure it's nothing." Natalia shook her head. "You gave up everything to get away from Pavia's drama. Now you want to run right back into the mess?"

Casey turned Natalia's words around in her head. "I can't move on until I know if anything happened. And I want to right things if I can. I'll text you when I get to Burbank."

Chapter Twenty-five

G one?" Tara narrowed her eyes. "What do you mean gone?" Shawn shrugged like it was taking every drop of self-restraint not to speculate six ways from Sunday. "I told you, there was some emergency—not medical—with her folks. She wanted to see you, but she must have had to leave for the airport."

Tara paced the length of the shop a few times, then stopped to stare at Shawn, as though more meaning might be hiding under the surface. "Gone." She resumed pacing.

"Only for a few days," Shawn said in a maddeningly placating way.

"It's the week before Christmas. No one who owns a shop and is in their right mind goes away the week before Christmas." A fact she thought Casey understood, even if it was her first year in business.

"Yeah, but family is the most important thing."

She shook her head. "Not if you want to stay in business. And unless your family is angling for you to fail, they know better than to ask."

"Maybe they don't know better. Or…"

"They want her to fail." Tara shook her head again. She had no clue if that might be the case. It made her realize how little she knew about Casey overall. Paired with how last night had gone down, it made her wonder if maybe Casey wanted it that way.

Shawn cringed. "Jeez, I hope not. Unsupportive family is the worst."

She'd never had a taste of that. Her mom—and her grandparents—were always there for her if she needed anything. Yeah, she'd lost her dad but she still had plenty of people who believed in her and would help at any time.

"You should call her."

Should she? This time yesterday, she would have, without hesitation. But with the way the night ended, it seemed like hearing from her might be the last thing Casey would want. "I don't know."

"She came looking for you before she left. If you don't call her, she'll think I didn't tell you."

Tara rolled her eyes. "Way to make it about you."

"I'm not. I'm trying different angles since you're being so annoying and stubborn about it for no apparent—"

The shop door swung open and Grandpa bustled in, a very large bee in his proverbial bonnet. "The porn shop is closed. What's going on?"

Tara looked at Shawn who seemed to have even less of a clue as to how to respond to that as Tara did. But in true extrovert form, Shawn pulled it together and said, "Casey had to go to California for a few days. Family emergency."

She had a passing thought that dashing home for family might win some brownie points with Mayor McFamily, but no such luck. Grandpa's brow furrowed and he scowled. "We can't go having shops closed the week before Christmas. It makes the town look bad."

For as pissed off as she was at Casey, the sheer hypocrisy grated on her, and she took the bait. "You can't go around wishing Casey's shop would close, then complain when it does."

Grandpa jabbed an index finger in her direction. "Don't get all smart aleck with me, little missy. You know as well as I do shuttered storefronts and fly-by-night businesses with inconsistent hours are the kiss of death in a town like ours."

"You're right. But family comes first, doesn't it? That's what you always say." A pretty easy point for her, but why was she hell-bent on defending a woman who'd fuck her one minute and barely give her the time of day the next?

"Well, if she's not a savvy enough businesswoman to hire backup, she has no business being in business."

Shawn coughed. "I'm her backup."

Grandpa balked, but it had nothing on the look Tara shot her.

Shawn lifted both hands, clearly wanting to avoid a conflict. "I offered to drop in if something urgent came up. I'm not taking shifts."

Grandpa shook his head. "I'll see you two later. I've lost my appetite."

He left without further comment, leaving Tara to glare and Shawn to shrug like it was no big deal. "Seriously, though. You should call her," Shawn said.

"I have work to do." Officially the weakest excuse ever.

"Did you two have a fight? I thought you were all hot and heavy and honeymoon phase."

She snorted at the description, then scowled. "I don't know what we are."

"Oh." Shawn let the word drag, like that explained everything.

"And I'm not going to figure it out standing here with you, so I'm going in there." She pointed at the kitchen. "Holler if you need me."

The door had barely swung behind her when Shawn called her name.

"What?" she yelled back.

"Call Casey."

Rather than reply, Tara mumbled under her breath. "I'll call her when I'm damn good and ready."

And then she got to work. Because no matter what else might be going on in her life, being in the kitchen was a place of solace. Of control. And in her world, those things might as well be one and the same.

After frosting refills for the shop cases to get through the rest of the day, she tackled the first special order on her docket. She had four such orders for tomorrow and six for the day after. Office parties mostly, along with a couple of holiday open houses and the local high school's Christmas concert. It felt like half the town had grown tired of the traditional cookie tray and jumped on the cupcake wagon. Which was perfectly fine with her.

She baked and frosted, frosted and baked. And as she often did, completely lost track of time. Not so much that she lost track of being equal parts annoyed with and worried about Casey, but really, little would be that distracting. It didn't help that Grandpa still seemed set against the Sweet Spot and, by extension, Casey herself. It made her want to dig her heels in. Only that meant making things awkward at family gatherings, which she hated. And it sort of felt like she was sticking her neck out for someone that didn't even consider her important enough to call before jetting out of town.

It was rude. It was obnoxious. And perhaps worst of all, it made her feel like a fool.

The door swung and Shawn's head appeared. "Think you can get me another couple dozen candy cane? We had a run and Mrs. Sims wants some for when her daughter gets home from college tomorrow."

Fortunately, she wasn't a complete sad sack, and her mind shifted gears instantly. "I don't have any peppermint frosting made, but if she can wait ten minutes, I can flavor a batch of vanilla and throw them together."

Shawn disappeared momentarily, then returned. "She says yes, please and thank you."

"On it."

And so it continued the rest of the afternoon and right up until close. Special requests, a flurry of customers, and slow but steady progress on her orders for the next day. Before she knew it, Shawn was standing in the kitchen and offering to help with cleanup.

"Are you all done out front?" Tara asked.

Shawn nodded. "It's going on eight."

"Damn."

"Wait, have you not taken a break all day? Did you not eat?" Shawn's eyes narrowed in a way that managed to be both caring and condescending.

"I got caught up in things." Not a lie, even if it was only half the truth.

"You didn't call Casey, either, did you?"

"In case you missed it, this is our busiest week. I was kind of occupied." Which sounded defensive and petulant, even to herself.

"I have a tub of hummus in the fridge. Sit with me a minute."

God, she'd take all the condescending over genuine worry, especially the kind that teetered on the edge of pity. "I'm fine. I just want to clean up and go home so I can shower and crawl into bed."

Shawn arched an eyebrow. "Don't make me sic Mom on you."

Tara groaned and let her head fall back. "I like her, okay? Like, really like her. And I thought the feeling was mutual, but now I'm not so sure."

"Forget hummus. You need something stronger. Come back to my place. We'll order takeout and open a bottle of wine."

There was little she could imagine wanting less than a heart-to-heart with Shawn about the sad state of her love life. "I love you, but no thanks."

Shawn sighed. "Are you really questioning everything because she had to go home for a family emergency and didn't get to see you before she left?"

"No."

"What, then?"

"Something was definitely up last night, but she didn't say a word." Which sounded like a weak argument when she said it out loud, but whatever.

"Okay." Shawn let the word drag, clearly sharing that opinion.

"Okay, so she'd rather be silent and sullen than tell me what's going on. How is that solid relationship behavior?" A much more reasonable argument and one Shawn surely couldn't counter.

"Because you'd never be silent and sullen over baring your soul and being vulnerable."

Touché. Damn it. "We're not talking about me."

"Yeah, but what's good for the goose is good for the gander."

Tara raised a brow. "I refuse to take you seriously when you start talking in Grandpa-isms."

Shawn let out a snort. "You refuse to take me seriously most of the time. What I'm saying is that it's hard to be vulnerable, especially in a new relationship. Casey might be scared of confiding in you, not uninterested."

It was a fair point, even if she didn't want to admit it. "How is saying 'I gotta go home for a family emergency' being vulnerable?"

"Maybe it's a mental health thing or a money thing and not a somebody-had-a-heart-attack thing."

She hadn't considered that. "Fine. You're right."

"I do love it when you say that."

Tara shook her head. "Don't be a jerk."

"I'm not. I'm just trying to positively reinforce a desired behavior."

"You are so freaking obnoxious."

Shawn shrugged. "So, you'll call her?"

"Yes, but I'm going to go home first so I can do it in sweatpants and with my feet up."

"Acceptable."

Tara gave her a bland look. "I'm glad you approve. Now, help me get this place whipped into shape so we can call it a night."

An hour later, she'd made it home and gotten that shower. She'd even managed to get a frozen pizza in the oven. She set the timer and flopped on the sofa with her phone. Maybe she'd been overreacting. Maybe Casey was embarrassed. Lord knew she wasn't proud of everything everyone in her family did. She could hardly blame Casey for wanting to keep her skeletons tucked neatly in the closet. Sure, it was the sort of thing they'd need to talk about eventually. They both would. Feeling slightly better about the situation, she tapped the screen, only to realize she'd missed a text from Casey.

Sorry I had to take off without talking to you. Dealing with some stuff. I'll call you tonight.

See? That was fine. Everything would be fine.

Chapter Twenty-six

Natalia hopped out of her car with a grim expression on her face and opened her arms for a hug. "Are you sure you're not making a mistake coming back here?"

Casey accepted the embrace. "No. But I have to try. Thanks for your help with—"

"Pavia's people? Ugh. I've spent the past three hours stroking egos to get people to talk. Maybe I should become a handler. I think I've got an untapped skill set." Natalia tipped her head toward the passenger seat. "Get in."

As they drove to Natalia's apartment, she rattled off the people she'd texted and the responses she'd gotten. Surprisingly, almost everyone she'd reached had said the same thing—they had no clue anything was wrong with Pavia. Nothing more than the usual, anyway. Natalia hadn't mentioned Pavia might be drinking again, only that she'd heard some rumors she wasn't doing well and was checking in. Not surprisingly, no one thought Pavia would be interested in talking to Casey.

"There was one other person I thought of. I don't have her number though." Natalia angled between two cars, jockeying her position up the onramp to the freeway, and then glanced at Casey. "Ingrid Larsen."

"Ingrid? Pavia stopped talking to Ingrid years ago." Ingrid had been part of Pavia's group of friends when she'd first gotten into acting as a teen. They'd been trouble together—party girls who tried everything—but Ingrid had managed to keep her nose a little cleaner and had never ended up on the streets like Pavia. Instead, she'd been on the cover of *Vogue* and had parts in multiple movies. She'd never landed a lead role but she'd done well for herself.

"I heard a rumor Pavia was at a club with Ingrid a month ago."

Casey processed the information. "I have Ingrid's contact info from when she auditioned for that part in *Roulette*. She might talk to me if I tell her it's something work related."

Natalia nodded. "That's what I was thinking. Of course the other thing you could do is knock on Pavia's door."

"Remember how she threatened to get a restraining order on me?"

"That was a publicity stunt. She begged you to come see her two days later. And then she showed up at your house the week after to 'talk things out.' She's full of shit."

"She's full of something..." Casey gazed out the window. They'd merged onto the freeway and cars were lined up as far as the eye could see, a hazy night sky above the sea of brake lights. "You know what I haven't missed? Traffic."

"Ten minutes and already you want to get back to Colorado."

"I like it there a lot," Casey admitted. "Although I seem to mess things up wherever I go."

"What do you mean?"

She shook her head, not wanting to get into the details of how she'd left things with Tara. "I'm only saying I'll probably screw things up there too eventually."

"The only thing you screwed up here was getting involved with Pavia." Natalia hit the brakes when a shiny black Porsche slid into the narrow opening between her and the pickup she'd been tailing. She cussed and rattled a few choice words in Spanish before glancing back at Casey. "Maybe I need to move to Colorado too."

"I've got an extra room," Casey said. "And I can get you a job working at a sex shop."

Natalia laughed. "God, that sounds amazing. My mom would kill me."

"Mine's not too happy either." Casey pulled out her phone. She sent a quick note to her mom letting her know she'd arrived and then glanced at Natalia. "I told her we'd swing by tonight."

"We?" Natalia's eyes lit up.

"Figured you'd want to see my mom more than an Uber driver would."

A smile spread across Natalia's face, but a moment later her forehead creased with lines. "What should I wear?"

Casey chuckled. "Knowing you, you'll pull out the sexiest outfit you have, put it on, and then get embarrassed ten minutes before we have to leave and change to a T-shirt and jeans."

Natalia shot her an offended look and then said, "Okay, probably."

"Honestly, my mom is going to be so focused on the Pavia problem, she's not going to think about anyone else. Ten bucks says she forgets to say hi to me."

Natalia slumped back in her seat. "But she's so hot and smart and—"

"Self-centered?" Casey laughed at Natalia's scowl. "I take it you prefer focused."

Which Lee Stevens also was. Traffic inched along and instead of continuing the conversation about her mom's attributes, Casey scrolled through her contact list until she found Ingrid's number. Ingrid wasn't listed by her real name—Casey had always made sure to use codes in her phone in case her contact list was copied. Her mom had taught her that trick. Now she stared at the number attached to the name: PVSIGLS. Pavia's Ingrid Larsen. She took a deep breath and then texted asking if Ingrid had time to talk.

Ingrid's response was immediate. *Sure. When?*

Casey tapped her finger on the edge of the phone case. Ingrid hadn't even asked why.

"What's up?" Natalia asked.

"I don't know… I've got a feeling about something. Do you mind if I call Ingrid now?"

Natalia motioned to the rows and rows of cars ahead of them. "We've got two miles to go in this mess so you've got at least a half hour."

Ingrid didn't answer the call but instead responded with a second text. *With someone. Can't talk now.*

"You've got a look. What's going on?" Natalia asked.

"Ingrid can't talk now." Casey stared at the phone screen for a moment. "I've always kind of wondered if Pavia and Ingrid had history. They were so close for a while."

"You think they dated?"

"Maybe?" She'd never asked because Pavia had a strict rule against talking about exes. "If so, I doubt Ingrid will want to talk to me about Pavia."

Natalia's lips pursed. "Then we go to Plan B."

"We have a Plan B?"

Natalia grimaced. "Not yet."

Casey's phone beeped with a new text. Ingrid: *Are you in town?*

Last Casey had heard, Ingrid still lived in Santa Monica. Not far from Burbank—unless there was bad traffic. Casey had lived there before the move to Colorado. She wondered how much Ingrid knew about her whereabouts now. If she'd been with Pavia a month ago, what were the chances she hadn't heard about Casey's relocation? She decided less was more and simply said: *Yes.*

Ingrid: *I'll be at Aces tonight.*

Aces was not the official name of the club. Pavia and her friends never called anywhere by the actual name if they were making plans. But Casey knew exactly which club Ingrid meant. She also knew anyone who was friends with Pavia—even old friends—wouldn't show up at a club before eleven.

"Want to go clubbing tonight?" It was the last thing Casey wanted to do but if that was where Ingrid wanted to talk, she'd make it happen. "Ingrid wants to meet up at Aces."

"Can we invite your mom? God, I'd lose it if I saw your mom on the dance floor. Can you imagine?"

"No." Not even a little bit. "My mom doesn't dance. But Ingrid Larsen does. Please will you go with me?"

"Fine." Natalia sighed dramatically. "Unless your mom asks me to stay for an after-dinner cocktail. Then you're on your own."

"I'll take it." Casey breathed out, feeling some relief at having at least a bit of a plan. She looked at Natalia again. "You're the best. You sure you don't want to move to Colorado with me?"

"With my luck, as soon as I moved there, you'd marry your baker." She shook her head. "Then I'd be even lonelier there than I am in this town."

Casey was struck by Natalia's tone. Her usual light sarcasm didn't cover the somberness. "You know what's nice? Being with someone you can relax around. Sometimes I think relationships are overrated and friendships are better."

Natalia met Casey's gaze. "Says the person who owns a sex shop. Is Tara only a friend? I thought she was more?"

"She is. More, I mean." Casey stared at the car idling next to Natalia's. "I think I'm falling in love with her."

"Why don't you sound happy about that?"

"No, I am. It's just…I don't have the best track record and she's kind of amazing."

"What are you worried about?" Natalia asked.

"Screwing things up somehow. I really like her."

"So don't screw up."

"Easier said than done."

Natalia turned her attention back to the traffic and Casey brought up Tara's text thread, reading over the messages she'd sent earlier. *Sorry I had to take off without talking to you. Dealing with some stuff. I'll call you tonight.*

None of it was a lie, but she was definitely omitting plenty. And she felt terrible she'd left without having a real conversation about everything she was facing with her family and Pavia. Still, she didn't want that conversation to happen over the phone.

Would Tara understand why she'd gone back to LA without an explanation? She weighed the question, wondering too if Tara felt their friendship had officially crossed the line into relationship territory like she did. If so, what did that mean for them going forward? As daunting as it was given her last go at marriage, the thought of sharing her future with Tara and making a life together in Rocky Springs felt entirely right.

"You know it might take more than a few days to convince Pavia to go to rehab," Natalia said.

Casey looked up from her phone, momentarily dazed. One minute she was in Colorado planning a future with Tara and the next the sight of LA's evening commute traffic smacked her with a dose of reality. Her past was still her present. She exhaled. "I can't leave the store for longer than a few days. I have a kid working six hours a day and that's only half the hours I wanted to be open this week."

Natalia didn't respond at first, her gaze focused on the Porsche in front of them. Finally she said, "What if I flew out there?"

"To Colorado?"

"Yeah. I could work at your shop. If you buy me a plane ticket, I'll work for free. It might be the only chance I get to work in a sex shop."

Casey grinned at Natalia's eyebrow waggle. "You'd really do that?"

"It sounds fun. Besides, you know I'd do anything for you. You're right about friendships being better than relationships most of the time." She paused. "But then again, I've never had a relationship that started as a friendship. Maybe you and Tara have the right idea."

Casey didn't admit how much she hoped that was the case. She also hoped Tara would understand everything when she explained why she'd had to come to LA. And, hopefully, it'd be okay that she'd waited to tell her the whole story until they were together again.

CHAPTER TWENTY-SEVEN

Casey didn't call that first night she was in LA. She didn't call the next night, either. Well, she did, but Tara was at her mom's for dinner and her grandparents were there and looking at one's phone was heavily frowned upon. But the cryptic message Casey left—alluding to things being tense but okay—was practically worse than not hearing from her at all.

She said as much in a text, and Casey's reply was a tepid apology and a promise to explain when she got home. Only she'd yet to commit to when that might be and, when Tara offered to look in on Aspen, Casey brushed her off with vague allusions to everything being under control. If she hadn't been so genuinely worried about whatever the hell was going on, she'd have been downright pissed.

It didn't help that work was off-the-charts busy. Under normal circumstances, she'd be delighted, hustling every waking moment and promising herself a nice little break in January when the inevitable New Year's resolutions and slump in weddings made for slow sales. It wasn't that she didn't appreciate the business, along with what it said about Coy Cupcakes' reputation. It was just…what?

It was that she'd imagined hustling through her days and tumbling into bed with Casey for hot sex and a good night's sleep. It was that she'd imagined talking Casey into sneaking away for a couple of days to reward themselves for a successful holiday season and recharge for the Valentine's Day surge. And now all of that felt uncertain. She didn't like uncertain. It left her antsy, irritable, and exhausted. None of which was made better by Shawn's nagging and the sinking feeling that she'd put way too much stock in anything and everything to do with Casey Stevens.

Tara said as much when she'd finally convinced Shawn to leave her to close up alone. No reason both of them had to suffer. So she sent Shawn off, flipped the sign to closed, and cranked up her wronged woman country playlist. She finally locked up a little after nine. Every surface gleamed and she'd practically sung herself hoarse. Of course, she'd spent the better part of fourteen hours on her feet and would definitely regret it in the morning. Whether she regretted it more than she regretted falling for the likes of Casey remained to be seen.

What a mess.

She turned in the direction of where she'd parked, which happened to be the direction of Casey's store, and her gaze landed on someone trying to break in. "Hey," she yelled before thinking better of getting involved.

The burglar jumped a mile. She should probably be grateful this was the extent of Rocky Springs's criminal element. But then she thought about the vandalism that had happened at Casey's shop before it opened, and a lick of anger coursed through her. "Who's there?"

She expected the culprit to run off, but the stranger turned and put both hands in the air like Tara was a cop. "I'm a friend of the owner. I have a key. I just can't get it to work."

The vague familiarity sharpened into something solid, though Tara couldn't for the life of her conjure the woman's name. "You're Casey's friend."

The woman nodded. "You're the baker."

Right. Images from Casey's first few weeks in Rocky Springs flashed in her mind. The woman was even more obsessed with her cupcakes than Casey had been. And that was saying something. "Natalia."

"That's me." Natalia flashed a thousand-watt smile and Tara wondered if she'd been born that beautiful or had gotten help along the way.

"What are you doing here?" The first of about a hundred questions that swirled in her mind, including whether that meant Casey was back and whether maybe Natalia and Casey were an item after all.

"I'm trying to help keep Casey's shop afloat while she's off dealing with her train wreck of an ex." Natalia kicked the frame of the doorway. "If I could get the damn key to work in the lock."

"Her ex?" She didn't want to know, but she probably needed to.

"Pavia. She's completely out of control and drinking again. Which wouldn't be a big deal if not for her horde of followers going after Casey's dad." Natalia let out a dismissive sniff. "And Casey is dumb enough to try to reason with her."

So so many more questions joined the mix. Did Casey still love her ex, despite all the drama? Or were they wrapped up in some creepy co-dependent spiral that Casey would never fully leave? Was this why Casey had gone all distant and sullen? And, if so, did that make Tara feel better or worse?

"Did she not tell you?" Natalia cringed.

Tara lifted her chin. "She did not."

"It's not personal. I promise. She's pretty mortified by the whole thing."

"I'm sure." And that was the crux of it. They might be fucking, but when push came to shove, Casey didn't consider her someone worth confiding in.

"Wait, did she not talk to you at all? She made it sound like she'd left things up in the air, but I didn't think she was that much of a blockhead." Natalia rolled her eyes. "She's hopeless."

Not the word Tara would have used but not completely off the mark. Stubborn, perhaps. Paired with sometimes clueless. Or maybe Casey knew exactly what she was doing. Maybe her priorities were perfectly clear and simply didn't include their relationship. Maybe this was all just a convenient excuse to let Tara know where they stood, which was miles apart.

"Tell me she at least called you." Natalia's words yanked Tara back to the frigid December air and the dark street and the world that had felt so tidy and certain before Casey waltzed into it.

She'd checked her phone before leaving the bakery but pulled it out anyway. She held it up, screen facing Natalia, to drive home the point. "One voice mail and a couple of noncommittal texts saying she'd explain when she got home. Otherwise, nada."

"You should call her."

"I did. Twice, in fact. She didn't pick up." A fact that felt even worse now, knowing who Casey had gone to California to see.

"She's in fixer mode. Also known as tunnel vision. It would do her good to be reminded of what she has waiting for her back here."

Tara pursed her lips, wondering if she should find a nice way to say "no way in hell" or just put it out there as is.

"I don't mean you should have to. Like, I'm not telling you what to do. What I mean is Casey could use someone in her corner right now. And she might be hopeless, but I have on good authority she's pretty far gone over you. She might not be able to say it, but it would mean the world to her."

Tara folded her arms and tapped her foot on the snowy pavement. "You seem more sure of Casey's feelings than she does."

Natalia tipped her head back and forth. "Sometimes."

"I'm not sure how much good that does me."

"She's working on it," Natalia said.

"Is she?" It came out more sarcastic than she'd meant but not more than she felt.

"Pavia did a real number on her. Built her up to be the hero, then exploded it all without a second thought. Publicly. I'm not saying that to give her an excuse, but she was way more traumatized by it than she lets on."

Tara prided herself on being a straightforward person, in her actions, but in her emotions as well. Having such a complicated swirl of feelings about Casey—not to mention her actions—left her unsteady. She liked feeling unsteady about as much as she liked being wrong. "I shouldn't keep you."

Natalia narrowed her eyes briefly at the abrupt shift. "Pretty sure it's the other way around. I think I might be standing here all night."

She blew out a breath, sort of wanting to storm off but knowing full well none of this was Natalia's fault. Hell, Natalia had given her more to go on than Casey had. She could appreciate that, even if it spelled disaster for Casey and her in the long run. "Here, let me help."

Natalia extended the keys without hesitation. "If you get this door open, you will have my eternal gratitude."

"Ours sticks the same way. I think they must have all been put in together." Tara slid the key into the lock and jiggled it. "Voila."

"You are a goddess. A lock-whispering, cupcake-baking goddess."

Well, at least one person thought that. "Do you need help with anything else?"

"I won't ask you to stick around tonight, but are there any tricks to locking it I should know? I'm only supposed to be making sure Aspen closed out the registers the right way so the software could do its mathematical magic overnight."

Tara shook her head. "No, that part's easy. And if you're back in the morning, Shawn and I should both be at the shop. Don't hesitate to pop in if you need a hand."

"Oh, I'll be popping in either way. I've been deprived and I have every intention of having a cupcake for breakfast."

She smiled instinctively, but sentiment backed it up. Whatever cluster of a situation she and Casey had going, Natalia had been honest with her, and had given her information she needed to figure out what to do next. And she'd dropped her life at the drop of a hat to help a friend. Natalia might be unequivocally team Casey—which was more than she could say about herself at this point—but Tara couldn't help but like her. "First one's on the house."

Natalia grinned as though Tara had offered something far more valuable than a four-dollar cupcake. "I'll accept only because I know I'll be paying for at least twenty while I'm here."

Tara softened even further. "You sure you're okay? I can stick around if you want."

"Nah. I'm more competent than my door unlocking skills would imply. And you should be home in case you decide to find it in your heart to give my sad sack best friend a call."

Was Casey a sad sack? Maybe in this instance. Even worse, sad sack with a hero complex. Tara could empathize with that, though it frustrated the hell out of her. She could give Casey the benefit of the doubt and at least try reaching out again. Whatever Casey decided to do with that was her business. And it would tell Tara what she needed to know about whether there was any point trying to sort out the rest.

Chapter Twenty-eight

When Pavia entered the café, heads turned, cell phones pointed, and Casey had to suppress a groan. One of many things she didn't miss was Pavia's need to be seen everywhere she went. And her version of evading notice was always the same— lightweight hoodie and big sunglasses. People recognized that look more than anything. A few turned not-so-subtly to ask whoever they were sitting with about the woman passing in front of them. "Isn't that Pavia Rossini?"

Casey couldn't actually hear what anyone said over the café's jazz music, but she imagined it. The online buzz would doubtlessly follow with everyone eager to rule in, or out, a Pavia sighting. Fortunately, Ingrid had requested a private table on the second floor which meant Casey could watch the scene unfold below with only an audience of one. The therapist. Simone LaFont, who came with high accolades, a promise for complete discretion, and a high price. Simone's attention wasn't on Casey however. She was focused on Pavia.

The stairs to the second floor were at the back of the café and one of the waiters stepped forward to motion upstairs. Pavia glanced up and Casey's heart raced. She knew Pavia wouldn't be able to see her—she'd positioned her chair behind a column on purpose—but she wished she practiced yoga and could control her breathing. Anything that might help. Funny how all the romances made it seem like it was a good thing when hearts raced at the sight of someone. In her case, it only reinforced how much her body dreaded this interaction.

Pavia passed temporarily out of view, and Simone turned her razor gaze onto Casey. "She's clearly intoxicated. This isn't unexpected, but it will potentially make our conversation more difficult."

How had the therapist picked up that Pavia was drunk? Casey hadn't seen any stumble or obvious sign. Before she'd decided to ask, Ingrid arrived. She slipped off her sunglasses, smiling graciously to the same waiter who'd pointed Pavia upstairs. Cell phones again flashed but Ingrid ignored them. Pavia always paused, angling her head just so for the shot. Ingrid acted like the cameras didn't exist. Ironic given she was the one who'd done all the modeling.

"Just like we planned," Simone said, her voice in a tone Casey knew was intentionally soothing. Except it didn't help.

Casey exhaled a slow shaky breath and nodded. They'd planned on Ingrid coming in last in case Pavia took one look at Casey and fled. Simone reached across the table to touch the back of Casey's hand.

"It's completely normal to be nervous, Casey. Are you okay to see this through?"

"Yeah," Casey lied. She wasn't okay. She was a wreck. Her right leg shook, as per usual when she was anxious and couldn't move, and her teeth kept trying to chatter. What was worse, her stomach acids surged like her insides were picking up the shakes too. She swallowed, thinking how uncool it would be to take one look at Pavia and vomit.

It would have been better if she didn't have to pretend to be the calm one in the situation. She wished, completely illogically, that Tara could be with her. She wanted to hold Tara's hand and know that someone was on her side. Tara wouldn't judge if she broke down in front of her ex. She'd understand.

"Fucking shit." Pavia stopped on the top step, the words coming out like a hiss. She ripped off her sunglasses and it struck Casey how different she looked. She'd never seen Pavia drunk or strung out and she was clearly both. She swayed, seemingly trying to make sense of the situation or to control some vertigo. She was wearing makeup but that didn't cover how red and puffy her eyes had gotten, while the rest of her looked unsettlingly gaunt.

"What the hell is going on?" She seemed to ask Simone the question but turned to scowl at Casey. "If you're the one who set up this so-called meeting—"

"Pavia, I'm Simone." Simone stood, adding she was a licensed therapist, and there to facilitate the conversation.

"This is bullshit," Pavia said, her tone seething. "Did Casey tell you I promised to get a restraining order if she tried contacting me?" Her tone raised at the last bit, and she focused on Casey as she said, "I can't believe you would pull a stunt like this." She spun but stopped short, like the sudden movement had thrown her off balance. Or maybe it was the sight of Ingrid, who now blocked the stairs.

Ingrid placed a hand on Pavia's wrist and Casey couldn't deny the motion was tender despite everything. Maybe because of that, Pavia didn't jerk away. Ingrid said something, the words inaudible to Casey but the meaning clear. *Give us a chance to help.*

They'd only have one chance. When Casey met up with Ingrid at the club, she'd known exactly why Casey had sought her out. And she'd been grateful—which Casey hadn't expected. Pavia and Ingrid had been dating, off and on, for the past nine months. It wasn't hard to do the math and recognize the overlap with the end of Casey and Pavia's marriage. But things with Ingrid had started years before that. They'd fallen in love as teens. Ingrid had balked at telling anyone, worried they'd both lose any future in acting. And then Pavia's world spun out of control.

The story hadn't surprised Casey. More it was a matter of pieces fitting together. All along Pavia had loved someone else. It didn't explain the affair Pavia had with her costar—the one who'd been married with three children—that had broken up their already faltering marriage, but it explained many other choices Pavia had made. And now, for better or worse, Ingrid still loved Pavia. If Casey could foster a reconciliation between them, it would help Pavia and go a long way toward creating a buffer between the life she'd built and the chaos she'd left behind.

"Pavia." Casey stood. She felt an odd kind of numbness when Pavia's gaze shot to hers, her body contorted with anger. From the deep scowl to the clenched fists, Pavia was ready for a fight.

"We only want to talk." For the first time since she'd landed in Burbank, the fear and self-doubt were gone. Pavia couldn't hurt her anymore, and even after everything that had been done and said she didn't want to see Pavia's life destroyed. "Will you sit down?"

She knew Pavia might leave and there was nothing they could do to stop her. But a minute passed and Pavia only held her ground.

"I hate you so much."

"I know." Casey nodded slowly. "And I'm sorry your world went to hell when I came into it."

Pavia let out a strangled laugh. She gestured to Simone. "You brought a fucking shrink?"

"Simone's really qualified and I think we need her. We need to talk about what happened. Get it all out. Then maybe we can both move on." She met Pavia's gaze and a familiar heaviness pressed down on her—the same feeling she'd had the last month they were together. All she'd wanted then was to leave and never look back. She'd said she'd never get into another relationship because of it. Tara had changed her mind on that and so many things. Thinking of Tara gave Casey a sense of steadiness and she pushed on.

"I still think you're a good person—even after everything. And I know you can do amazing things when you're the one in control. But things are out of control and you know you can't argue that."

Pavia shook her head, but Casey didn't stop. "Ingrid loves you. I don't think you want to hurt her, but that's what you're doing." She paused, trying to gauge Pavia's response. Cold eyes simply stared back at her.

"Today could be a restart, Pavia." Simone's voice cut in, calm and resolved. She nodded at each one of them, lastly Casey as if to encourage her to finish.

"We want you to be healthy and happy," Casey said. "And that means sober. Ingrid wants that for you more than anyone."

Pavia's eyes zipped to Ingrid. The two stared at each other for a long painful moment before Ingrid whispered, "I love you, but I can't handle this anymore."

Pavia cussed and started for the stairs. When Ingrid reached for her, Pavia shot back, "I can't believe you're on Casey's side."

"I'm on your side, Pavia." Ingrid's voice cracked. "I didn't do anything to stop you last time. I only stood by and watched. I'm not making that mistake again."

"So, what, you want to send me to rehab?"

"I can't stay with you if you keep going on like this."

Pavia seemed to clutch the railing as if she'd fall without it. "Are you saying you want to break up?"

"No." Ingrid took a deep breath. "I want you to go to rehab. I want you to get clean and stop drinking."

Pavia cussed but that didn't seem to phase Ingrid. "I know you can do it. I watched you do it once. The whole world did." She shifted closer to Pavia, taking her hand from the railing and clasping it. "The first time everyone abandoned you. Including me. But you got up and started all over again. All on your own. I don't want to watch you lose everything you've achieved."

"What have I fucking achieved?" Pavia ripped her hand away. She gestured at Casey. "Ask her. The only thing I want is more followers."

Casey leveled her gaze on Pavia. "We both said some crappy things to each other."

"You want to turn this back on me?"

"No. I want to move on." Casey looked over at Simone and the therapist's nod pushed her to go on. "And I want to apologize. I know my parents screwed you over. I read the contract yesterday. The clauses they snuck into the fine print were manipulative and self-serving."

Fortunately, the contract issues seemed to be the extent of it. She'd asked everyone she could think of and there seemed to be no truth to the other allegations against her father. And Pavia had never directly said anything had happened—it'd only been rumors created by her fans. Rumors she hadn't bothered to correct.

Pavia closed her eyes for a moment. "I've got such a fucking headache. I need a drink."

"I ordered you a double espresso." Casey pointed to the waiting mug. "Your favorite. Can we sit down and talk?"

Pavia shook her head, but Simone spoke up. "Pavia." She motioned to the two open seats like they were truly only there for the coffee. "Come sit. We're only going to talk."

Definitely not Simone's first rodeo. Casey's unease about the whole intervention lifted when Simone had spelled out the logistics as they'd chatted the first time on the phone. Now she saw the effect of the steady professionalism on Pavia as Simone coached her. "Please, Pavia. We're all here only wanting to help."

Ingrid touched Pavia's arm and whispered, "Please."

Casey felt a tug in her chest. Ingrid's love for Pavia was undeniable. It was written all over her face. If only Pavia could see it.

"Ingrid, Casey ordered you an almond latte." Simone held up her drink. "We have the same order."

Ingrid whispered something to Pavia and finally Pavia turned to meet Ingrid's gaze. Casey held her breath, hoping. When Pavia took Ingrid's hand, Casey exhaled.

There was no one better than Pavia to show the world that two steps forward could be followed by a stumble, a faceplant, and then getting back up again. Pavia could start life over a second time and then a third.

Ingrid reached out to take Pavia's other hand. She brought both to her lips and kissed the knuckles gently. "I'm in this with you," Ingrid murmured. "You're not alone this time."

Pavia's tears started then, followed by Ingrid's. Casey couldn't hold back either. All the pain and hurt had to come out. Then they could find a way forward.

When they left the café a full two hours later, Ingrid walked on one side of Pavia and Casey on the other, holding her arm. Simone, who Casey now considered therapist extraordinaire, led the way to the waiting SUV. A driver had been arranged to take the three of them directly to the rehab facility. Simone would follow behind in her own car and stay on to get Pavia settled.

Ingrid asked Casey to stay on one more day. She agreed mostly because Ingrid had sounded so forlorn and lost. Ingrid's mental health was something Simone had spoken about—and Casey's too. She'd given them both strict instructions to set up appointments with their own therapists. Casey almost laughed. Therapy was definitely overdue. But she left the café with a feeling of hope. What lay ahead wouldn't be a picnic for either Ingrid or Pavia. But now they had a chance.

As for her, all she wanted was to get back to Rocky Springs and back to Tara. The longing grew even stronger when she took out her phone and noticed a missed call from Tara. She couldn't call but she texted. *Sorry I missed you. Had my phone on silent.* She had so much to tell Tara. Too much to contain in a text. *You have no idea how much I want to talk.*

Chapter Twenty-nine

Tara strode into the cantina with purpose, determined to eat her feelings rather than do something more destructive with them. With the breakfast crowd clear and the lunch throng yet to descend, the tiny eating area was quiet and not a soul stood in line. Juan, so often hidden away in the kitchen, sat on a stool behind the register with a clipboard. Tara smiled, knowing those moments well. "I should always come in at weird times. No wait and I get to see your handsome face."

Juan looked up, mirroring the smile. "Hey, you."

"I need a burrito, stat."

The smile vanished, and his eyes narrowed with concern. "Yeah. What a mess, huh?"

Accurate, but how did he know? "Was Shawn in here?"

"Something is wrong with Shawn, too? Aw, man, when it rains it pours, huh?"

Her own eyes narrowed, but in confusion. "Wait. What are you talking about?"

"Casey and that actress. Her ex." He shook his head. "Interventions are no joke."

"Huh?"

Juan scratched his temple. "I don't keep track of celebrities and influencers and stuff, but my cousin sent it to me because the article mentioned Rocky Springs and he wanted to know if I knew Casey. Pretty wild."

The more he said, the less she understood. Well, not entirely. If what Natalia said was true and Casey went to LA because her ex was drinking again, an intervention would make sense. But it didn't explain how Juan knew about it. Unless Casey had confided in literally everyone but her. Which honest to God wouldn't surprise her at this point, but still. "What article?"

"Oh. Shit. Did you not see it?" Juan cringed. "I assumed you knew about it."

Wanting to know paled in comparison to the utter humiliation of not knowing. Whatever put that look on Juan's face would be bad, but the pity masking as concern had to be worse. Before she could tell him not to bother, he tapped at his phone a few times and held it up to her. The headline took up half the screen. "Love Wins: Pavia's Back to Rehab."

Underneath the loud black typeface was a picture of Casey with Pavia. It was cropped funny, but there was no mistaking Casey's arm around Pavia. And Pavia leaned into Casey like her life depended on it. Tara closed her eyes for a second and willed herself to disappear.

Unfortunately, teleportation wasn't a thing and when she opened them, Juan stood there with that infuriating look of sympathy on his face. "So, is she like gone, gone?" he asked.

Tara shrugged.

Juan frowned. "She seemed really happy here."

"I don't know." Clearly, she didn't know anything.

"The article makes it sound like they're getting back together, but you know how those celebrity sites are. Anything for more clicks."

"Yeah." Casey had talked about how much she hated that world, but maybe old habits died hard. She certainly had more history with that life than the one she had here. Tara didn't want to believe it had all been some grand publicity stunt, but it wasn't outside the realm of possibility.

"Do you want to talk about it?"

Juan's gentle tone made Tara's jaw clench. "I really, really don't."

"Okay, then. Let's talk burrito. What'll it be?"

She looked at the menu, then at Juan. "Actually, I don't think I'm that hungry after all."

He came from behind the register and put a hand on her arm. "Aw, Tara. I'm sorry."

She shook her head, but he pulled her into a hug anyway. The tenderness had her throat constricting and tears threatening. "I gotta go."

Tara didn't give him the chance to try to convince her otherwise. She bolted, heading straight for her car, where she could cry alone like a normal person. And did she cry. Basic tears at first, with little sniffles thrown in. But instead of the quick release she anticipated, letting it out only seemed to fuel the torrent of emotions, and she wound up hunched over the steering wheel sobbing like someone had died. It was utterly out of character and yet she was powerless to stop it.

When it finally let up, she rooted around in her center console for some tissues. She wiped her eyes and blew her nose and willed herself to feel better. It didn't work, but she managed to replace helpless and devastated with low-grade rage, especially after pulling up the article and reading all the insinuations and speculations for herself.

Rage felt like an improvement, so she clung to it, punching her steering wheel a few times for good measure. When her fists started to throb, she stopped and let out a string of cuss words. It felt good, so good she almost felt hungry again. Too bad going back to the cantina would require talking to Juan. That was a level of pulling herself together she knew better than to attempt, or fake. She'd have to make do with the sandwich fixings she kept at the bakery.

She drove over, beating Shawn there and letting herself in without flipping the sign to open. After making a quick grilled cheese and eating it without really tasting it, she put on her apron and hat and started the first batter of the day, fueled by the mix of adrenaline and doing something she could control.

She paused mid-sift, realizing she hadn't preheated the oven, and decided to put some more mileage on her wronged and revenge-seeking song library. Not that she'd actively seek revenge, of course. But it was nice to contemplate.

"That bad, huh?" Shawn stood in the doorway, wincing.

Tara looked up from the pan she'd half-filled. "I didn't hear you come in."

"How could you with the music blasting at jet engine levels?"

She grabbed her phone and hit pause. "Sorry."

"Don't apologize. But maybe turn it down a little before we open?"

She unpaused and adjusted the volume. "Better?"

"Much." Shawn stopped at the counter, surveying the collection of dirty mixing bowls. "Do you want to talk about it?"

"Did you see?" Had everyone seen but her?

"See what?" The puzzled look made it clear Shawn wasn't bluffing.

Tara rolled her eyes. "Google Casey and Pavia. And no, I don't want to talk about it."

The combo was enough to send Shawn backing out of the kitchen. Tara resumed scooping batter and mumbled select swear words under her breath—some directed at Casey and more than a few at herself.

She managed to get into a groove, especially when it came to frosting. Something about the rhythmic squeeze and swirl of a piping bag put her in a trance, almost like how she imagined meditation would feel. She didn't quite forget the fact that everyone she knew would be asking her what happened, or the way Casey and Pavia looked in that picture. It became more of an annoying murmur at the edges of her mind, though, rather than sitting front and center.

"Uh, Tara."

"What?" She looked up, annoyed to have her concentration broken.

"There's someone here to see you," Shawn said, disappearing without further explanation.

Since it might be one of her brides or corporate clients, she couldn't very well ignore them. Or tell Shawn to tell them to buzz off until after Christmas. So she took a deep breath and blew it out slowly, locking away her irascibility and fixing her brightest and most professional smile on her face.

She strode into the bakery like she was thrilled to see whoever it was and stopped short. Not even her most practiced smile stood a chance against what she saw. Casey stood there, looking sheepish and exhausted but utterly gorgeous, clutching a bouquet of white roses. "Hi," she said.

Tara turned on the ball of her foot and went back the way she came. Nope.

Given Casey's recent behavior, she thought she might get away with it. Left to stew in peace while Casey slinked off with her tail between her legs. Or maybe Casey wouldn't even slink. She'd swagger, thrilled that she could tie up the loose end of their dalliance so easily. Go back to her shop or her ex who might not be her ex anymore or wherever the hell else she wanted to go that was as far away from Tara as possible.

"You have every right to be mad at me."

She let out a dismissive sniff. "I don't need you to tell me that."

"I'm not getting back together with Pavia. I know it's all over the internet that we're a couple again, but I can't think of anything I want less." Casey took a breath. "And if you saw the picture that keeps being reposted everywhere, that was after her intervention. She was on her way to rehab."

Tara nodded and tried to look disinterested.

"Her actual girlfriend was standing on the other side of her. She's a model. I'm not sure why they didn't play up that angle."

Another nod.

"I guess I might not be famous, but my parents are. So there's that. And our breakup was so ugly and public, and all her fans blamed me for everything." Casey chewed her lip for a second. "But that doesn't matter now. What matters is that you need to know I have no romantic interest in her whatsoever. I care about her as a human being, and I care about the damage she was trying to do to my parents' company, but that's it. I promise. And if there's anything I need to do to prove that to you—"

Since it seemed like Casey might be willing to carry on like that all day if left to her own devices, Tara took a deep breath of her own. "You honestly think that's why I'm upset?"

To her credit, Casey looked genuinely confused. "Isn't it?"

"You lied to me, Casey."

Casey flinched as though she'd been slapped. "I didn't."

Tara folded her arms. "Family emergency?"

Casey shook her head vigorously. "Maybe not the whole truth, but definitely not a lie. It was my mother who called and basically demanded that I come home and deal with Pavia before things got even more out of hand."

For some reason, the half-baked logic made her angrier. "Seriously."

"I posted that picture of me with the blue ribbon from the window display contest and Gary Jenkins did his homework. He managed to link me to my folks and Stevens Productions. Then he reposted a bunch of crap that wasn't true. Pavia's trolls took everything and ran with it. Especially after Pavia started dropping hints about suing Stevens Production for putting shady stuff in her contract with them." Casey's head dropped and she stared at the floor. "Which turned out to be at least partially true."

Tara fought the grimace she could feel forming on her face. What a freaking train wreck. "That sucks."

Casey returned her gaze to Tara. "That's putting it mildly. Pavia was completely off the rails, and my parents were legitimately implicated. I was afraid of what she might do, to them but also to herself."

Honestly, she couldn't imagine dealing with a person like that. Even at her lowest, she'd never gone down the rabbit hole of substance abuse. And for all that her ex had been a self-absorbed flake, she'd never been a physical danger to anyone. "I get it."

"Good." Casey visibly relaxed. "I'm sorry about the whole mess. Getting away from drama is the reason I moved here, but I guess I couldn't escape it completely."

Tara nodded, the sad reality of the situation sinking in.

"So, we're okay?"

"No." They were so far from it.

"No?"

"Even if we don't split hairs over the technicalities of lying, you kept all of this from me. Which is pretty gross in my book, but now you're saying it's been going on for God only knows how long." She shook her head at how much that hurt.

"I didn't know how to tell you. And I didn't know it was going to turn into such a big deal. I'm sorry."

"That's not good enough." Even if she wanted it to be.

"What would be good enough? What do you want?" Casey's eyes were pleading.

"I want you to trust me enough to tell me hard things, to confide in me. I want a relationship that's real enough to handle that." Which was funny to say, given how much she hadn't been looking for a relationship.

"I want that to. And I want to tell you things."

"Only you didn't. And now how am I supposed to know if things are fine or if you're holding important things back?" She shook her head. "I can't be with someone I don't trust."

"Please don't say that." Casey took a step toward her but stopped. "I want to fix this."

"I don't think you can."

"So, that's it? We're done?"

For all that she'd tapped into her anger, it abandoned her in an instant. What remained was a heart that hurt way more than it should and a desperate need to be alone. "We can't end what we never really started, right? You said all along you weren't ready for a relationship. I just should have believed you."

Casey waited a beat but didn't speak. Tara forced herself to sit in the uncomfortable silence, not sure whether she was more afraid of saying something unnecessarily mean or starting to soften. Fortunately, Casey didn't linger, and Tara didn't have to muster the words to ask her to leave. She went quicky and quietly, leaving Tara with the aloneness she wanted so badly. Only it didn't make her feel any better. The truth of the matter was she couldn't remember a time she felt worse.

CHAPTER THIRTY

"Who turned off the Christmas music?" Aspen stopped in front of Casey. "I thought you were okay with the instrumental mix."

"It started to sound too happy."

Aspen squinted at her. "You know, I never would have guessed you'd be all bah-humbug when I started here."

"People surprise you." *Especially people you think you're in love with.* She motioned to a box with items she'd tagged and sorted while Aspen was on lunch. "Mind stocking some shelves?"

"You want me to put codes in the computer?"

"Already done."

Aspen looked at her with surprise. "Already? Damn. No rest for the Santa-haters, huh?"

"I don't hate Santa."

"You sure?"

"I mean, I always thought the story was a little weird. Big guy running around in red pajamas, sliding down people's chimneys. Who even came up with that? And those elves? Creepy little dudes watching us while we sleep?"

"Okay, bah-humbug." Aspen laughed. "For the record, I love Santa. And all the elves."

"Well, thanks to people like you, this shop has a good chance of staying afloat." Casey held up a set of bells meant to be attached to harnesses for kink fun and gave them a shake. "Ho ho ho. See? I've got Christmas spirit." She motioned to the box. "You know what's almost as fun as stuffing someone's stocking?"

"Getting the merch out on the shelves? On it." Aspen's enthusiasm was either real, or they ought to consider acting. They picked up the box but then glanced back at Casey. "I know it's not really my place to ask but… Since you've come back from California, I haven't seen Tara come around. And you haven't really being smiling. Like at all. Everything okay with you two?"

Casey forced a smile and pointed to her lips. "Better?"

Aspen shook their head but didn't push. As soon as they turned away, Casey let the swell of emotion hit. She missed Tara more than she wanted to admit. But there was no reason to talk about it. Not to Aspen, and not the day before Christmas Eve.

Unfortunately, the shop wasn't as busy as she thought it would be—which left more time to think about everything she'd done wrong with Tara—but she was determined to get through the day. And the next one. Then it would be Christmas, and she'd have all the time in the world to think. It would be the first Christmas she'd be spending alone, and the shop would be closed so she wouldn't have any distraction.

"Oh, I like these." Aspen had managed to get one book on the shelf before they were distracted by a package of greeting cards. The theme was "The Twelve Days of Christmas" and each card featured an elf in a scene with one of the twelve days' gifts. "When did these come in?"

"A couple weeks ago."

"Huh. I must have missed them. Too bad it's too late now for anyone to buy them." Aspen flipped the package over. "I love the one with the elf running away from the seven swans. And the one with all the maids? That elf looks super naughty."

Casey had bought the cards with Tara in mind. Not thinking she'd give the cards to her but thinking of the first time they'd gone out together—when Tara had offered to meet her for a drink to tell her the inside scoop about Gary and the window contest and the Christmas market. When they'd left the pub, Casey had thought how easy it'd be to date Tara. How much less complicated Tara was than Pavia and all the other women she'd dated. Tara's laugh had seemed so carefree that night. She pictured Tara standing by the jewelry store, the elves in the window holding up rings and bracelets, and the memory made her throat tighten.

Casey looked away from Aspen and the cards and glanced around the space. With no customers and with the paperwork all caught up, there was nothing for her to do. "I'll be in the back taking a break. Holler if we get busy."

She hadn't slept well for days, and closing her eyes for a moment was more appealing than lunch. She sank down on the settee, only to be reminded of what she'd done with Tara in the same spot. Instead of any rush of arousal, the thought only made her chest ache.

She pulled out her phone and brought up the last line of text she'd sent to Tara. Reaching out now was pointless, but she wanted to anyway. The problem was, she didn't know what to say. Another apology? She tossed the phone down with a groan. If another apology would help, she'd pay for Santa himself to deliver it.

"Knock knock."

Kit was not who she expected. Then again, she hadn't been expecting anyone. Only hoping. But Tara wouldn't be walking through her door anytime soon. "Hey." She straightened, but when she went to stand, Kit held up a hand.

"You look comfortable there. And, honestly, kind of like shit. When was the last time you slept?"

Casey ran a hand through her hair. "Last night. For a couple hours."

"And were you wearing that shirt?"

Casey tugged at the wrinkled fabric. "No. But it may have been on the bottom of my laundry pile. The clean clothes pile, not the dirty one. Do I smell?"

"Not from here." Kit didn't seem to want to come any closer. "Shawn's up front talking to Aspen. You would not believe what Shawn's mom put on her Christmas wish list." Kit paused for a fraction of a second before saying, "Something fun from the Sweet Spot. And she didn't specify what. Shawn's the only one in the family brave enough to take on buying that gift."

Shawn's family. Tara's family. Casey clenched her jaw to hold back the tears that threatened. Of course Tara wouldn't be the one to pick something out for her mom from the Sweet Spot. "There's a hand lotion and a vanilla mint foot cream she likes—if Shawn wants to get something tame. I know because she came in two weeks ago to tell me how happy she was with it. And it's a Colorado company. I put together a gift basket with a bunch of their items that's been selling well."

"I'll mention that to Shawn." Kit continued to stare at Casey like she had no intention of doing so at the moment, however. "You didn't respond to my text."

"No." Casey dropped her chin. "I haven't really been responding to anyone."

"Because you're hoping Tara will text you."

Casey didn't answer. Kit hadn't asked, she realized. It was obvious. "I keep thinking there's gotta be something I can do to make her reconsider, but I don't know what. I want a serious relationship with her. I should have told her so many things before."

Kit pointed to the settee and Casey moved her feet off the end. Kit sat and swung an arm around Casey. The half hug was more contact than Casey had received since Pavia's intervention, and she took a shuddering breath as her body threatened a full breakdown.

"Remember way back in September when I asked you to come visit me here in Colorado?"

Casey nodded.

"I'm sorry."

"Why are you sorry?"

"I think it might have been a mistake. You left everything you knew and ran headfirst into a maelstrom. All the crap with Gary Jenkins and having half the town against you. Now you're in the news again because of Pavia."

Casey forced a smile. "I don't think coming here was a mistake."

"Even though you breaking up with Tara is making the gossip rounds?"

"Except she broke up with me. Or...decided she didn't want to date me ever since we weren't in a relationship yet anyway. I probably would have dumped my ass, too."

"Are you sure about that?"

Casey squinted at Kit. "Which part?"

"I think she's regretting pushing you away. You didn't hear it from me but she's not sleeping well either."

"What are you saying?"

"I'm saying you could give her time and I think you two could be friends again."

"I don't want to be only friends."

"Then don't give her time. Find a way to convince her that you want a serious relationship with her and that you're ready to fight for it."

Casey shook her head. "I'm not a fighter. If Tara doesn't want me, I'm not going to push it. That's not who I am."

"What if Tara wanted you to fight? What if she wanted you to throw all in?"

Casey tried to process what Kit was asking. Did Tara want that?

Kit set her hand on Casey's knee. "Try to get some sleep. You really look like hell."

"Thanks."

Kit hugged Casey again. "Don't worry. Tara still thinks you're cute."

"Doubtful."

"Want to know one more secret you did not hear from me?" Kit stood. "Tara said she was mad at you for being the hottest woman she's ever had sex with."

Casey couldn't help smiling. It wasn't much, but it was something. "You really think she wants me to fight back?"

"Not fight back, no. You're thinking about it wrong." Kit hesitated. "If you want a relationship to work, you have to be willing to go through the hard parts, right? You have to fight for the relationship. Show her you're serious about wanting her."

Wasn't it too late? She didn't ask but the question circled even as Kit left. The truth was, she hadn't tried fighting for Tara or for their relationship. Because she didn't fight. She stood back and let other people make the big decisions—even decisions that pertained to her. Then she did her best to smooth the fallout. Moving to Rocky Springs, she realized now, was all about smoothing the fallout with Pavia and with her mom as well. But she wanted the move to be a new beginning. Something she did all on her own. Maybe part of that new beginning meant doing things differently.

An idea materialized and she stood quickly. "What if..." She hurried out and her gaze landed on the packet of cards for the twelve days of Christmas. "Maybe it's possible."

"What's possible?" Aspen asked after handing the customer her bag.

The customer, a woman in her sixties with a warm look to her, eyed Casey. Both she and Aspen seemed to be waiting on the answer.

She didn't say what was in her head. Instead, she asked, "Do you think people have to fight for a relationship? Like, two people together. Not fighting each other but... Is it sometimes about showing up and fighting to make it work?" She felt silly asking. At her age, shouldn't she know these things? Still, she wasn't sure, and she wanted more than Kit's advice before she went through with what she was thinking.

Aspen scrunched up their brow, but the customer said, "Love is a battlefield, honey."

CHAPTER THIRTY-ONE

Shawn gave Tara's shoulder a gentle shove. "Go back to the kitchen. Surely there's something you should be baking or frosting or something."

Tara folded her arms and lifted her chin. "Trying to get rid of me?"

"Yes."

She frowned, not surprised by the sentiment so much as Shawn being so blatant about it. "Damn. Tell me how you really feel."

"You're miserable and it's literally radiating off you. You're scaring the customers."

"Am not. Scaring customers, I mean." Because she knew better than to even try to argue the miserable part.

"You should have seen the look Mr. Winters shot me after you'd boxed up his order. He was traumatized."

She'd never been particularly good at faking emotions. Bottling them up, sure. But being with Casey—and feeling like she could be herself—had gotten her out of practice. Great. One more reason to be mad at Casey. Not that she needed one. The list was plenty long.

"Tara McCoy?"

She looked up as Shawn hooked a thumb her way. "That one," Shawn said.

The guy held up a small bonsai tree. "Delivery for you."

He handed Tara the ceramic pot and left as quickly as he'd arrived. Tara looked it over. Other than a sticker on the bottom of the pot identifying the local flower shop, there was nothing. No card, no note, no indication who it was from or why. "That's weird."

"Yeah, I would have gone for roses," Shawn said.

"What makes you think it's from Casey?" And what made Shawn think Casey would send her roses or anything else?

"Who else would be sending you something on Christmas Eve?"

Fair question. "Maybe a customer. There's no card, though. Maybe it fell off. Do you think if I call the shop, they'll tell me who ordered it?"

Shawn shrugged. "My money's still on Casey."

She was mulling that possibility and trying to decide how to feel about it when the bakery door opened and Wisteria, from the local food market down the block, came in with a basket of pears. "Special delivery," she said.

Tara looked at Shawn, who merely raised a brow.

Wisteria handed the basket to Tara. "These are for you. But I'm definitely getting cupcakes while I'm here."

Unlike the bonsai, the basket had a card tucked inside. Shawn noticed and stepped closer. "What can I get you?"

Tara snatched the envelope and pulled out the card. It had a whimsical drawing of a partridge in a pear tree. Inside, she recognized Casey's handwriting instantly. Her heart started racing so fast, it took a second to get her gaze to focus.

It's quite difficult to get one's hands on a pear tree at this time of year, so this is the best I could do. Not perfect, but I'm hoping you'll think it was a good try. I want to try again with you. Or maybe I should say try harder. I'm hoping you'll let me.—Casey

She read the note a second time, then a third. The meaning didn't change, and her pulse continued to pound in her ears. She scanned the room, looking for the catch. Or maybe she was looking for Casey. All she saw, though, was Wisteria leaving with a box of cupcakes.

"Are those from Casey?" Shawn asked.

Tara nodded.

"Not sure what she's going for, but it feels like she's trying." Shawn chuckled. "A for effort?"

Trying. She thought back to that conversation she and Casey had about favorite foods and how much it said about whether people—girlfriends—paid attention. "I think she remembered pears are my favorite."

"They're not bad in the fruit category. Not really peak romantic gesture though."

She was about to argue that it was plenty romantic, then remembered she didn't want romantic gestures from Casey. Especially not thoughtful ones. But she was spared having to say that when Kit came in bearing a gift bag.

Tara breathed a sigh of relief. Shawn would be distracted for at least the next half hour, and she could obsess in peace about whether to acknowledge Casey's overtures or ignore them. Only Kit walked right past Shawn and came up to her. She held out the bag. "This is for you."

"Oh." Surprise quickly gave way to embarrassment. "I didn't…I don't…"

"Don't worry. It's not from me," Kit said. "I'm only the messenger."

She knew immediately that whatever it was, it had to be from Casey. "Uh, thanks."

"Who are you playing messenger for?" Shawn asked.

Kit jerked her head in the direction of Casey's shop.

"Of course." Shawn looked to Tara. "Please tell me it's something even more random than a basket of pears."

As much as she didn't want to do this with an audience, she stuck her hand in the bag and pulled out its contents: two bags of Dove dark chocolates. She smiled in spite of herself.

"Hey, chocolate is an improvement," Shawn said. "There might be hope for her yet."

The card had the same whimsical artwork as the first, only it featured a pair of turtle doves in matching top hats.

I almost went with turtles, but I remembered you're a purist when it comes to chocolate. I respect that, even if I don't understand it. I respect so much about you—who you are, who you want to be, how you make your way through the world. You've been so good for me. I'd like to be good for you, too, and not just a passing thing.—Casey

Tara let out a sigh. What was she supposed to do with that? The words were even more thoughtful than the gift, and they tugged at each and every heartstring she had.

"I'm supposed to give you this, too." Kit took an envelope from her pocket and handed it to Tara. "But I was supposed to wait until you'd opened that."

She slipped the card from the envelope. Three hens, as expected. Only these were dressed like can-can dancers. It managed to be adorable and a little naughty, which felt like the most Casey thing possible. Tucked inside was a gift certificate for a special French-themed dinner at the fancy hotel in town.

I've been assured the poulet will be out of this world, but you can order whatever you'd like. I thought it might be a nice treat for you and your mom. I'd love to be your third wheel, obviously, but understand if you'd rather take Shawn. Maybe one day I'll get the chance to go there with you.—Casey

"What is it?" Kit asked.

She held up the certificate. "Fancy French dinner."

Shawn nodded. "Ooh. Still random but stepping up her game."

She hadn't shown Shawn the cards, wasn't sure she wanted to. The truth was she wasn't sure what to do with any of this. If part of her melted at the care Casey had put into it, the other part bristled at the fact that Casey was falling back on gifts and apologies rather than wanting to talk things out. Of course, she'd been pretty clear she didn't want to talk the last couple of times Casey had texted.

"I gotta go, but I'm dying to know how this turns out." Kit turned to Shawn. "Text me when the next thing arrives?"

"Next thing?" Tara and Shawn asked in unison. Though, to be fair, she shouldn't have been surprised.

Kit shrugged and gave Shawn a quick kiss. She'd no sooner left than Miguel from the Handwork Co-op stopped in. "Merry Christmas Eve," he said, as jovial as any Santa.

"And a merry Christmas Eve to you." Shawn thrust an arm in Tara's direction. "Let me guess, you have a delivery?"

He gave her a quizzical look. "How did you know?"

Shawn grinned. "Lucky guess."

Miguel handed Tara a box tied with bright red ribbon and let Shawn talk him into a couple of cupcakes to keep him going until closing time. She opened the box and found four hand-carved wooden birds inside. She'd admired them the last time she and Casey strolled downtown after closing time.

I confess I spent more time watching you than window shopping. But I know these made you smile then, so I'm hoping they make you smile now. Especially after I seemed to go so far out of my way to make you sad.—Casey

And so it continued. An Olympics-themed keychain made from five interlocking rings. An ethically sourced down vest she'd coveted but couldn't justify. A spa day at Swan Lake. And the maids a milking took the form of eight pints of whatever custom flavor Tara wanted to think up from the local ice cream shop. Each gift came with a perfectly personal note referencing something they'd done or talked about or wanted.

"Please tell me we're about to be visited by nine ladies dancing," Shawn said after the owner of the ice cream shop had gone on her way.

Tara tried for a withering stare but didn't quite pull it off. Because for all she knew, they were lurking on the sidewalk waiting for their turn. Fortunately, that didn't happen. What did happen was a visit from Rick, who owned the jewelry store.

Shawn let out a low whistle. "Damn. Woman is hell-bent on making the rest of us look bad."

Tara shook her head but didn't disagree. She'd never dated anyone who attempted even a fraction of what Casey had pulled off today. And she'd certainly never fallen hard enough to attempt something like it herself. "It's too big to be jewelry."

"Well, don't keep me in suspense."

The music box was small and delicately carved. It was just like the one she'd had as a kid. The one Shawn had knocked off the dresser during a bout of horseplay and broken when they were kids. Only she hadn't told Casey that story. She opened the lid, expecting a pink tutu-ed ballerina. Instead, a tiny ice skater in a red dress turned perfect layback spins.

Nine seemed like overkill, so I settled on this one because she reminds me of you. That day you took me ice skating will be one of my favorite memories of my first winter in Rocky Springs. You wanted me to feel the Christmas spirit, but what stayed with me is the way you felt in my arms. I really hope I get to feel that again.—Casey

For the first time since the parade of presents began, Tara teared up. Because damn it all if she didn't love that memory, too. Not only the memory. The whole package. Being with Casey was the best thing that had happened to her since coming home. For all that she'd said they couldn't end what they'd never really started, she'd done a hell of a lot more than start falling for Casey. She'd gone and fallen all the way in love with her.

She scrubbed a hand over her face and wondered if she was supposed to wait for all twelve days or go show up on Casey's doorstep now. Before she could decide, Aspen strode in, looking like they were on a mission and their life depended on it. Tara held out her hand in anticipation, and Aspen set the envelope in her outstretched palm. She opened her mouth to say something, to give Aspen a message to give to Casey, but they didn't give her the chance. They booked it out of there like their hair was on fire. Despite the emotional roller coaster that the day had turned into, she couldn't help but laugh. Nor could she blame Aspen for not wanting to take any chances of getting stuck in the middle.

Since she had the card in hand, she opened it. A four-by-six photograph fell out. She picked it up and discovered a picture of what appeared to be a teenage Casey in an elaborate ice-skating costume and full stage makeup.

This is the closest I ever got to being a lord a leaping. I didn't just have a professional skating coach, I got hauled into a production of The Nutcracker on Ice. *There weren't enough boys and I already hated dresses, so I got to play the Mouse King. I've never shown this picture to anyone I met as an adult. I know I have a lot to learn in the talking about my feelings department, but I'm counting this as a moment of vulnerability.—Casey*

Tara laughed. And laughed. And laughed some more. Something about the absurdity of it made such a perfect foil to the sensitive note that preceded it.

"Now what?" Shawn asked.

Tara shook her head. "I have to go."

"Please say you're going next door to kiss and make up."

"Something like that."

"Thank God." Shawn stuck both hands in the air. "What should I do if a slew of pipers and drummers show up?"

At this point, she hardly cared. All she wanted was Casey. "Enjoy the show and don't hesitate to lock up without me."

CHAPTER THIRTY-TWO

All you have to do is walk in the bakery, play a bit, and give her this." Casey held out the card to the pale-faced teenage boy toting a bagpipe.

"I'm not sure if this is a good idea. Bagpipes are more for playing outdoors, you know?" He eyed the bagpipes like the instrument might mutiny. "And there's usually others playing with me."

"Like ten other pipers?" When the boy gave her a questioning look, Casey shook her head. She didn't have time to find ten more people willing and able to play a bagpipe. "You don't have to play a whole song. You could blow one note and that'd be enough. It's really about giving her the card."

"Why can't you give her the card?"

"Because I'm trying to show I'm ready to fight for our relationship."

"With bagpipes?" The boy looked more dubious.

Casey groaned and glanced at the bakery door. No sign of Tara yet, but she was running out of time. She also had no other lead on a musician if this kid backed out. "I guess I could go in with you, but I'm not sure how she's feeling about all of this. She might still hate me."

The bagpiper scrunched up his nose. "You're sending me to play bagpipes for a girl who hates you?"

"I'm not sure she hates me. I'm hoping she thinks I made a dumb mistake." And she'd hoped to give Tara space to respond rather than showing up with the cards herself. "Look, I'm not much for being in the spotlight either. I get being nervous." She met the boy's gaze. "But Aspen said you were good, and they don't give compliments unless they're deserved." Technically, Aspen had only said they knew of a bagpiper and drummer who might be available—two teens who lived in the same apartment complex as they did and kept the whole neighborhood awake practicing.

"Seamus, you totally got this," the drummer girl said. She was a few years younger than her brother but had apparently gotten all the brave genes. For the past twenty minutes she'd been eagerly tapping out rhythms to show Casey she was qualified for a paid gig.

"Bagpipes are supposed to be for battles," the boy said. "Not for getting someone to like you."

"Okay, I get that, but could we make an exception?" Casey reached into her pocket for another twenty-dollar bill. "This is going to be way less scary than marching into battle." Less scary for the bagpiper, anyway. He wasn't the one trying to get a girlfriend back.

The bagpiper eyed the twenty, biting the edge of his lip. "It's not about the money."

Casey sighed and lowered her hand. It was a quarter after three. The bakery closed at four, but Tara might leave early. And it was Christmas Eve. She could walk out any minute. Likely her last two cards wouldn't change Tara's mind if the others hadn't.

"What if we go in together?" the drummer asked her brother.

Casey nodded encouragingly. "That would work. Bagpipes first, then drums. You two hand off your cards and you're done. Easy, right?"

"Easy-peasy." The drummer reached for the twenty and added, "They send drums into battles, too, but I'd rather play in a bakery. I bet I can get a cupcake."

Casey couldn't help laughing. "I'll buy you both cupcakes if you go in there and play."

"Or you could give the performance right here."

Casey turned at the sound of Tara's voice.

She smiled at the two teens but didn't meet Casey's eyes. "I've always thought bagpipes were cool. And, Mina, I had no idea you were a drummer."

"I have other hobbies besides eating cupcakes." Mina grinned and tapped her sticks together. "Tell me when you're ready, Seamus."

The bagpiper took a deep breath, eyes focused on a crack in the sidewalk. When he lifted the pipes, the first few notes were tentative. Then Seamus launched into a ballad and Mina joined in. The noise was deafening, but familiar. Casey couldn't recall the name, but she also couldn't hear herself think. She glanced at Tara, wondering if Tara would even talk to her after this was over. But Tara was tapping her toe and smiling. When Mina started marching around Seamus, Tara clapped her hands together.

She caught Casey's eye and her smile faltered. She didn't seem upset, but her look made Casey's heart clench. They held each other's gaze, a dozen questions running through Casey's mind. Was it foolish to hope Tara would consider giving them a second chance? Or a real first chance? The music stopped and Tara applauded. Casey joined in and the teens bowed.

"Oh, what about the cards?" Seamus asked.

Casey held them up. "I think I can deliver these myself."

"We could play a few more songs if you want," Seamus said.

Mina added, "Seamus knows the Highland Wedding song."

"I'm not sure we're ready for wedding songs," Tara said. "But you two were amazing. Thank you! I've had so many surprises today but I think this one was my favorite."

Both kids happily accepted another couple of twenties from Casey and took off, trading high fives as they went. When Casey looked over at Tara, the worries and questions she'd managed to tamp down rose up again.

Before she could think of what to say, Tara said, "We need to talk." She pointed to the Sweet Spot. "Okay with you if we go inside? It's a little chilly out here."

Casey opened the door and waited for Tara, flipping the sign to closed after she'd passed. The only one in the shop was Aspen, who looked up from the counter, eyes tracking between her and Tara.

"Should I take a break?"

Casey nodded and as Tara wandered to the book section, Aspen grabbed their coat and was out the door, murmuring a not-so-subtle "good luck" as they passed Casey. Tara didn't seem to notice, however. She'd picked up a "how to" book on difficult conversations in relationships and was thumbing through the pages.

"Have you read this?"

"No. I probably should." Casey walked over to where Tara stood. The truth was, she hadn't opened any of the relationship books she sold.

"You think you should read it because you sell it or because conversations are hard?"

"Yes?"

Tara nodded but her attention seemed to be focused on the text. Casey shoved her hands in her pockets to stop herself from tossing the book aside and pulling Tara into an embrace. Standing three feet away made the ache of not being able to reach for her all the harder to bear. Finally, Tara looked up and said, "I think I should read this too."

"Together project?" She didn't try to hide the hope in her voice.

"Casey, I—" she broke off, waited a beat, and started again. "I didn't know what to think about us this past week. I went from hoping we had a chance, and even imagining a life together, to convinced we had no future. And convinced I'd been played."

Casey swallowed, Tara's words hitting her square in the chest. "I'm sorry. I screwed up not telling you what was going on. And, honestly, it makes sense you didn't want to listen when I tried to explain."

"Yeah, I wasn't in a good place." She closed her eyes and shook her head like she was shaking off the feeling. "I know you didn't mean to hurt me. I'm realizing I have issues I haven't completely worked through. My ex would do stuff like that all the time—not tell me exactly what was going on and get pissed if I acted like I didn't trust her." She paused, meeting Casey's gaze. "I know you aren't her. But I need someone who can be transparent with me."

"Totally fair."

"That's not all I need though."

Casey waited, heart lodging in her throat. Was Tara going to say she needed someone who she could never be?

"When I told you things were over, you turned and walked out. You didn't even look back. And I know it was my fault for making you leave, but—"

"I didn't try to fight for us." Casey took a deep breath. "There's a lot of things I wish I'd done better. I should have explained what was going on with my parents and Pavia before I even left for California. I should have made time to talk to you on the phone while I was there dealing with everything. And I should have done a better job apologizing and listening to you after."

"All those things." Tara sniffed. "That's what I needed."

Casey hesitated but then asked the one question she needed Tara to answer. "Do you think we still could have a chance?"

"I've been asking myself that all day. And ever since you walked out of my bakery I've been asking myself if I made a mistake cutting you off." She glanced at the book she was still holding, closed it, and placed it back on the shelf. "Everything you sent—the cards, the gifts—all of it was so sweet."

"But?" Casey wished she could tell what Tara was thinking. "I have two more cards. Tickets to a concert at the Red Rocks amphitheater and…well…another silly memory I wanted to share. Not because it's important, really, but because I want to share myself with you. And I was hoping that if I shared, you might want to as well."

Tara's lips pursed. "I'm not great at sharing things about myself, but after that adorable picture of you dressed up as the Mouse King, I think I owe you one. Ask me anything."

Casey's mind spun. *One question.* There were dozens of things she wanted to know about Tara, but she was stuck on the question she'd already tried asking. Did they have a chance? "Would you consider going on a date with—"

"Yes." Tara took a step closer. "Yes, I would."

Casey's heart bounced in her chest. "I know I have issues I need to work on, but I want a real relationship with you. More than anything."

"We both have things we need to work on, but do you mind if we skip to the kissing part for a minute? Because I really need to kiss you."

Casey was certain she needed to kiss Tara even more. She closed the distance and as Tara's lips met hers, a warmth spread through her.

Tara's arms circled her neck, and she shifted forward, deepening the kiss. Kissing Tara felt so right.

She wanted to promise to read all the relationship books and go to all the therapy sessions. Anything and everything it took to make things work. She wanted to make Tara happy in all the ways she could. Her hands settled on Tara's hips, and she thought she could be happy simply holding Tara like that forever. One kiss moved into another and then another before Tara pulled back.

"I think maybe we need to slow down."

"Yeah. Okay." It was the last thing Casey wanted to do, but she stepped back and willed her libido to ease up.

"I'm not saying I don't want to keep kissing you, but I've discovered falling into bed with you is easier than having hard conversations, and I don't want to make the same mistakes twice."

"Right. I agree."

Tara touched Casey's lips, a smile forming on her own. "You trying not to pout is kind of adorable."

"I'm not pouting." Not entirely anyway. "I completely agree that we should have a plan this time. It's just…"

"You start kissing me and you stop thinking?" Tara laughed. "I've noticed. Which is why I'm trying to do the thinking for us both. How long before Aspen comes back?"

"Five minutes. Maybe." Aspen hated taking breaks. They usually went to the café across the street and hung out with the baristas, but the café would be closing soon.

"I'm guessing you probably don't want to leave them alone here on Christmas Eve." Tara's brow furrowed. "And I'm supposed to go to a family dinner at six."

"Aspen can handle closing." It wouldn't give them long, but she'd take it. "We could go to my place—or somewhere else if you think that wouldn't be a good idea."

"Do you think you can focus on talking if there's a bed within ten feet of us?"

Casey opened her mouth to say "of course" but before the words came out, she knew that wasn't the truth.

Tara shook her head knowingly. "Right. I'm in charge of keeping us on task. Which means, you probably should stop looking at me like you want me undressed and under you."

"That obvious?" Casey dropped her chin. "I do want to talk. You just make me also want to do other things."

Tara laughed and the sound was so light and easy and so perfectly Tara. Casey wanted to wrap her up in an embrace and kiss her again. But, she reminded herself, a conversation needed to happen first. She owed Tara her focus on that. "Let me text Aspen and I'll pull my car around. You can stay here in the shop where it's warm."

Aspen didn't ask questions, and Casey told Aspen it'd be fine to close up early. She didn't feel guilty leaving. Some things were more important than work.

The car ride was quiet. Casey thought of a dozen things to say, carefully considered each one before discarding it and hoping Tara would start talking first. When she pulled up to her house, Tara got out before she could open the car door for her, and she wondered if Tara was upset. Maybe reconsidering the whole idea. Tara waited for her to unlock the front door, then stepped inside and took off her boots and coat without looking at Casey.

"Would you like something to drink?" Casey asked, hanging her own coat on the hook next to Tara's and trying not to think about how nice it would be to see their coats side-by-side every evening.

"Tea would be nice."

"I'll get water boiling." Casey started to the kitchen but only made it a few steps before Tara caught her hand, entwining their fingers. She looked at their linked hands and then to Tara.

"I want to change my mind."

"You don't want tea?"

Tara stepped forward, wrapping her arms around Casey and kissing her. Not a light peck but a full-on kiss, and when her lips parted, her tongue met Casey's. In the next moment, Tara's hands slipped under Casey's shirt. Cool fingers against her warm skin sent shivers through her. Good shivers. She didn't hold back a moan when Tara's hands moved to her back, stroking up and down, lips brushing against her neck.

Casey's body responded eagerly but her conscience nagged. "Am I supposed to stop you so we can talk?"

"I spent the car ride thinking how I wanted to do other things." Tara kissed her again, then pulled back abruptly and said, "But do you know how mad I was at you? I need us to be on the same page going forward."

Casey nodded, her attention divided between Tara's words and Tara undoing her belt.

"If I'm doing this with you, I need to trust you'll tell me things."

Another nod as Tara pulled Casey's belt through the loops and tossed it on the ground.

"We both have to tell each other what's going on. It's one thing keeping something to yourself if it doesn't affect the other person," Tara paused, midsentence as she worked loose the top button on Casey's jeans. She reached for the zipper and continued. "But it's another thing entirely to not tell someone when you're meeting up with an ex-girlfriend."

"Yeah. Definitely. Completely agree." Casey looked down at her open jeans and Tara's hands pushing them low on her hips. "Is this how that book recommended having tough conversations?"

"This is all me. You're paying attention, right?" She kissed Casey again, grazing her thumbs over the front of Casey's boxers. "I want to continue this conversation in your bedroom."

"Me too. But I'm not sure I can fully listen with your hands on me."

"You better try."

Casey would have promised to try but Tara's mouth was on hers again. Arousal took over and she caught hold of both of Tara's hands. "If you want to tell me something, and expect me to pay attention, now's the time."

"Or else?" Tara's eyebrow arched.

"Or else the only thing I'm gonna be paying attention to for the next hour is your body." Casey kissed her hard, giving in to her desire. She pulled back and met Tara's eyes. "Last chance."

"I'm not letting you off the hook, but I know we're both distracted." Tara moved into Casey's next kiss. They stumbled their way to the bedroom, trading kisses and helping each other out of their clothes. When they got there, Tara only let Casey go long enough for her to push back the covers.

They tumbled onto the bed, Casey moving on top and Tara not arguing. She kissed her way down Tara's neck, then took one full breast in her hand and pulled the nipple between her lips. Tara moaned, "More," and Casey gave her what she asked for.

She let her other hand roam over Tara's belly, down her thigh and up again, straying close to Tara's center but holding back. She wanted to have all of Tara at once and at the same time wanted to savor every brush of skin, every ragged breath between kisses.

She shifted lower, kissing below Tara's belly button, along the side of her chest, and the rise of her hip. She continued down one leg and then the other with her hand before pushing Tara's thighs apart and settling between them.

"I want to do all the things you need," she murmured. "Like have open conversations and trust each other and—"

Tara cupped Casey's chin, closing her mouth as she did. She traced her thumb over Casey's lips. "I can't believe I'm saying this, but I need your mouth to be doing other things than talking."

Tara's words pushed her arousal into overdrive. She licked Tara's finger, and then dipped her head and kissed the inside of Tara's thigh. "I really want to do all the things you need."

She slid her tongue along Tara's slit and Tara tensed for a second and then pushed up. Casey found Tara's clit, lavishing everything she'd been holding back, until Tara pumped her hips. When Casey slid her fingers inside, two then three, Tara moaned and bucked faster. The sounds Tara made, how good it felt touching her body again, all pushed her to give more than ever. She didn't let up until Tara's nails sank into her shoulders. Then she pressed her tongue hard on Tara's clit and rode out the climax, loving how Tara soaked her hand and made a mess of the sheets.

It was minutes later before Tara let her pull her fingers out. She licked them and Tara only shook her head, the movement lazy from everything Casey had done to her.

"You," Tara said.

"What about me?" Casey shifted up to lie fully stretched over Tara's body. She kissed her gently and then closed her eyes, feeling her body relax for the first time in too long.

"As amazing as you feel on me, you better not fall asleep."

"Why not?" Casey forced her eyes open. "Oh. Because we're still supposed to have that conversation?"

Tara smiled. "No. Because you're going to roll on your back and let me kiss you every place I want."

"I am, huh?" Casey grinned.

"Or we can have that conversation."

"That's a hard decision." Casey chuckled and rolled onto her back, laughing more with Tara's ribbing about how she'd have to open up and talk sooner or later. *Sooner or later.* It wouldn't be easy when it happened but at least now Tara was giving them a chance. A chance for both a sooner and a later.

FROSTED BY THE GIRL NEXT DOOR

CHAPTER THIRTY-THREE

Tara jolted awake with the sensation of being late for something incredibly important. But also with the sense of not knowing whose bed she was in or what day it was. The details hit her all at once. Casey's bed. Christmas morning. And other than her mom's house in a few hours, nowhere to be.

She took a deep breath and her pulse slowed. Not the best way to wake up, perhaps, but she couldn't imagine waking up to anything better. Including—or maybe especially—Casey dead to the world beside her.

She'd never made it to her mom's the night before. What began as an attempt to talk things out, to start building the foundation of trust they'd sort of skipped over when they tumbled into bed the first time, had given way to tumbling into bed once more. She blamed too much pent-up desire. And it was only a pause in the conversation, not a way of avoiding it.

But for all that difficulty keeping their hands off each other, they'd talked after, and it was the talking that had her bowing out of Christmas Eve dinner. Talking about fun childhood memories, but also the less fun ones. Talking about the emotional wounds of failed relationships and not just the superficial details. Talking about hopes and dreams and fears and what attempting a real relationship might look like. Then they had sex again and talked some more, eating boxed mac and cheese on the sofa because it was the only food Casey had in the house.

It was a bit of an emotional hangover, she realized, that had her waking the way she had. The cost of doing several months of sharing in the span of a single night. Not that she regretted it. As much as it had been less than ideal, she couldn't bring herself to regret any of it. Because coming through it gave her hope that if she and Casey could weather that, they could weather anything and make things work.

"Why is your brain going a mile a minute at some ridiculously early hour on Christmas morning?" Casey's arm tightened around her as she nuzzled into Tara's neck.

"What makes you think my brain is going a mile a minute?" She wasn't denying it, obviously. Just curious how Casey could tell.

"Your aura vibrates." Casey kissed where she'd been nuzzling.

Tara chuckled. "I thought I was sleeping with the sex shop hottie, not the owner of the new age hippie store down the block."

Casey pulled back enough to make eye contact, her sleepy-eyed smile cute and sexy at the same time. "You think I'm a hottie?"

"Obviously." She poked Casey lightly in the ribs, making her squirm.

Casey blinked a few times, and her gaze intensified. "Seriously, though. Are you okay?"

"I'm so much more than okay." Tara kissed her. "I'm perfect."

"Well, I can't argue with that."

Tara shook her head. "I didn't mean I'm perfect. I think we established last night that neither of us are. But I feel perfectly happy in this moment."

Casey nodded. "Important clarification. For what it's worth, I'm pretty blissed out myself."

"Would you still be blissed out if I asked you to come to dinner at my mom's later?"

Casey's smile didn't falter, but her body tensed just enough for Tara to notice. "Are you sure that's a good idea?"

"Well, after bailing last night, there's no way I can get away with not showing up today." Her mom would be sad, and Shawn would never let her hear the end of it.

"Oh, you should definitely go. I just don't want you to feel like you have to invite me if it would make things awkward."

With Grandpa in peak patriarch mode, it might very well be awkward. But she couldn't imagine leaving Casey home alone on Christmas. Even more, she wanted Casey there. If they were going to make a go of being together, that would need to include family functions, uncomfortable or otherwise. "What if I promise to stand up to my grandfather?"

Casey's smile did falter then. "Oh, shit. I wasn't even thinking about him."

It might not have been the best moment to giggle, but she couldn't help it. "He's all bluster. And even then, it's only when he's trying to be all big man mayor."

Casey cringed. "You're not helping."

"My mom adores you, you know. Shawn, too."

"Your mom has met me like once," Casey argued.

"Twice and she had lots of opportunity to see that you made me happier than I've been since moving back."

Casey pouted. "Until I made you miserable."

"Yeah, but everyone loves a kiss and make up story. Especially at Christmas." She bit her lip before adding. "We're practically a Hallmark movie."

That broke the tension, and Casey laughed. Like, really laughed. "Well, when you put it that way."

She kissed Casey again, and it occurred to her that she didn't think she'd ever get tired of kissing Casey Stevens. "Come on. I'll make you coffee."

After some coffee, some truly terrible protein waffles Casey passed off as breakfast, and a little more fooling around, they got in the shower together. Which, of course, led to more fooling around and a genuine risk they'd be late for dinner. Especially since they had to stop at Tara's for her to put on something other than the clothes she'd worn to the bakery the day before.

By the time they pulled into her mom's driveway, Grandpa's pickup already sat in the driveway. Along with an assortment of vehicles belonging to various aunts, uncles, and cousins who'd put in an appearance at the McCoy Christmas dinner.

"You didn't tell me your family was huge." Casey's voice held genuine nerves.

"Not huge. Probably less than a dozen people this year, with some of my cousins having kids and starting their own traditions."

Casey coughed. "My family Christmas consisted of exactly three people. Assuming my parents weren't on location and we actually had one."

"You're going to do great," Tara said, channeling maybe a bit more confidence than she felt.

"It's fine. I'm fine. And I'm happy you wanted me to come along. Truly."

Since it wouldn't do either of them any good to get sentimental before setting foot inside, she shot Casey a wink. "The more people there are milling around, the less likely Grandpa will set his sights on you."

"Good point." Casey squeezed her eyes shut. "Or maybe I'll wait here."

"Come on, scaredy pants. Fortune favors the brave." She gave Casey's knee a squeeze. "And if you survive the day, I'll make it worth your while when we get home."

Casey raised a brow.

"Your place. You know what I mean."

Casey nodded, but a smile crept over her face. Like she was imagining what it might be like to go home to a home they shared. It was probably too soon to go down that path, but Tara's mind had already toyed with the idea. She shook off the ripple of not entirely unpleasant anticipation. Definitely a conversation for another day.

Inside, the air smelled like Christmas. Woodsmoke, but laced with fresh pine. Cinnamon and citrus. And a ham right out of the oven. Tara stole a glance at Casey, who seemed to be doing her best to take it all in. Of course, there was the wall of sound to accompany all the aromas. At least four conversations were going, and that was just the kitchen. Christmas music, too, coming from the smart speaker she and Shawn had gotten Mom for her birthday. She'd forgotten how overwhelming it could be for the uninitiated. "Smile, nod, and hold my hand. You'll be fine."

Casey nodded and stayed close as they wound their way to the far counter where Mom was transferring green beans from a sauté pan to a serving dish. "Well, look who decided to grace us with her presence," Mom said.

Tara kissed her mother on the cheek. "Sorry about last night, but I made up for it by bringing company today."

Tara stepped to the side and Casey stepped forward, sheepish smile firmly in place. "Merry Christmas, Mrs. McCoy."

Mom's eyes lit up. She set the pan down and pulled Casey into a hug. "Oh, you're here. I'm so glad."

Casey looked surprised but not put off by the sudden display of affection. "Thank you for having me, especially so last minute."

Mom released Casey from the embrace but held both her arms. "You are always welcome here on one condition."

Tara narrowed her eyes slightly. Mom had never done the aggressively protective parent thing, so it seemed like a strange time to start.

"You must call me Debbie."

Casey chuckled and it only sounded a little nervous. "I can do that."

"Good. Now you two go get yourselves a glass of something festive. Dinner will be ready soon."

Casey offered to help in the kitchen and was promptly rebuffed. Tara pulled her along, promising it was mom prerogative and not anything personal. They made the rounds and Casey was a champ at getting introduced to people she didn't know. It helped that everyone knew her store and pretty much everyone had either been in or heard glowing things about it. She even managed to be gracious when Tara's uncle commented about how Casey had taken twenty years off his marriage.

After finishing the full circuit, Tara couldn't put off the inevitable any longer. Hopefully, Casey had picked up enough good vibes to withstand whatever bluster Grandpa dished out. She pointed to where he and Grandma sat on the loveseat in the living room and gave Casey's hand a squeeze. "Don't worry. I got you."

Casey gave a tiny shake of her head. "Just let him say whatever. It's Christmas and the last thing I want is a scene."

Well, they'd have to wait and see what whatever entailed. She had no intention of letting him belittle Casey, or her business. "I promise I won't yell."

Casey looked more alarmed than assured by that promise, so Tara simply grinned. She took the lead and leaned in to kiss them both on the cheek. "Merry Christmas, Grandma and Grandpa."

Casey echoed the sentiment, without the kisses.

"Grandma, this is my girlfriend, Casey."

"Oh, I know," Grandma said with a smile for Casey. "Good to see you here, hun."

It felt like a win, but Grandma was the easy one. "Grandpa, you remember Casey." She cleared her throat. "She owns the Sweet Spot, next door to the bakery."

Tara was so busy watching her grandfather, she almost missed the delight on her grandmother's face. "It's a darling little shop," Grandma said. "My friend Mildred and I were in last week and this lovely young woman took such good care of us. What was her name?"

She couldn't imagine a scenario where Grandma was openly discussing a visit to the sex shop with Grandpa sitting right next to her. But it was happening. Casey, on the other hand, didn't seem at all thrown. "Natalia?"

"Oh, yes. That's her." Grandma clicked her tongue. "Spent half the time we were there raving about Tara's cupcakes. And the other half making some excellent recommendations."

Casey slid into gracious business owner mode. "I'm so glad you had a positive experience. That's what we're all about."

Tara stole a glance at Grandpa, fully expecting to find him on the brink of a tirade. Instead, she found him staring at her grandmother with a mischievous gleam in his eye. And then he seemed to realize all three of them were looking his way and quickly stood. He stuck out a hand. "We're glad to have a business like yours in Rocky Springs."

If Casey was even half as shocked as Tara, she didn't show it. She accepted the handshake and gave Grandpa what Tara could only describe as a gentleman's nod. "Thank you, Mr. McCoy."

Tara scrambled for a graceful conversational shift but was spared having to come up with one when a couple of the kids ran over to show off the things Santa had brought. She and Casey made a quiet escape, and Tara pulled her down the hall to hide for a minute in her childhood bedroom.

"Oh, my God. Did that seriously happen?" she asked.

Casey's casual smile belied the absurdity of how that conversation had gone. "It did."

"Can I be super sex positive and still desperately not want to know what my grandma brought home that put that look on my grandpa's face?"

Casey chuckled. "I think that's reasonable. Like I don't need to know to appreciate a satisfied customer."

"Completely. But could you not use the word satisfied right now?"

"I thought it was only dildos that you didn't want me to say."

"That too." She grimaced. "I feel bad saying this but I hope I never find out what my grandma bought at your store."

"It's perfectly okay to embrace things in theory—like your grandparents getting it on—and really not want to know the specifics."

"Thank you." Tara let out a heavy sigh.

"Is something else wrong?" Casey asked.

"I was all ready to stand up for you." She could feel herself pouting and didn't try to stop. "You went and did all the grand gestures, and I haven't done any."

Casey took both Tara's hands in hers. "You listened. You gave me another chance. That's all I wanted. Oh, and you gave me several spectacular orgasms."

"Yeah." It was a big deal, obviously, but not grand like Casey's twelve days of Christmas in one. "But you got me a bagpiper."

"A very nervous bagpiper." Casey grinned. "I'm glad you didn't refuse the gifts. I was afraid you might."

Given that Casey had them delivered by her friends and fellow business owners, she wouldn't have. But the sentiment—that they might have missed their chance—wasn't lost on her. "For what it's worth, it wasn't about the gifts."

"I know."

"I'm glad you decided to show me the real you."

Casey nodded. "Same. And I'm glad you liked what you saw."

"Oh, I like what I see very much." She put a hand on Casey's chest and looked into Casey's eyes.

"Would it be okay if I kissed you here?"

"I'm not sure I'd be okay if you didn't."

Casey's lips brushed over hers, the sort of sweet kiss you'd give someone in their childhood bedroom. Tara slid one hand onto Casey's shoulder and the other into her hair. She traced Casey's bottom lip with her tongue and used Casey's gasp of surprise to slip inside. Casey's arms came around her and she was more than a little tempted to take the kiss horizontal.

A loud knock at the door disabused her of the notion. Poor Casey looked like she'd been caught with her hand in the cookie jar. "Don't worry, it's only my mom."

"How do you know?" Casey asked. "And how is that supposed to make me feel better?"

"She's the only one who knows we're in here." Tara shrugged. "And it's the special knock Shawn and I had back when we were kids and thought we were subtle."

Casey chuckled. "Ah."

She held out her hand. "Come have Christmas dinner with me and my wacky family?"

Casey took it and brought it to her lips. "I'd be honored. Come home with me after?"

"I can't think of anything I'd rather do."

CHAPTER THIRTY-FOUR

H ow is it so bright out?" Casey shielded her eyes, but it did little to help with the glare. Sunshine glinted off every snow-capped surface.

"Not used to Colorado sunshine yet?" Tara smiled. "Want my hat? I know how you feel about my sunglasses."

"I like your sunglasses on you. They're a little too…sparkly for me."

"Are you saying you aren't queer enough to pull off sunglasses this fabulous?" Tara pulled her sunglasses down far enough to give Casey a sexy look over the rims.

Casey laughed. "Maybe."

"Considering I know where your tongue has been all morning, I know you're plenty queer enough." Tara bumped Casey's shoulder. "We can agree to disagree on the sunglasses, but I really don't need the hat."

Casey shook her head, squinting but determined. She had sunglasses and a hat back at the house, but she'd been so eager to get outside and enjoy the morning, she'd only remembered her jacket and scarf.

"Have you always been stubborn?" Tara asked.

"Always."

"Hmm." Tara linked arms with her. "I feel like that should have been disclosed when we first met."

"I'm pretty sure me deciding to still open my sex shop after that town hall meeting where you all tried to run me out—and then me ignoring Gary Jenkins with his posters riling up those Rocky Springs family values folks—was a big clue on the whole stubborn thing."

"True. You officially have a track record of being stubborn. Too bad you're so sexy and I'm too stubborn to let go of you now."

Tara lifted the brim of her hat as an offer. "Want this hat anyway?"

"Nope. We're almost there."

"Mmhmm. And it'd be a nicer walk if you weren't blinded."

Casey loved their pseudo argument. Which was weird. She'd never liked arguing or fighting but there was no pressure this time. Tara clearly thought she was being difficult, but she wasn't mad. Wasn't saying Casey was dumb. Wasn't yelling. All of the above had happened in past relationships over things just as inconsequential as forgetting a hat, but Tara was different. And she was different with Tara.

"I feel a little bad for saying we should walk." She'd thought it'd only take twenty minutes to get to the diner from her place, but it was pushing that and they were still several blocks away. "Are you warm enough?"

"I'm perfect." Tara shifted closer, her grip tightening on Casey's arm. "And it's beautiful out. I'm glad we aren't stuck in a car."

"We'd already be eating omelets and hash browns if we'd driven."

"Okay, no being logical and stubborn. That's too much for ten in the morning."

Casey laughed. Looking out her bedroom window that morning, the world had felt magical. Fresh snow blanketing everything in crisp white, the sun shining overhead, the sky a dazzling blue and Tara naked and curled against her asking if she was hungry. She'd heard Tara's stomach rumble and suggested breakfast burritos—their favorite. Unfortunately, Tara broke the news that the Cantina was closed for Christmas week and suggested omelets at the diner instead. Casey had grumbled that she wasn't getting out of bed if she couldn't have a green-salsa-laden burrito, but Tara had tickled her sides until she got up. The truth was, she wasn't thinking about food. She was thinking about how amazing it was to be in such a perfect place with such a perfect woman and not wanting anything more than exactly what she had in her arms. Although that and a breakfast burrito wouldn't be horrible.

Tara motioned to a shop that sold Colorado tourist kitsch. "Mountain Gnome is open."

"I heard they only take three days off every year." Still, given the snow and the lack of tourists on a Sunday morning the day after Christmas, Casey was surprised they were open this early.

The Mountain Gnome marked the spot where houses gave way to the five blocks of downtown. The heart of Rocky Springs. With the snow and the holly-lined street posts and the ornaments strung on the bare-branched trees, the little mountain town truly looked like a Christmas card. Three blocks up, over the bridge and on the left, was Coy Cupcakes. And right next door was the Sweet Spot. Casey still couldn't believe her shop was part of it all.

"I know we're almost to the diner, but can we take a quick detour?"

Casey wondered what Tara was thinking as she motioned again to the Mountain Gnome. "Sure."

Casey had met the couple who owned the shop at the last meeting of the Rocky Springs Business Association. They'd bragged about their three days off a year rule and insisted the other shop owners should follow their example. Tara had rolled her eyes and Casey had loved her for it. But now here they were, walking into the Mountain Gnome while both of their businesses were closed.

Tara greeted the gray-haired man working the counter by his first name—Henry—and then asked him how he'd enjoyed his Christmas. She didn't let go of Casey's arm while they chatted, and Henry's brow stayed furrowed nearly the entire time. Nearly. But Tara put on the charm and the next thing Casey knew, Henry was coming out from behind his counter and walking them over to a stack of hats.

"I think this one would work real nice." Henry picked out a cowboy hat and set it on Casey's head, adjusting it and then giving Casey a firm nod. "Have a look." He pointed to a mirror opposite the hats.

Casey turned and caught her reflection. She laughed and started to take the hat off, but Tara caught her hand. "It looks good on you. You sure you don't like it?"

Casey looked at the mirror again. She couldn't help smiling. "I look like I'm twelve again pretending to be Butch Cassidy."

"You look more like the Sundance Kid of that pair. But fine. Next." She took the cowboy hat off Casey and placed a derby style hat on her head.

Casey took one look and shook her head. "Nope. No way."

"I want to get you a hat. You're going to have to decide on one." Tara continued offering hat after hat—ranging from a bucket hat to a bowler to a sun bonnet. Finally, Tara handed her a dark green ballcap with a mountain stitched on front above the words Rocky Springs.

Casey tried it on and turned to Tara. "What do you think?"

Tara pressed her lips together. "It's more important what you think. The cowboy hat looked good too."

"I'm not a cowboy. Not a Butch Cassidy or a Sundance Kid." Casey grinned. She checked her reflection again and adjusted the brim. "I like this one. It's more me."

Casey's eyes tracked to Tara's reflection in the mirror. She'd seemed to have something on her mind when she'd woken Casey that morning, and now she had the same look again. Whatever she really thought about the hat, Casey was certain she was holding something back.

"But I really don't need a hat," Casey said, starting to take it off.

Tara stopped her hand. "I know you have one at home and you could buy this yourself, but I want to buy it for you. Please? It's nothing compared to everything you got me for Christmas."

Casey let Tara take the hat over to Henry to pay and then place it back on her head. It wasn't until they stepped outside that Casey turned to ask Tara if something was wrong. But she didn't get the words out because Tara started talking before she could.

"I know I'm being weird. And I know you're concerned. You've got that look you get." Tara took off the sunglasses she'd put on a moment earlier and swiped at her eyes. Casey realized a beat later it was because she was crying.

"Tara, what's wrong? Shit. I swear sometimes I have no idea when I'm screwing everything up."

"You didn't screw up."

But she must have, or Tara wouldn't be crying. "Did I say the wrong thing last night? When I told you how much I liked being with your family? Was it too soon to say that?"

"No. Oh, Casey." Tara shook her head and her jaw clenched. She swiped again at her eyes and sighed. "Why am I so bad at this?"

"You? You're not bad at anything."

"Yes, I am. I'm bad at lots of things but somehow you don't see it. And I appreciate that. Very much." She sniffed and reached for Casey's hand. "I'm not good at talking about feelings." She gave Casey's hand a squeeze and continued, "I love you in that hat. I love that you picked the one that says Rocky Springs out of all the choices. And it looks like it was made for you." She cleared her throat. "Although, I wish I'd gotten a picture of you in that sun bonnet."

Casey wanted to laugh it off, but Tara's comment was a deflection, and they'd agreed not to avoid the hard conversations. "Before the hat—this morning—something was wrong."

"Nothing was wrong." Tara dropped her gaze to their linked hands. "I was trying to hold myself back from saying something. Something I want to tell you but something that might change things with us. Please, don't worry. I see you worrying. You're so sweet and caring and I hate that people have taken advantage of that."

Casey's throat tightened. She didn't know what to say. "Tara, tell me what's wrong. Please. And then maybe we can—"

"I love you." She lifted their clasped hands. "That's what I've been trying not to say. But I want to say it. So there." She nodded. "I love you. I love that you picked that hat. I love how you are with my family. I love how you make me feel. God, I love you in bed. And I love how much you love my cupcakes."

Casey stepped forward and kissed Tara. She didn't care if Henry with his furrowed brow could see. She didn't care if anyone walking by stopped to stare. She deepened the kiss, wrapping Tara in an embrace and not caring about anything except the three words that had her floating. When she finally pulled back, she laughed.

"You're laughing?" Tara tipped her head. "I tell you that I love you, and you kiss me like you'd rather kiss me than breathe, and then you laugh?"

"I can't help it," Casey said. "I feel so good. And I'm in love. And the woman I love, loves me back. And I own a sex shop. I think I'm the luckiest person alive."

Tara laughed then too.

"I love you. So much." Casey kissed her again. "I want to spend the rest of the day with you. And then the next day. And all the others too."

"I like that plan." Tara snuggled closer for another kiss. "I don't really want to let you go back to work tomorrow. You know, Coy Cupcakes is closed all week. The Sweet Spot could be too."

"You want me to deprive Rocky Springs of sex toys for the New Year? What is everyone going to do? Stay up and watch a ball drop when they could be sucking on birthday-cake-flavored edible bras? Think of the titties."

"Titties is a terrible word. I think I'd rather you say dildo."

"Oh, there'll be dildo sucking too. You wouldn't believe how those things were flying off the shelf this past month."

"You know, I've never been so glad that a sex shop went in next to my bakery." She kissed Casey. "Let's get breakfast. Then I want to take you back home and keep you in bed for the rest of the day."

"Back home? Like our home?" Casey knew Tara understood her question. "Just so you know, I'd be okay with you moving in anytime. Very much okay, in fact. I love waking up with you."

"I love waking up with you too." Tara smiled. "But you're going to need to be patient. I'm not a U-Haul girl."

"Totally get it. I hate supporting big corporations when we could find a smaller family-owned moving company."

Tara placed her index finger on Casey's lips. "Be patient with me. I'm not going anywhere."

Casey felt the words in her heart. She knew Tara was telling the truth and when they looked into each other's eyes, she knew it was forever they were both thinking of. "I think you know this, but I want to say it out loud. I'm not going anywhere either. I found the place I want to stay. I love it here. With you."

CHAPTER THIRTY-FIVE

The following November.

"Are you sure this is a good idea?" Casey asked, cupcake in each hand.

Tara took both cupcakes and set them exactly where she wanted them in the half-decorated display window of the Sweet Spot. "Is that your way of saying you don't want my cupcakes in your window?"

Casey laughed. "How do you make that sound dirty?"

"It's a gift." She turned and made a suggestive circle with her head. "You wanna put your cupcakes in my window, hot stuff?"

"I don't even know what that means, but my answer is yes. If you ask me like that, it doesn't matter what it is. My answer will always be yes."

She'd sort of expected the sex to cool off after a year, at least a little. But things with Casey only seemed to get better. They'd moved in together over the summer, they'd adopted a cat, and the sex continued to blow her mind. And every morning, they went to work next door to one another, dropping into each other's shops for light lunches, discussions about what to have for dinner, and the occasional quickie on the settee in Casey's stockroom. It wasn't easy one hundred percent of the time, but it was damn near perfect.

"What? Was that not the right thing to say?"

She shot Casey a stern look.

Casey, hands now free, lifted them in defense. "Right. I know. I'm not supposed to immediately assume something is wrong. Sorry. Old habits die hard."

"You're adorable, and I love you."

Casey shook her head. "You're not supposed to find me adorable. You're supposed to find me sexy and rugged."

She pressed her lips together for show but didn't really try to suppress the smile. "I'm sorry. I didn't get the memo."

That got her a full-on pout.

"Fine. You're very sexy. Very rugged."

"That's not what I meant." Casey grinned. "But thank you."

"What did you mean?" She reached around Casey for another cupcake and put it in place.

"I meant that while I'm thrilled to have your cupcakes in my window, maybe you don't want my cupcakes in yours."

She'd either lost track of the euphemism or Casey wasn't making any sense. "Huh?"

"Your cupcakes." Casey picked up a pair frosted with a red and white candy cane effect. "My cupcakes." She tipped her head at the stack of better sex guides.

"Oh." Tara let the word drag. "You mean actual cupcakes. And, well, naughty bits."

"Yeah."

They'd agreed to come up with collaborative window displays highlighting both the bakery and Casey's shop. Not to toot her own horn, but the design was brilliant—playful and all about enjoying the sweet things and simple pleasures. Casey had a few risqué elements in hers, but the items Tara had picked to go in the Coy Cupcakes window were squarely PG. "The cupcakes of yours I'll be showing off are pretty tame, even by Rocky Springs standards."

"Technically, yes. But you're still, you know, hitching our wagons together."

Tara laughed. "I'm not sure if that's the best sketchy metaphor I've heard all day or the worst."

Casey ran a hand through her hair. "Let's go with the worst. I'm already batting a big fat zero over here."

"Aw, honey. I'm sorry for teasing you. Especially while you're trying so hard to be sweet."

"Trying." Casey gave her a gentle poke in the ribs. "People know we're together, but officially aligning our businesses is going to turn off some people."

She knew Casey's concern was genuine, but she'd stopped worrying about that sort of thing and wasn't about to start again now. "I'll sacrifice the closed-minded jerks who might otherwise buy cupcakes if you'll accept being boycotted by the keto crowd."

That broke the tension, and Casey laughed, too. "When you put it that way."

It was an easy sentiment to embrace since karma had so nicely nudged Anna Jenkins to divorce her husband and take him to the cleaners. She'd taken over the Western store and become a vocal supporter of the Sweet Spot. There hadn't been even a whisper of protest in months. "I'm glad we're in agreement. Now, help me get this gingerbread boudoir finished so we can go work on my cupcake orgy."

"It's not an orgy. You have to stop saying that." Casey shook her head, but the smile didn't leave her face.

They'd agreed to set up a romantic ski lodge look for her window. But having just a pair of kissing cupcake characters felt boring, so they'd added lots, and Tara had insisted on calling it an orgy ever since. "Now who's the prude?"

"Who knew getting you comfortable with saying dildo would open the floodgates?"

Tara waggled her eyebrows. "I like the way you open my floodgates."

Casey managed a disapproving look for about two seconds before cracking. "What am I going to do with you?"

"Give me a kiss, then grab those gumdrops for me." She pointed at the bag.

"Yes, boss."

Tara turned her attention back to the display, if for no other reason than the sooner they finished it, the sooner they could go home and get naked. She stuck out her hand behind her, only no gumdrops landed in it. Instead, something round and metal. She closed her fingers around it. She spun around. Only instead of a sheepish Casey standing there, she found a somewhat terrified looking one on one knee. "Casey?"

"Hi." Casey gave a tentative smile.

"What are you doing?" She had a pretty clear guess, but it didn't quite seem possible. Or real.

"I thought about reprising the twelve days of Christmas, but I didn't want to wait that long. I also wasn't sure I could come up with twelve new ideas."

Was it an early present, then? But why was Casey on her knee? Tara slowly opened her hand and, sure enough, a ring sat in her palm. But not just any ring. A gorgeously simple band with a perfectly set emerald-cut diamond.

"You've made me the happiest I've ever been. I love you. So damn much. And I love who I am when I'm with you. I want a whole lifetime of working next to you and coming home to you and everything else. If you'll have me."

Little rendered her speechless, but Casey did in that moment. Of course, it was hard to find words around tears, even if they were tears of joy.

"Will you marry me, Tara?"

She started with a nod but managed a yes. Well, several. Many. "All the yesses," she said eventually.

Casey took the ring from Tara's hand and slipped it on her finger. Tara grabbed Casey's hands and hauled her to her feet. And then the clapping started. Muffled, because it was through the window, but definitely clapping. As in, multiple people clapping.

She shifted her gaze without turning her head. Sure enough, they'd gathered a small crowd. Aspen stood front and center. Mom was there, too, along with Shawn and Kit. "Is that your doing?"

Casey shook her head. "I knew there was a chance people would see us, but I didn't plan on an audience. I mean, what if you'd said no?"

"Did you really think I might?"

Casey grinned. "No."

A rather impatient knock came at the glass. Shawn.

"I think they want to see the ring," Casey said.

"Nah. I'm pretty sure they want us to kiss."

"Oh." Casey chuckled. "Or that."

"Well, Casey Stevens, you've been open for over a year. What's the number one rule of running a successful business?"

Casey shrugged. "Fall in love with the baker next door?"

God, she loved this woman. This sweet, sexy, occasionally dorky, amazing woman. "I think that might be a one-off situation."

"Hmm." She seemed to seriously ponder the question. "I don't know."

She stole another glance at the crowd watching them. Any flashes of self-consciousness evaporated in the sheer perfection of this moment. "Give the customers what they want."

"Right. Let me get on that."

Casey's arms came around her, and Casey's lips covered hers. Not unlike the thousands of kisses they'd racked up at this point, and yet completely different. Because while the others may have hinted at forever, implied it even, this one came with a promise. A promise they were making together, and one Tara couldn't wait to keep for the rest of her life.

The clapping started up again, along with a few whoops and whistles. Casey took her time, though, and Tara didn't mind one bit. Kissing Casey was one of her absolute favorite things in the world.

When Casey eventually pulled away, Tara turned to face the window and flashed her left hand. Everyone ate it up. "You know, maybe we should just reenact this moment as our entry in the competition. We'd be a shoo-in."

Casey laughed. "Yeah, but if we did that, I couldn't take you home for a proper celebration."

She made a show of considering the options. "Does celebrating include champagne and a nice dinner or naked and in bed?"

"Yes," Casey said without hesitation.

"Yeah, I want that. Ribbons are overrated." Not that they wouldn't finish their displays and make a good showing either way.

"Besides, I've already got the best prize."

Tara's mind raced through all the things she'd wanted for her life when she moved back to Rocky Springs. Success, sure, but also a support network. She'd assumed that would be her family. Nowhere on her list of goals was a relationship—and she'd definitely not planned on getting engaged. Funny how getting to know one stranger could change so much. "No, you don't. I do."

"I guess we'll have to call it a tie."

Hard to argue with that. "A tie."

"Come on. I think there are some people that want to congratulate us."

As much as she didn't love being the center of attention, she didn't mind this once. Even if her mind was already on the private celebration she and Casey would have at home. They stepped out of the window and started toward the door, but Tara grabbed Casey's hand.

Casey gave her a quizzical look. "What? I didn't embarrass you too much, did I?"

She shook her head. "I love you. I mean, I say that a lot, but it feels extra important to say in this moment. I really, really love you."

Casey nodded, as though sensing the weird surge of urgency. "I love you, too. And you know what else?"

"What?" Tara asked, wondering what could possibly be as important as that.

"I can't wait to have your cupcakes at our wedding."

About the Authors

Aurora Rey is a college dean by day and award-winning lesbian romance author the rest of the time, except when she's cooking, baking, riding the tractor, or pining for goats. She grew up in a small town in south Louisiana, daydreaming about New England. She keeps a special place in her heart for the South, especially the food and the ways women are raised to be strong, even if they're taught not to show it. After a brief dalliance with biochemistry, she completed both a BA and an MA in English.

She is the author of the Cape End Romance series and several standalone contemporary lesbian romance novels and novellas. She has been a finalist for the Lambda Literary, RITA®, and Golden Crown Literary Society awards but loves reader feedback the most. She lives in Ithaca, New York, with her dog and whatever wildlife has taken up residence in the pond.

Jaime Clevenger lives in a little mountain town in Colorado. Most days are spent working as a veterinarian, but time off is filled writing, reading, swimming, practicing karate, and goofing off with their wife and kids (both two- and four-legged). Jaime loves hearing a good story and hopes that if you ever meet, you'll share your favorite. Feel free to embellish the details

Books Available from Bold Strokes Books

Accidentally in Love by Kimberly Cooper Griffin. Nic and Lee have good reasons for keeping their distance. So why does their growing attraction seem more like a love-hate relationship? (978-1-63679-759-5)

Fatal Foul Play by David S. Pederson. After eight friends are stranded in an old lodge by a blinding snowstorm, a brutal murder leaves Mark Maddox to solve the crime as he discovers deadly secrets about people he thought he knew. (978-1-63679-794-6)

Frosted by the Girl Next Door by Aurora Rey and Jaime Clevenger. When heartbroken Casey Stevens opens a sex shop next door to uptight cupcake baker Tara McCoy, things get a little frosty. (978-1-63679-723-6)

Ghost of the Heart by Catherine Friend. Being possessed by a ghost was not on Gwen's bucket list, but she must admit that ghosts might be real, and one is obviously trying to send her a message. (978-1-63555-112-9)

Hot Honey Love by Nan Campbell. When chef Stef Lombardozzi puts her cooking career into the hands of filmmaker Mallory Radowski—the pickiest eater alive—she doesn't anticipate how hard she falls for her. (978-1-63679-743-4)

London by Patricia Evans. Jaq's and Bronwyn's lives become entwined as dangerous secrets emerge and Bronwyn's seemingly perfect life starts to unravel. (978-1-63679-778-6)

This Christmas by Georgia Beers. When Sam's grandmother rigs the Christmas parade to make Sam and Keegan queen and queen, sparks fly, but they can't forget the Big Embarrassing Thing that makes romance a total nope. (978-1-63679-729-8)

Unwrapped by D. Jackson Leigh. Asia du Muir is not going to let some party girl actress ruin her best chance to get noticed by a Broadway critic. Everyone knows you should never mix business and pleasure. (978-1-63679-667-3)

Language Lessons by Sage Donnell. Grace and Lenka never expected to fall in love. Is home really where the heart is if it means giving up your dreams? (978-1-63679-725-0)

New Horizons by Shia Woods. When Quinn Collins meets Alex Anders, Horizon Theater's enigmatic managing director, a passionate connection ignites, but amidst the complex backdrop of theater politics, their budding romance faces a formidable challenge. (978-1-63679-683-3)

Scrambled: A Tuesday Night Book Club Mystery by Jaime Maddox. Avery Hutchins makes a discovery about her father's death that will force her to face an impossible choice between doing what is right and finally finding a way to regain a part of herself she had lost. (978-1-63679-703-8)

Stolen Hearts by Michele Castleman. Finding the thief who stole a precious heirloom will become Ella's first move in a dangerous game of wits that exposes family secrets and could lead to her family's financial ruin. (978-1-63679-733-5)

Synchronicity by J.J. Hale. Dance, destiny, and undeniable passion collide at a summer camp as Haley and Cal navigate a love story that intertwines past scars with present desires. (978-1-63679-677-2)

The First Kiss by Patricia Evans. As the intrigue surrounding her latest case spins dangerously out of control, military police detective Parker Haven must choose between her career and the woman she's falling in love with. (978-1-63679-775-5)

Wild Fire by Radclyffe & Julie Cannon. When Olivia returns to the Red Sky Ranch, Riley's carefully crafted safe world goes up in flames. Can they take a risk and cross the fire line to find love? (978-1-63679-727-4)

Writ of Love by Cassidy Crane. Kelly and Jillian struggle to navigate the ruthless battleground of Big Law, grappling with desire, ambition, and the thin line between success and surrender. (978-1-63679-738-0)

Back to Belfast by Emma L. McGeown. Two colleagues are asked to trade jobs. Claire moves to Vancouver and Stacie moves to Belfast, and though they've never met in person, they can't seem to escape a growing attraction from afar. (978-1-63679-731-1)

Exposure by Nicole Disney and Kimberly Cooper Griffin. For photographer Jax Bailey and delivery driver Trace Logan, keeping it casual is a matter of perspective. (978-1-63679-697-0)

Hunt of Her Own by Elena Abbott. Finding forever won't be easy, but together Danaan's and Ashly's paths lead back to the supernatural sanctuary of Terabend. (978-1-63679-685-7)

Perfect by Kris Bryant. They say opposites attract, but Alix and Marianna have totally different dreams. No Hollywood love story is perfect, right? (978-1-63679-601-7)

Royal Expectations by Jenny Frame. When childhood sweethearts Princess Teddy Buckingham and Summer Fisher reunite, their feelings resurface and so does the public scrutiny that tore them apart. (978-1-63679-591-1)

Shadow Rider by Gina L. Dartt. In the Shadows, one can easily find death, but can Shay and Keagan find love as they fight to save the Five Nations? (978-1-63679-691-8)

The Breakdown by Ronica Black. Vaughn and Natalie have chemistry, but the outside world keeps knocking at the door, threatening more trouble, making the love and the life they want together impossible. (978-1-63679-675-8)

Tribute by L.M. Rose. To save her people, Fiona will be the tribute in a treaty marriage to the Tipruii princess, Simaala, and spend the rest of her days on the other side of the wall between their races. (978-1-63679-693-2)

Wild Wales by Patricia Evans. When Finn and Aisling fall in love, they must decide whether to return to the safety of the lives they had, or take a chance on wild love in windswept Wales. (978-1-63679-771-7)

Can't Buy Me Love by Georgia Beers. London and Kayla are perfect for one another, but if London reveals she's in a fake relationship with Kayla's ex, she risks not only the opportunity of her career, but Kayla's trust as well. (978-1-63679-665-9)

Chance Encounter by Renee Roman. Little did Sky Roberts know when she bought the raffle ticket for charity that she would also be taking a chance on love with the egotistical Drew Mitchell. (978-1-63679-619-2)

Comes in Waves by Ana Hartnett. For Tanya Brees, love in small-town Coral Bay comes in waves, but can she make it stay for good this time? (978-1-63679-597-3)

Dancing With Dahlia by Julia Underwood. How is Piper Fernley supposed to survive six weeks with the most controlling, uptight boss on earth? Because sometimes when you stop looking, your heart finds exactly what it needs. (978-1-63679-663-5)

Skyscraper by Gun Brooke. Attempting to save the life of an injured boy brings Rayne and Kaelyn together. As they strive for justice against corrupt Celestial authorities, they're unable to foresee how intertwined their fates will become. (978-1-63679-657-4)

The Curse by Alexandra Riley. Can Diana Dillon and her daughter, Ryder, survive the cursed farm with the help of Deputy Mel Defoe? Or will the land choose them to be the next victims? (978-1-63679-611-6)

The Heart Wants by Krystina Rivers. Fifteen years after they first meet, Army Major Reagan Jennings realizes she has one last chance to win the heart of the woman she's always loved. If only she can make Sydney see she's worth risking everything for. (978-1-63679-595-9)

Untethered by Shelley Thrasher. Helen Rogers, in her eighties, meets much-younger Grace on a lengthy cruise to Bali, and their intense relationship yields surprising insights and unexpected growth. (978-1-63679-636-9)

You Can't Go Home Again by Jeanette Bears. After their military career ends abruptly, Raegan Holcolm is forced back to their hometown to confront their past and discover where the road to recovery will lead them, or if it already led them home. (978-1-636790644-4)